MW01126293

**ISBN: 978-1-947863-22-4 (Paperback edition)**
**ISBN: 978-1-947863-23-1 (Hardcover edition)**
**ISBN: 978-1-947863-24-8 (Kindle edition)**
**ISBN: 978-1-947863-21-7 (Audio edition)**

**Library of Congress Control Number: 2024936706**

This is a work of fiction. Names, characters, dialogue, places, incidents and opinions expressed are the product of the author's imagination or are used fictitiously, and any resemblance to actual persons, living or dead, business establishments, events, or locales is entirely coincidental, and not to be construed as real. Nothing is intended or should be interpreted as expressing the views of the U.S. Navy or any other department or agency of any government body.

Cover art and design by bookcoverart.com

The appearance of U.S. Department of Defense (DoD) visual information does not imply or constitute DoD endorsement. The United States Department of Defense's Prepublication & Security Review cleared this manuscript for public release on April 15, 2024.

Printed and bound in the United States of America.
First printing June 2024.

Published by Kirby Publishing, LLC
Lacey, WA 98503

Visit www.tomcarrollbooks.com for more information

# TOM CARROLL

# SHANGHAI PROTOCOL

Book three of the COLT GARRETT series

*Writing a novel was more challenging than I thought and more rewarding than I could have imagined. I was warned that writing my third novel would be even more difficult. None of this would have been possible without the help of a large group of old and new friends who took the time to help me when I needed it most. That is true friendship.*

*The Copyreading Team. I'm grateful to the friends who agreed to read through the pre-publication edition to help me find my errors: David Stocks, Roger Spealman, Bill Webb, Jim Carroll, Michael Evans, Laurie Carroll and Mike Robbins.*

*The Experts. A special thanks to the group of naval, military, intelligence, and aviation experts who tolerated my endless questions and attempted to ensure the novel's technical elements approximated reality: Commander Bill Webb, USN (Ret); Captain Roger Spealman, FedEx Express; Former Deputy Chief Glenn Cramer, Washington State Patrol, Commander Randy Unger, USN (Ret), and Lieutenant Colonel Gene Vey, USAF (Ret).*

*To Troy Kirby for his continued guidance and support through the publishing maze and for helping me turn my ideas into stories.*

*And to Ivan Zann at BookCoversArt.com for yet another great cover.*

*For Calvin Lee Rowe*

*"Be extremely subtle, even to the point of formlessness. Be extremely mysterious, even to the point of soundlessness. Thereby, you can be the director of the opponent's fate."*

*-Sun Zu, The Art of War*

*"A nation can survive its fools, and even the ambitious. But it cannot survive treason from within. An enemy at the gates is less formidable, for he is known and carries his banner openly. But the traitor moves amongst those within the gate freely, his sly whispers rustling through all the alleys, heard in the very halls of government itself."*

*-Marcus Tullius Cicero*

# Prologue

### Russian Antonov 148-300 over Eastern Russia

The Russian Air Force captain scanned the instrument panel of the large transport aircraft as it flew east over the desolate Russian landscape. Even at 35,000 feet, the pilot could see details of the land below, void of any sign of humanity. He was proud to serve his country as an Air Force pilot and couldn't imagine doing anything else. These long-distance flights were the best part of his job. They allowed him hours to think about the more significant issues of his life. He was about to comment on the uninhabited terrain below when he noticed his young copilot had buried his nose into the trashy romance novel he kept in his flight bag.

"Lieutenant," began the captain, "I realize this aircraft can fly itself, but your duties as copilot still require you to monitor the navigation and systems displays to ensure the computers don't kill our passengers and us. Put that garbage away, and don't make me tell you again!"

The high-wing and modern Antonov 148 was a twin turbofan regional jet airliner manufactured in Ukraine for commercial use. This aircraft had been specially modified as a business jet for the Russian Federation's Ministry of Defence. With its autoland instrument landing system, fly-by-wire flight controls, and multiple flat-screen displays, the AN-148 could nearly fly itself. With only two passengers and five crew on board, the plane could easily fly between its home airfield in Moscow and Shanghai without a refueling stop.

"Very sorry, Captain. But speaking of our passengers, who

do you think they really are, and why are they going to Shanghai? The manifest lists them as Passenger One and Passenger Two. The man looked intense with that wicked scar on his face and that Makarov pistol on his belt. But did you check out that babe in the dark jacket and skirt? And those long, delicious legs? Oh, my God! I wonder what her story is." He pushed several console buttons to select the passenger compartment surveillance system, projecting an image of the female passenger's legs on one of the cockpit's glass display screens.

"Turn that off, Lieutenant," ordered the captain. "I'd prefer you focus on our fuel calculations rather than that woman's legs. None of our business why we are flying these people to Shanghai. Don't want to know what they will do after we land. We are to remain with this aircraft and be ready for further instructions. So, rework those fuel consumption calculations and stop your stupid fantasies about that woman!"

The copilot realized he better focus on his job. He returned the well-worn paperback to his flight bag and entered revised fuel data into the flight computer. He wasn't concerned about the Antonov having enough fuel for the trip when he filed the flight plan, but they had experienced major unexpected headwinds, and they needed to be sure. After double-checking his work, he yawned and extended his arms above his head. "The fuel still looks good for Shanghai, with enough to spare. Need to visit the toilet. Back in a few, Captain." He unbuckled his seat harness, exited the cockpit, and entered the main cabin. After using the cramped restroom, he was about to return to the cockpit, but a thought occurred to him. He decided to turn right instead and speak with the mysterious passengers.

"Good morning. I'm Lieutenant Sidorova, your copilot. Looks like we will be arriving on time. Please let me know if I can do anything to make your trip more pleasant." He leaned down and placed one hand on the attractive woman's shoulder and his other on her knee. "I have a bottle of vodka in the crew's compartment," he whispered, "if you are interested."

Lieutenant Sidorova was shocked and excited as the woman deftly slid her hand between his legs and caressed his manhood. But then his excitement turned into alarm as the woman increased her grasp and slowly put a vise grip on his testicles. "Good God!" he cried as he dropped to his knees. When he thought the pain couldn't worsen, he passed out and collapsed unconscious on the cabin floor.

"Well, Admiral Orlov. I want to compliment you on such a practical demonstration of the vasovagal fainting technique. I hope you have not permanently damaged the poor young man. After all, he was only trying to make your acquaintance."

Rear Admiral Sofia Orlov curled her lip. She would have preferred to make this trip without the human guard dog from the SVR, but it had not been up to her. "No worries, Major. The boy should be awake momentarily, seriously regretting his insolence." As if on cue, Sidorova began to moan and rub his aching groin. He slowly recovered and rolled to a sitting position.

"I am so sorry, madam. I meant no disrespect. Please do not report my actions to the authorities," he pleaded.

"We are the authorities, you stupid peasant! Bring me that bottle of vodka, now!" she hissed.

The young lieutenant carefully stood and then stumbled to the crew's compartment in search of his bottle of vodka.

Major Kalishnik shook his head. "It is hard to believe the aircrew did not discover our true identities. I'm impressed that the Ministry of Defence can keep some things secret, if only from our own forces." Kalishnik knew something about security with his background as a major in the Russian Foreign Intelligence Service or, more commonly, the SVR. The successor to the infamous KGB, the SVR matched and occasionally exceeded its predecessor's reputation for ruthless tactics and stratagems. SVR was tasked with civilian intelligence and espionage activities outside the Russian Federation. It sometimes coordinated activities and operations with its military counterpart, the GRU. Rear Admiral Sofia Orlov commanded the military spy agency's second directorate, which focused on the Americas, the United Kingdom, Australia, and New Zealand. Kalishnik closely studied the stunning woman seated directly across from him. About forty-five years old, quite young for a rear admiral. Short brunette hair with large, dark eyes to match. A tall Ukrainian beauty with an hourglass shape and flawless alabaster complexion. Kalishnik could well understand the young lieutenant's attraction to the admiral and her amazing legs. Too bad that this mission would be over so soon.

"Major, perhaps we might spend some time discussing our upcoming meeting? Assuming you are finished undressing me with your eyes."

Embarrassed at being caught leering at the senior naval officer, Kalishnik reached for the pen and pad of paper on the table, looked the admiral in the eye, and said, "Of course, of course. At your service."

Sofia was about to start the briefing when Lieutenant Sidorova returned and silently placed a bottle of Stolichnaya Elit vodka and two glasses on the small table. She picked up the slender bottle. "Must have cost you a week's pay, Lieutenant. How generous of you."

The young copilot nodded nervously. He limped back to the cockpit and knocked on the locked door.

The pilot unlocked the door, and both officers took their seats. "Welcome back. You have been gone for quite some time. Feeling all right?"

"Fine, sir," responded Sidorova. "At least I think I will be in a few hours." He was about to make up a story about stomach problems when he saw the exaggerated smirk on the pilot's face. And then, he noticed the cabin surveillance system was still displayed on the cockpit screen. He could see the woman and the man with the scar and realized the captain had seen everything.

Back in the passenger compartment, Admiral Orlov started her briefing once again.

"After we arrive in Shanghai, Chinese Communist Party security forces will escort us directly to our meeting downtown. No stop at immigration or customs. This visit and our meeting are strictly off the record."

Kalishnik had been briefed by his superior that Admiral Orlov would be meeting with senior CCP officials but not that the meeting would be covert. He was about to ask why but then thought better.

"I will meet with Chinese Minister of State Security Sun Ping to discuss our two countries' joint interests regarding the American threat. The O'Kane Doctrine, spearheaded by American Defense Secretary Colton Garrett, has drastically limited Mother Russia's ability to exert global influence. The Chinese offer us a path to mitigate American economic sanctions. We might eventually agree to share resources, assets, and information to circumvent American interests and policy more effectively, particularly in the Pacific."

"But, Admiral, the Chinese? Does Moscow honestly believe these people can work with us? Although Alexander Pushkin wrote about politics and difficult bedfellows, history has proven the Chinese can never be trusted."

"Difficult times, Major." Sofia opened the bottle of vodka and poured herself a glass. "And the quotation you mangled was not Pushkin's. In The Tempest, William Shakespeare wrote, 'Misery acquaints a man with strange bedfellows.' Would you like a glass of vodka, Kalishnik? This is exceptional!"

He nodded. "But are you saying we might need to share some of our illegal agents buried deep within the American government and military? The SVR has worked for decades to nurture and grow those collection networks. I cannot imagine my headquarters would authorize sharing those precious assets with the Chinese."

"Your superiors have already done so, Major. My challenge is to ensure we receive something of equal or greater value in return. Desperate times, like I said, Kalishnik. Russia is not the power we once were. We must evolve to survive."

"Yes, Admiral, but—"

"But what?"

Sofia looked at the SVR major, but he was staring out the airplane's window at a fighter jet that had just joined on their starboard wing. She could tell it was a fully armed SU-27 air superiority fighter with the markings of the Kazakhstan Air Force.

"We must have just entered Kazakhstan air space. The Sukhoi interceptor is yet another reminder of how times have changed. All of this used to be Soviet air space."

Major Kalishnik took a long sip of vodka and looked again at the lethal fighter. "Yes, many things have changed. But we are still Russians, Admiral, and that will never change." Sofia hated to agree with Kalishnik, but in this case, he was right.

The Kazakhstan fighter escort broke off several hours later as the Russian transport aircraft crossed into Mongolian airspace. The aircrew and passengers watched as the Gobi Desert passed beneath, miles of pale orange sand for as far as the eye could see. Sofia stared out of the window. "The Himalayan range keeps moisture away from the Gobi, creating a rain shadow where vegetation cannot survive. Did you know that? In 1275, Marco Polo crossed the Gobi and wrote, 'This desert is reported to be so long that it would take a year to go from end to end, and at the narrowest point it takes a month to cross it.' The famous Silk Road. That part, at least, you must know."

Kalishnik wondered about the senior intelligence officer who seemed to be distracted by the history of the Gobi Desert when, in his opinion, she should be thinking about the meeting with the Chinese. He decided to observe the beautiful admiral more closely and include his concerns in his report. Before long, another fighter joined on the Russian plane's wing. Looking very similar to the Kazakhstan jet, this one had the markings of the People's Liberation Army Air Force, or more commonly, the Chinese Air Force.

"That's a Chinese Shenyang J-11, Admiral. It looks just like our SU-27s."

"Yes, Kalishnik, we gave the Chinese the design. Many years ago, we were trying to help a struggling communist nation. Now, it appears we are the ones who need help."

## Shanghai, People's Republic of China

The Chinese characters that represent Shanghai are "upon" and "sea," together meaning "On the Sea." What an appropriate name for this enchanting city. People have inhabited the Yangtze River delta for over 6,000 years, first as a fishing village and trade center. More recently, it has become the home of more than 24 million people and the most populated city in the world. The Port of Shanghai is home to the world's busiest container operation, and the city has a global reputation for being a leader in economics, business, and finance. The Shanghai Stock

Exchange competes with other exchanges as a leader in market capitalization, a remarkable achievement for a city in a communist country.

Perhaps one of the lesser-known facts about the city is its importance to the Chinese Communist Party. In 1921, the First National Congress of the Chinese Communist Party was held in a downtown residence where fifteen men met to build a movement. That site is now a small museum celebrating the birth of Chinese communism, welcoming nearly two million visitors annually. Today, it was closed so that representatives of two global powers could privately meet and discuss how they might join forces to defeat a common enemy.

"Admiral Orlov, Major Kalishnik, welcome to the People's Republic of China and my favorite city, Shanghai. I am Sun Ping, minister of state security. On behalf of the Chinese Communist Party, I sincerely hope this meeting between our two great nations will be the first of many to come. Please sit and make yourselves comfortable. Perhaps some tea? Your journey has been long."

Sofia and Kalishnik sat at the ornate gold-leafed table in the center of a modestly furnished conference room. Minister Sun sat directly across from the two Russians. The three were alone after Sun's security team left the room.

"I thought it would be wise to limit our conversation to as few as possible," said Sun. "Extremely sensitive matters, and we must be cautious."

Sofia glanced around the room and assumed that at least a dozen hidden microphones captured every sound. "I completely agree, Minister Sun. We are not recording this meeting and will not take any notes. You have my word." She did not share that Major Kalishnik had a total recall and a photographic memory. Everything seen and said during the meeting would be reduced to a formal written report during the flight back to Moscow.

Sun set his teacup down and motioned around the room. "It is hard to imagine that the Chinese Communist Party was formed in this very room. A small group of Chinese men sitting around a table like this started a historic movement. It was truly a pivotal moment for mankind. Don't you agree, Admiral?"

Sofia looked around the room. She decided not to mention that one of her countrymen, Vladimir Nikolsky, a primary architect of the movement, had also been in the room that day in 1921. Another day, she thought and decided to change the subject.

"In your view, Minister Sun, how has China become a world power in such a relatively short period of time?"

Sun narrowed his eyes and looked intently at the Russian admiral. "If by 'world power,' you refer to our growth in economic power, I believe there are two principal reasons."

He placed his teacup on the saucer, interlaced his fingers, and continued.

"First, we have prioritized capital investment on a massive scale, aggressively encouraged foreign investment, and redirected our domestic savings resources. Second, China has focused on increasing worker productivity. While we do remain significantly behind the capitalists in this regard, we have something they lack: an unlimited supply of cheap, nonunionized labor. Our comrades typically work six days per week, twelve hours per day."

Sofia was completely surprised by the conciseness and complexity of Sun's response. In her experience, leaders didn't typically consider economics a power source. She was about to ask another question when he raised his index finger.

"But I believe there is a third reason for our recent economic success against the capitalists: our deeply held belief in the sacredness of nationalism. We have put China first, and all our policies reinforce this concept. For some reason, Western nations have recently suppressed their historic instincts of self-defense and patriotism. This recent behavior of self-loathing in the West is most puzzling to us. For example, contrast our nationalism with America's—what can you call it?—anti-nationalism. China celebrates our history and culture, while the United States questions its immoral past and many malfeasances. Even their educational institutions reinforce and propagate this narrative, and as a result, the country is tearing itself apart. Americans are extremely distracted, and their distraction has served us well."

"But all nations must examine and acknowledge their past to move forward." Sofia was thinking about atrocities committed by the Stalin regime. "Russia renamed Leningrad and Stalingrad after the Soviet Union's demise. We tore down statues. We evolved."

"Admiral, please do not insult my understanding of world history by comparing the acts of Stalin and Lenin with those of Jefferson and Lincoln. The Americans have taken self-loathing to an unimaginable extreme, dividing their nation. Should China highlight our practice of binding women's feet or the influence of the Han Chinese within our society? Ludicrous! Self-destructive!"

Sofia realized Sun held strong opinions about American culture, and she decided to include his statements in her report. His comments might prove a gold mine for analysts developing the man's psychological profile. Glancing at her wristwatch, she shifted the conversation to the purpose of their visit.

"Minister Sun, our time here is limited. The Russian Federation desires to move forward with a specific initiative to operationalize several concepts of mutual benefit to our countries. For some time, the Americans and their allies have been interfering with our internal affairs and, as such, have infringed upon our sovereignty. They have downplayed the importance of the United Nations and its security council, preferring to push their definition of democracy on our two nations. As you know,

China and Russia have rich traditions in our forms of democracy. We stand together to proclaim that China and Russia, rather than America, should determine the right path for our citizens."

Sun nodded as he listened to the Russian admiral. He had heard all this before and wondered why the Russians had traveled so far to restate long-held positions. "Yes, this is all well known. We are particularly concerned regarding what the Americans and British are doing in the Pacific. New alliances forming, and they are not in the best interests of our two nations. Japan and India continue to cooperate with the Americans, and they have been exercising their sea power. We do see this as a direct threat to our sovereignty. You're right."

The Russian admiral leaned forward and pressed her hands on the table. "These exercises are most disturbing. The Indian and American navies have been conducting readiness drills in the Indian Ocean, and we know that other bilateral operations are planned. The American defense chief, Garrett, has been convincing his president to reaffirm their country's support of the Quadrilateral Security Dialogue, which, as you well know, is an informal but strategic alliance between the US, Japan, Australia, and India. We see that alliance as essentially an Asian NATO. We believe there's a chance that President Hernández may publicly announce her support for the alliance when she visits San Francisco in April to attend the United Nations celebration. In summary, Garrett appears to be determined to upset the status quo in the Pacific, and, thus far, we have been unable to find a way to bypass him."

"Unable to bypass Mr. Garrett, or unable to kill him?"

Sofia paused while Major Kalishnik nervously cleared his throat. "Yes, as you know, we have made several unsuccessful attempts to eliminate Colton Garrett. Our thinking now is that a better approach to achieve our joint goals would be to effect a change in leadership above Garrett's level."

Sun sat upright and stared at Sofia. "The only person above the US secretary of defense is the American president. What makes you think you could be successful in that endeavor?"

"Minister Sun," asked Sofia, "may I assume you have the utmost trust in those recording this meeting? What I am about to share with you is most sensitive."

Sun was about to deny the meeting was being recorded but quickly reconsidered. He nodded and then held his right index finger up while he reached under the table and pressed a hidden button. "Proceed, Admiral."

Sofia stood from her chair and walked to the window overlooking the street below. "We are aware of your program that targets local politicians and other officials who appear to have the potential for higher office. You assist with campaign fundraising, political guidance, and other resources. Through this program, you've gained influence and, in some cases, control over a group of well-placed government officials in Western nations. How am I doing so far?"

Sun sat expressionless and replied, "All this you could have discovered by reading Western newspapers or watching cable television stations. But continue."

Sofia turned from the window and walked to the adjacent wall to admire a painting. "We also have similar operations in some Western nations. We are willing to share our resources with you in exchange for access to your resources. In effect, to create a pooling of these combined intelligence resources to further our joint goal to restrict American influence in the Pacific. Perhaps even alter American policy to our mutual benefit. Are you interested in discussing this further?"

Sun pressed another button under the table. "Perhaps you should contact your aircraft and advise them that you have agreed to have lunch here before returning to the airport. I will have some food brought in, and then we can continue our most pleasant conversation."

### Aeroflot Cargo Terminal, Shanghai International Airport

"Admiral, I was surprised that you disclosed to Sun the extent of our knowledge of Chinese political infiltration of Western governments. I assume you received prior approval from higher authority?"

Sofia leaned back into the aircraft seat and watched the ground crew finish refueling the Russian jet in preparation for the long flight back to Moscow. It would be many hours before she could climb into the bed in her Moscow apartment. "Of course, I had prior approval. Do you take me for a fool?"

Sofia momentarily enjoyed the terror on the major's face as he carefully considered his reply. He was on treacherous ground with a powerful woman, and he must have known it. "Calm yourself, Major Kalishnik. My question was rhetorical. The whole point of this mission was to gauge the CCP's interest in more active resistance against the Americans in the Pacific. And I think we received a crystal-clear answer."

Several hours later in the flight, Kalishnik handed Sofia a stack of typewritten pages. "I have created this summary of our meeting in Shanghai for your review."

Sofia carefully read and then reread the entire file. After making several edits and adding an executive summary, she handed the document to the major for final printing. She wanted to be prepared to present the paper soon after landing in Moscow.

"Here's the final version, Admiral. If you don't need anything else, I'll try to get some rest before we arrive."

Sofia held the document and looked at the cover, "Russian Federation and People's Republic of China Joint Understanding." This one document could be responsible for altering the power balance in the Pacific. Knowing that securing the agreement with the Chinese would likely propel her career forward, Sofia decided the accord needed a better title. After several attempts, she ultimately settled on a more fitting name. On the document's cover, she penned the words "Shanghai Protocol."

# Day One

## Russian Military Intelligence HQ, Khodinka Airfield, Moscow, the Russian Federation

The chief of the Main Intelligence Directorate of the General Staff, Armed Forces of the Russian Federation (GRU), Admiral Kornilov, sat at his massive oak desk reading the detailed personnel file of Rear Admiral Sofia Orlov, Russian Navy. He had spent nearly an hour reading through the thick paper file while scribbling notes on a sheet of paper.

"Ukrainian-born, raised in Odessa by her parents," Kornilov commented aloud. "Graduated from the Makarov Pacific Higher Naval School in Vladivostok and commissioned as a junior lieutenant. Selected for intelligence work and identified as one with high potential. Fluent in English. Represented the Russian Federation in the 2002 Olympics in Salt Lake City, placing eighth in the women's downhill. Postgraduate work at the Kuznetsov Naval Academy in St. Petersburg, followed by a tour at the Military Academy of the General Staff in Moscow. And now responsible for our Second Directorate and its focus on the Western powers. An impressive resume for a woman of only forty-three!" The three-star admiral and spymaster removed his reading glasses and looked at the attractive one-star navy admiral standing before his desk.

"Impressive. Please be seated, Rear Admiral Orlov."

Sofia nodded, sat in the upholstered chair, and crossed her legs. Glancing around the intimidating corner office, she noticed it was adorned with mementos of the man's distinguished career,

17

including photos of the old admiral with more senior admirals and Politburo members. The lack of family mementos in the expansive office wasn't surprising for a man of Kornilov's stature. But Sofia had heard the headquarters rumors regarding the admiral's political aspirations, that he had sacrificed his personal life for advancement within the navy and the party. She smoothed her black uniform skirt and patiently waited for the GRU director to continue.

"I'm pleased you've been assigned to our headquarters here at Khodinka Field, Admiral Orlov. May I call you Sofia? And I am impressed that your first major assignment has been so successful. Did Major Kalishnik hinder your efforts in any way in January? My SVR counterpart insisted his agency was represented on your trip to Shanghai. I could not think of a reasonable objection other than I don't want the SVR sticking their nose into our GRU business."

"Sofia is fine, Admiral Kornilov. And no, Kalishnik was not a bother at all. His mnemonic skills were of great value in documenting the discussions with Sun, but I am certain an equally thorough version has already found its way into SVR headquarters. Do you have any questions about my background before I brief you on our concept of operations?"

Kornilov scanned his hand-written notes. "Just one. I can't help but wonder if you took advantage of your time at the Olympics to practice your English?"

"I did," Sofia answered. "The Canadian and American boys were more than willing to spend time with me in the Olympic Village bars. Not that they were very interested in women's downhill."

The older man looked at the appealing woman across from him, with her high cheekbones typical of a classic Ukrainian beauty. He could well imagine what the boys found interesting about Sofia Orlov. "Yes, I am sure it had nothing to do with your downhill prowess. Now, please proceed with your brief."

"As I have outlined in my report, Admiral, this operation will require the combined intelligence assets of both Russia and China." She uncrossed her legs, pressed them together, and enjoyed the discomfort on Kornilov's face before continuing. "The operation, if successfully executed, will result in the death of the American president and her defense secretary, Colton Garrett. Vice President Carlisle will assume the presidency, and the current national security advisor, Travis Webb, will be nominated and easily confirmed as defense secretary. Our significant influence and leverage over both men will ultimately result in America and its allies reversing their aggressive posturing in the Pacific and a more accommodating environment for Russian and Chinese interests in the region."

Admiral Kornilov removed his glasses and slowly massaged his forehead. "And you feel this event in Seattle offers the best opportunity for this? Why?"

Sofia shifted in her chair. "As you know, our goal is to prevent President Hernández from attending the event in San Francisco, which celebrates the 77th anniversary of the founding of the United Nations in that city. We suspect she will reaffirm America's support of their Pacific alliance while there."

"Yes, yes, of course she will." Kornilov was intimately familiar with the Quadrilateral Security Dialogue, America's thinly veiled attempt to extend their Pacific influence. "But I asked you about Seattle."

Sofia was mildly bothered by the man's impatience, but she smiled and continued. "Yes, sir. We know security will be extremely vigilant in San Francisco, with all the other foreign leaders attending the United Nations celebration. Hernández will make a brief layover in Seattle several days before the celebration

19

to meet with defense contractors and repay some political favors. It seems the Chinese have several well-placed operatives in the Seattle area. They recently shared that they have compromised several elected officials who will prove vital to our success should the operation be approved. Minister Sun was hesitant at first to disclose these remarkable resources. Still, I convinced him that our mutual goal of changing American policy was worth the sharing of some secrets."

Admiral Kornilov had thoroughly read Sofia's report, but he wanted her to personally brief him so that he could decide if she could execute the plan. The opportunity to prevent President Hernández from recommitting America to the Quadrilateral Security Dialogue and simultaneously eliminating Colton Garrett at the Department of Defense was too good to pass up. Sofia appeared to be up to the challenge.

"Excellent, Sofia. It seems you are the perfect choice for this mission. Of course, we have been aware for years that the Chinese Communist Party has been using local and state officials in America to advocate on the PRC's behalf at all levels. The Chinese believe these minor government officials enjoy great autonomy from their central government. It is the same with their people-to-people exchanges and business associations. For some reason, the Chinese have been much more successful than we have in the ground execution of this indirect method of political influence, particularly in North America. I am amazed that even when one of their operations becomes public, the American press appears to discount the importance of intelligence penetration. I suspect it has something to do with the enchantment of Asian culture. I wish we could be so successful."

"Yes, Admiral, but we have had our successes as well—incredible, well-placed assets at the highest levels of government. Carlisle and Webb are just the two best examples. And as my report indicates, we will need to share these resources with the Chinese for this plan to be successful. Assuming, sir, that I have your permission to move forward?"

Sofia watched the elder admiral close his eyes and rub his forehead once more. He stood from his desk and slowly walked to the windows overlooking the field below. Kornilov clasped his hands behind his back and leaned forward until his forehead rested on the bulletproof glass pane. He could feel the Moscow cold through the window, and at last, he made the most crucial decision of his career.

"Let's move on this, Sofia. You have my permission to contact our officer in Washington and assign Carlisle and Webb their respective tasks. Your Shanghai Protocol is approved!"

## Northbound Interstate 270, Maryland

Interstate 270, known to locals as the Washington National Pike, is a major, six-lane highway that begins at the Capital Beltway near Bethesda and runs north to Frederick, Maryland. The commuter traffic was heavy this cold, early spring morning, and the frost threatened to damage the pink cherry tree blossoms that lined the well-manicured boundaries of the busy highway. Colt was reminded of his college days in Seattle, of the Yoshino cherry trees that decorated the paths of the University of Washington campus. The trees had been planted more than 90 years ago, and the vibrant pink blossoms supposedly symbolized birth, death, beauty, and violence. When he was a student, Colt read somewhere that the blossoms also represented the short but colorful life of the samurai. That was decades ago, long before Defense Secretary Colton Garrett would find himself in an armored black Suburban on his way to a high-level meeting at

Camp David.

A 125-acre retreat for the president of the United States, Camp David was initially constructed as a camp for federal workers by the Depression-era Works Projects Administration in 1938, but President Franklin D. Roosevelt ordered it remodeled into a presidential retreat and promptly renamed it Shangri-La. The retreat is nestled in the hills of the Catoctin Mountain Park and more closely resembles a hunting lodge than a national security facility. Dwight D. Eisenhower changed the name again to Camp David in 1953 to honor his father and son. Officially known as Naval Support Facility Thurmond, Camp David had been the site of many famous international accords. The US Navy and US Marine Corps provide guest support services. And, of course, the US Secret Service was responsible for the president's safety whenever she visited.

"I sure am going to miss the fringe benefits of this job! Armored limo rides to business meetings and an executive protection detail to ensure I get there safely! Cambridge Shipping will pay me much better, but, man, I'll seriously miss these perks!" Garrett's executive assistant, Lenny Wilson, had recently accepted a management position with an international shipping company and would be leaving federal service at the end of the month. The two men had developed a close, personal relationship, and Colt was sad to see him go.

"I hate to break it to you, Lenny, but the Suburban and protection detail are for me. If you were going to the meeting alone, you'd be driving your minivan, and your protection detail would be your dog, Brady!" Lenny knew all too well that his boss and friend needed protection. On more than one occasion, Colt had been the target of assassination attempts.

"Right, boss. But I'll still miss it." Lenny enjoyed his government service and the satisfaction of serving his country.

But the former merchant marine officer yearned for the less political world of corporate shipping, a place where success was measured by a company's profit margin rather than the latest polls or opinion page articles. It was time to think about his family's future. College tuition and living expenses for three kids would be expensive. If he didn't make the break now, it might never happen. And besides, he was ready for a new challenge.

Colt glanced at Lenny beside him. "If it matters, I think you're doing the right thing. You need to spend more time at home with your wife and kids. That's time you can't get back. I know from experience."

Lenny knew Colt was speaking from his heart. The man's wife had died while the couple was working on repairing their marriage, and Colt's daughter lived on the West Coast. Colt's son was stationed on the East Coast but focused on his career. Lenny was about to share his regrets about leaving Colt for the new job when the driver, special agent Brian Smith of the Army's Criminal Investigative Service, cleared his throat.

"Secretary Garrett, you asked me to tell you when we were thirty minutes out, sir."

"Thanks, Brian." Colt opened a folder and asked, "Is the cone of silence engaged?"

"Yes, sir. The system is operational." The cone of silence was Colt's nickname for the highly sophisticated security system that ensured conversations within the vehicle could not be heard outside the SUV.

"Lenny, I want to walk through our meeting with the president regarding China's recent actions in the Pacific. Travis Webb will be there, of course. And the president's chief of staff. The objective is to go over all the issues and develop an approach for a new national security policy in the region. The president thought holding the meeting at Camp David might ease the tensions between Defense and the National Security Council and get us all on the same page."

"By tensions between Defense and the NSC, you mean between you and Webb!"

Lenny knew the history between National Security Advisor Travis Webb and the defense secretary. Webb previously had been deputy defense secretary when Colt was undersecretary for policy. When the former defense secretary unexpectedly died, Travis was forced to resign when some racially offensive photos from his college days surfaced, and Colt was appointed secretary. Later, Travis was appointed deputy national security advisor and then NSA when his predecessor died from a heart attack. Travis Webb still held a serious grudge against Colt because he believed the defense department should have been his. And there was one other issue with Travis Webb. Colt and Lenny suspected Travis might be the source of a security leak within the national security community. A leak that resulted in one of the assassination attempts on Colt's life.

Colt motioned to the driver in the front seat and shook his head. "I think that NSA Webb is a fine man, Lenny. We see things differently at times."

Lenny smiled and rolled his eyes. "Right, boss. That's what I meant." He knew better than to talk about such sensitive matters as a potential mole in front of a protection agent. Maybe it was time to get into another line of work. To deftly change the subject, he asked Colt, "When will the president arrive at Camp David, sir?"

Colt looked at the new Rolex GMT-Master on his wrist. The stainless-steel watch with the red and blue bezel had been his latest gift to himself. Although scores of more accurate quartz watches could dramatically exceed the Rolex's ability to display two time zones simultaneously and cost a fraction of the Rolex,

Colt preferred the classic over the merely functional. The watch suited his personality perfectly.

"She should be boarding Marine One in a few minutes and arriving before us."

## 1600 Pennsylvania Avenue, Washington DC

María Hernández silently watched the two Sikorsky H-60 helicopters descend. Visually similar to the more common black Army Blackhawks and gray Navy Seahawks, the livery of these aircraft included a two-toned paint scheme comprising white on the upper fuselage and green on the lower portion. Nicknamed Whitetops, they were flown by Marine Helicopter Squadron One naval aviators based at Marine Corps Air Facility, Quantico. This wasn't the first time that María wondered if she'd made the right decision not to accept the appointment to the Naval Academy at Annapolis and instead attend Rice University and then grad school at the London School of Economics. Her best friend, Chris O'Leary, had gone to Annapolis and then to the more than a two-year program to earn her wings as a naval aviator. Chris loved flying rotary-wing aircraft, preferring the low-level flying and stick and rudder environment over highly automated fixed-wing models. Despite their career choices, the two women had maintained a close friendship for decades. Last Christmas, Chris gave María a coffee mug with the inscription "Wings are for Amateurs." Now a colonel, Chris O'Leary commanded Marine Helicopter Squadron One, which had more than 800 Marines and 35 helicopters; she believed she had the best job in the world. She deftly lowered the collective in her left hand while adjusting the anti-torque pedals to compensate as the bird softly touched down on the plush green turf.

"My life certainly would have been different if I'd gone to Annapolis," María said as she watched the helicopter's blades slow and then stop spinning. A side door opened, and a Marine sergeant climbed down and placed a small platform beneath the chopper's steps.

"No question about it, President Hernández. You aren't the first president to wish they'd chosen a different trajectory, but you should feel proud of how spectacular this term has been. With more than 72 percent job approval—that's the latest from RealClearPolitics—you'll quickly secure the nomination without challenge. Then, you can use the general election to establish your agenda for the second term."

White House Chief of Staff Eric Paynter knew much about what presidents thought. A holdover from the Harrison administration, those within the Beltway considered him the insider's insider. The White House Communications Agency assigned him the codename CHASER because of his previous profession as a San Francisco personal injury attorney. His reputation in town as a man of political ruthlessness and predator cunning was well deserved. One of the reasons he resigned from his law firm was that the industry had shifted to make employment law even more profitable. Eric admired the president as she looked out of the Oval Office windows. Probably the best-looking boss I've ever had, he thought. President María Hernández stood 5 foot 7 and weighed an athletic 128 pounds. A striking brunette with shoulder-length hair, she had large brown eyes that men found mesmerizing. And a figure to match. Eric Paynter, by contrast, stood barely more than five feet tall and had the physical characteristics typical of an elderly doorman. His most remarkable feature was his face, which members of the White House press corps described as identical to the presidential version of Teddy Roosevelt, down to the round wire-rimmed glasses.

"Eric, let's spend a few minutes discussing the Camp David agenda before we board Marine One. Much easier to talk here."

The always-prepared chief of staff pulled a chair closer to the president's desk and opened a thick paper file. "As we've discussed, Madam President, our goal for this short trip is to get consensus among your senior defense policy advisors on how best to deal with the challenges posed by the Chinese in the Pacific. The advisors are divided into two schools of thought. Secretary Garrett and the joint chiefs believe we should continue our efforts with the other major Pacific powers to build an integrated force to counter regional Chinese aggression. You've been briefed on their sovereignty claims over vast Pacific areas. Garrett believes that the military exercises with the other members of the QUAD should not only continue but expand to all domains of operations." The QUAD was an unofficial term for the combined forces of Japan, Australia, India, and the United States, mainly when operating in combined exercises in the Pacific. "Your national security advisor, State, and some in the intelligence community espouse a contrary policy view. They feel we should scale back any Pacific activity the Chinese would perceive as aggressive. They're particularly concerned by the recent overtures between the Chinese and Russians to develop a shared perspective of what they call Western aggression in the Pacific. They see this potential alliance as a much greater threat. I know the vice president has been trying to get you to see things in this contrary view, but I have no idea why the man's sticking his nose into this fight. He usually doesn't expend effort unless there's something in it for him."

María had selected Joseph Carlisle as her running mate for the same reason every presidential candidate since Abraham Lincoln had done it: to bring in additional support to the ticket. She didn't like or trust Joe Carlisle and had made it clear to her chief of staff that she intended to replace the man in the next election. She knew that Eric strongly felt that Colt Garrett would be a good candidate as her running mate. On several occasions, Eric stressed Garrett's foreign policy expertise and good reputation with the media. But María wasn't confident he'd bring additional votes to the ticket. Wasn't that why one picked someone as a running mate? Garrett wasn't exactly a favorite of her party's leadership, who preferred someone more loyal to their political goals and agenda.

The national security advisor was Travis Webb, a Southerner who had become famous when photos of his fraternity days at Vanderbilt surfaced and caused former President Harrison to remove him as deputy secretary of defense. Travis eventually finagled his way into the NSC staff, and then Harrison appointed him NSA when Jonathan Unger suffered a massive coronary. Travis was one of those people who always seemed to land on their feet, regardless of baggage. He seemed to know everyone in the city but had no friends. María didn't understand why President Harrison appointed Travis as NSA. She didn't trust Travis Webb either and had been looking for an excuse to replace the man at the right time.

"Well, Eric," responded the president, "it should make for an interesting meeting." She turned back to the view of the South Lawn. "Okay, we probably should go now." And then María repeated her favorite Arnold Schwarzenegger line, "Let's head for the chopper!"


## The LeDroit Society, Washington, DC

Becci Quinn found her work as executive director of one of Washington's most highly regarded charitable foundations enjoyable and surprisingly rewarding. In just a few years, she had revitalized the previously unknown foundation into one of the most successful in the country. Formed to improve the welfare of children in the more neglected communities in the nation's capital, the foundation had also developed a reputation for attracting many of Washington's elite as donors. The LeDroit Society had recently been recognized by Charity Navigator with the highly coveted four-star rating, proclaiming to the world that it "Exceeds or meets best practices and industry standards across almost all areas. Likely to be a highly effective charity." Key to the foundation's high rating was that a hundred percent of donations were dedicated to its clients, made possible because its operations were funded by an obscure trust based in Finland—a trust established by a shell company secretly created by Russian Military Intelligence, the GRU.

Russia has a long history of funding and influencing organizations in the United States. In 1919, Russia was influential in creating the American Communist Party, support which continued through the Great Depression and the Cold War. There were rumors of Russia covertly funding several organizations advocating for US nuclear disarmament. Scores of naïve and unsuspecting Americans were exposed to and furthered Russian misinformation and manipulation as they participated in various social and political activities. All in the name of making the world a better place. Becci Quinn knew Russia was funding the foundation because she was a GRU agent.

She was a major in the Russian intelligence agency and had successfully transformed the tiny non-profit foundation into a primary intelligence source for her country of birth. If she continued to provide Moscow with high-quality and actionable intelligence, her promotion to lieutenant colonel would be assured. Ironically, Washington's elite fought to get an invitation to any of Becci's exclusive fundraisers. She never ceased to wonder at the lengths some people would go to rub shoulders with the city's major power brokers. Patrons could, at once, benefit from virtue signaling when they donated to her foundation and get a significant federal income tax deduction. If they only knew that they were also furthering Russian initiatives in America.

Becci, a highly trained and ruthless intelligence operative, was well-equipped to tackle comprehensive intelligence collection techniques. Still, her forte was developing human intelligence sources—Americans willing to share their country's greatest secrets. Recruiting national security advisor Travis Webb had been Becci's crowning achievement.

## The Laurel Lodge, Camp David, Maryland

Not counting the military barracks, the Laurel Lodge is the largest structure at Camp David. It has been remodeled several times since its original construction. It houses three large conference rooms where the most important meetings at the presidential retreat are held. British Prime Minister Winston Churchill was the first foreign leader to visit the presidential retreat, crafting war strategies with President Roosevelt in 1943. In September 1978, President Jimmy Carter, Egyptian President Anwar Sadat, and Israeli Prime Minister Menachem Begin met for nearly two weeks to produce the Camp David Accords. In keeping with the retreat's informal and rugged atmosphere, guests typically wear casual attire during their stay at Camp David. Colt was amused by the practice of dignitaries and senior government officials dressing down for what, in some cases, was perhaps the most important meetings of their career. Denim and boots were more common than wool suits and oxfords.

The Camp David staff had meticulously cleaned the main conference room in preparation for the president's meeting but had somehow missed a large, ornate spider web that spanned one of the large vertical windows at the room's end. Colt wasn't aware of how long he'd been staring at the spider and her beautiful web when someone kicked him under the table. He looked up and noticed everyone seated at the large conference table was staring at him, including the president.

"Secretary Garrett, did you hear my question?" asked the irritated president. Colt picked up his pen and began making notes on the paper pad before him. After a few seconds, he responded, "Yes, Madam President. Just gathering my thoughts." He calmly thought back over the past few minutes when he was much more interested in the spider than in what Vice President Carlisle was saying. He and Carlisle had a challenging relationship dating back to when the vice president had served under his command. The former admiral, now vice president, sought every opportunity to challenge Colt's expertise in foreign affairs and national defense issues. Today's meeting was about US defense policy in the Pacific regarding China and Russia. Even though Colt, of course, hadn't been paying attention to Carlisle's rant on the subject—he'd heard it so many times before that he felt he could repeat it word for word. He took a reasoned chance that the president had asked for his opinion of the vice president's position.

He placed his pen down, clasped his hands together, rested his elbows on the table, and leaned forward. He looked around the table to see the president seated directly across from him, with Carlisle sitting on her left. Eric Paynter, White House chief of staff, was placed on her right, and beyond Eric was NSA Travis Webb. Chairman of the Joint Chiefs of Staff General David

Schmidt was seated to Colt's right, while CIA director Michele Walker was on his left. At Colt's far left was the director of national intelligence, Janine Chun, the former US Representative from Texas.

"Madam President," Colt began, "I'm very familiar with the vice president and the NSA's position regarding our exercises with the other QUAD nations. Defense and the Joint Chiefs believe we must continue to oppose China's increasing claims of sovereignty over vast areas of the Pacific. We must protect our sea lines of communication to allow commerce and other maritime traffic to navigate freely. Our Pacific allies firmly support this position, and our exercises demonstrate our resolve to remain a major regional player. I remain unconvinced that if we were to reduce our posture in the Pacific and disengage with our allies, China and Russia would withdraw their objections and not continue their aggressive actions in the region. Nature abhors a vacuum, and I believe if we change course now, we risk the Chinese becoming even bolder with their territorial demands. Now is the time to reaffirm our commitment to the Quadrilateral Security Dialogue. And your upcoming attendance at the United Nations celebration in San Francisco would be the appropriate public venue to announce our position."

Colt knew that the majority of the president's advisors preferred a more conciliatory approach to China, but he knew in his gut they were dead wrong. As a historian, Colt could list the times that a policy of appeasement or misunderstanding led to hostilities or war. Churchill's *The Second World War* and John F. Kennedy's *Why England Slept* addressed the issue. China and the United States made crucial miscalculations during the Korean War, which turned the conflict into a prolonged and deadly struggle still ongoing. The Vietnam War proved that a nation could easily back into a war without a clear and broadly understood foreign policy.

The vice president looked down the table at Travis Webb and cleared his throat. "It seems our defense secretary is determined to continue to poke China in the eye, blithely unconcerned about the consequences. We have common ground with China on several issues, not the least of which is fair trade. Our economies are inexorably linked, and the intelligence community supports a more reasonable approach to our activities in the Pacific. Madam President, you've mentioned your plan to reaffirm our commitment to the QUAD when you visit San Francisco. Travis and I think this decision should be reconsidered. Even the ODNI agrees." The ODNI, or Office of the Director of National Intelligence, was established in 2004 after the September 11th terrorist attacks. The Intelligence Reform and Terrorism Prevention Act created the new agency to oversee the seventeen-organization American intelligence community by improving integration and information-sharing. Many in the CIA felt ODNI was a superfluous organization that didn't add value and only served to reduce the esteem and influence of the CIA. The jealousy between the two organizations was inevitable, and conflict regarding intelligence estimates was common.

CIA Director Michelle Walker set her ceramic coffee cup on the table loud enough that everyone turned to her. "Not all intelligence agencies concur with that assessment, Mr. Vice President," she said. "I've seen the ODNI's paper on this issue, and the CIA holds an opposing view. We believe that naval exercises with our allies in the Pacific demonstrate a firm resolve to maintain the status quo and do not at all communicate a posture that might invoke a reaction from the Chinese. We recommend that the United States reconfirm our commitment to the QUAD, and the United Nations anniversary in San Francisco would be a timely opportunity to support the alliance publicly."

The meeting continued for several hours until Eric Paynter whispered into the president's ear. María seemed to think for a moment, and then she gathered the papers in front of her into a leather padfolio. She stood up, and it was clear the meeting was over. Everyone came to their feet. "Thank you, folks. I want you to know that I appreciate you joining us here today and sharing your positions on our activities in the Pacific and our allies in the region. I need to think about this a bit more this evening after dinner. Let's plan to get together again tomorrow morning before returning to the city. Colt, would you remain for a few moments? I have a question about the defense appropriation."

After everyone left the conference room, María Hernández walked to the end of the room and closed the door. She motioned to the small table, and Colt joined her. "I wanted you to know right away that I'm not going to change my mind about reaffirming the QUAD. Michelle's idea about using the UN celebration to announce our decision is sound."

"I'm glad to hear that, Madam President. I sincerely believe this is in our best interest, and San Francisco would be the perfect place to make the announcement. I'm also looking forward to our stopover in Seattle. It's important to show administration support for some of the high-tech firms in the Pacific Northwest."

"Can you join me for a walk after dinner, Colt? I have something else I'd like to discuss. And we can get in some steps!"

## Camp David Trail

The sun had just begun to set at the secluded presidential retreat, with the sky turning a deep shade of red with scattered white cauliflower-shaped cumulous clouds. White-tailed deer grazed on the lush undergrowth vegetation and scoured the tulip poplar tree trunks up as far as their necks could reach. President Nixon's wife Pat, who enjoyed walking the Camp David trails, had mentioned to Nancy Reagan, "Without Camp David, you'll go stir crazy." President Nixon, who found shelter from the storm there during the Watergate scandal, wrote, "I find that up there on top of a mountain, it is easier for me to get on top of the job."

"I just love it here," President Hernández said as much to herself as to Colt as they walked alone on the winding trail through the woods, except for the discreet but ever-vigilant protection of the president's security detail that walked several paces behind the president. The two Secret Service special agents were dressed as casually as the retreat's guests, but they were armed and prepared for any threat to the chief executive, codename ROUGHNECK. It was rumored that the White House Communications Agency had assigned the president the codename due to her background in the oil and gas industry. But Colt thought it was because of her reputation for dealing with a problematic Congress. Colt's codename was PATRIOT, an ironic nod to his dislike of the New England NFL team. One of the USSS agents spoke softly into a voice-activated mic, "Team Alpha with ROUGHNECK and PATRIOT on the Aspen Trail." Others in a nearby operations center closely monitored the radio traffic and video images transmitted from a loitering drone. "Roger, Alpha. Control out."

"Madam President, you mentioned earlier that you had something on your mind. What can I help you with?"

"Well, Colt," began the president," I've been talking with Eric about Travis Webb. I'm not sure why President Harrison appointed him after Jonathan died, but I've decided to replace him, and I wanted to get your perspective on that and to get your thinking about whom you'd like to see as his replacement."

Colt was taken aback by the president's candor regarding

Webb. He hadn't realized that the White House shared his negative opinion of the man.

"To be frank, I just don't trust him," Colt replied. "As I'm sure you know, we've had our differences, but my concerns go well beyond the personal." Colt shared his doubts about the national security advisor with the president as they walked down the paved path. He turned to be sure the security detail was far enough behind and continued. "For the past few months, the Pentagon's been attempting to trace the source of several intelligence leaks. While the investigation is still underway, Webb has surfaced on a short list of potential suspects."

The president continued to walk silently as she considered what Colt had just said. The implications of her national security advisor leaking classified intelligence were disastrous to national security and her campaign for a second term. She was about to ask Colt a question when the two closest agents grabbed her arms and rushed her toward the Aspen Lodge. "Control, Alpha acknowledges and is moving ROUGHNECK and PATRIOT to Aspen." Colt struggled to keep up with the protection detail as they hustled the president across the grass field and into the safety of the presidential lodge. Once inside, the team moved down a flight of stairs and through a heavy security door into what appeared to be a secure set of rooms below the president's living quarters. María and Colt rested on a sofa while the protection team contacted the operations center on telephone sets attached to the room's wall.

"What's going on, Jason?" asked a rattled María after she drank from a water bottle one of the agents had given her.

"Madam President," the senior agent responded, "a small, single-engine airplane entered the prohibited airspace over Camp David. The pilot didn't respond to FAA warnings, and two F-16s from the 121$^{st}$ Fighter Squadron out of Joint Base Andrews were vectored to intercept."

Colt could hear low-flying jets overhead despite being in an underground bunker. He knew the Air National Guard had air defense responsibilities over the continental United States. Pilots had busted the restricted airspace before, so he hoped this pilot had just made a stupid error that would result in a warning, monetary fine, or a revoked pilot's license.

The agent hung up the phone and unlocked the security door. "All clear, Madam President. Just some Joe Cessna out trying to impress his date with a low pass over Camp David. His radio was out, so he didn't respond to the controller's warning. I guess a pair of F-16s dropping flares in front of him finally got his attention. The Air National Guard is escorting him to a military field where the FAA will have some questions for him. Not a good way to end a date!"

The president and Colt stood up and thanked the agents. María turned to Colt. "Mr. Secretary, I don't know about you, but I could use a drink. Care to join me upstairs?"

## The Birch Cabin, Camp David

The Birch Cabin was just a few hundred yards from the president's quarters in the Aspen Lodge. The small, modest structure featured two bedrooms, two baths, and a large living room that opened to a paved patio. The living room featured a beautifully maintained vaulted ceiling and a large stone fireplace. Colt and Lenny sat facing the fire in high-back brown leather armchairs with their feet resting on matching ottomans. The furniture reminded Colt of what he guessed would have been found in a Manhattan nightclub in the 1930s. The chairs might have been that old.

"I wonder how many people have sat exactly where we're sitting now, Lenny. Feet up, a nice fire, and enjoying a fine bourbon."

Lenny Wilson looked over at Colt. "Probably more than you can imagine, boss. I do hope they clean between guests!"

Colt considered the dignitaries that must have stayed in the cabin over the years and smiled at Lenny's joke. "Good point. I suppose somebody will sit in this same chair someday and hope they cleaned up after us!"

Lenny poured another two fingers of bourbon into their glasses. "So, how did you end up having drinks in the president's cabin? I want to get the story straight if anyone asks. Or should I stick with what happens at Camp David, stays at Camp David?"

Colt chuckled and was reminded how much he would miss having Lenny as his executive assistant, confidant, and friend. "As I said, nothing happened. I think the incident with the plane spooked her, and she needed to calm her nerves a bit. She's the only one in that big lodge. I was surprised the first gentleman didn't accompany her on this trip."

The first gentleman was María's husband, Ethan Davis, codename RATTLER. Most people thought he was assigned the codename because he earned his MBA at Florida A&M. A few suspected it was because of his reputation among White House staff as a snake. Ethan lived separately from María in their home in Houston, where he was president of Hernández Oil. It was common knowledge within the Beltway that their marriage was in serious trouble and had been only maintained for María's political benefit. Some said the couple's decision not to have children was at fault. There were also stories circulating that Ethan felt emasculated as the president's spouse, relegated to speaking to church groups, advocating for disadvantaged people, and decorating the White House for holidays and state dinners. It was a far cry from his responsibilities running a major petroleum corporation, even if his father-in-law founded and chaired the company. It's better to be a big fish in a small pond than a small one in the most enormous pond.

"You'd be the only one in Washington that would be surprised RATTLER didn't make the trip. You've heard the rumors, boss."

"Of course, I have. We just don't have to spread them." Colt got up from the chair and walked to the restroom.

Lenny could tell he had pushed the issue too far. Something may have happened in that lodge after all. He decided to change the subject. After Colt returned, he noticed Lenny was texting on a new phone.

"Isn't that the new iPhone with the high-res camera? I didn't know they had been released yet. When did you find it?"

"I didn't find it, boss. It was given to me. After accepting the Cambridge International job, they issued it to me. All the execs get them. Cambridge even covers the monthly service costs. And check this out."

Colt read the text on Lenny's new business card aloud. "Lenard G. Wilson, Director of Operations, Cambridge International." He handed the card back to Lenny.

"Really nice. A new phone number, too?"

"Yep. 857 area code. I'll be moving the family to Boston. Good for the kids to be closer to my mom." Lenny looked at his other phone. "Boss, it sounds like the Veep and the Creep couldn't convince the president to cancel her trip to San Francisco or change her mind about the QUAD. I bet they're plotting how to take another run at POTUS in the Hemlock Cabin right now."

"Lenny, I warned you several times about referring the vice president and the NSA with those terms. Besides, God only knows if we're being recorded right now."

"Oh, crap! You think so?" Lenny began scrutinizing the living room's light fixtures and wall art.

"Probably not," said Colt, but he secretly enjoyed the fear that the idea of remote monitoring put into his old friend. Lenny finally sat back down in his chair and turned to Colt.

"Tell me about those granddaughters of yours. Will you get to see them when you stop over in Seattle?"

Colt's daughter Allie and her husband Kyle lived in Gig Harbor, Washington, where they owned a small but growing tech consulting firm and were raising a family. Colt's twin granddaughters, Abigale and Angela, were twenty-two months old, and Colt wished he could spend more time with them.

"I hope so. Allie says the girls are changing daily, and we try to video chat on Sundays. But I want to be in their lives. I know these days go by too quickly. I've missed too much already."

Lenny knew his boss had struggled with loneliness since his wife had passed a few years ago. The twins would have been a great distraction, but they lived on the other side of the country. Colt had briefly considered running for Congress, hoping to spend more time in the Northwest, but decided against starting a political campaign when he realized he'd still be spending time flying between coasts. Colt planned to resign as defense secretary at the end of the president's first term and move into the seventy-foot motor yacht he purchased after he sold his home in Olympia. The phenomenal housing market gave Colt a windfall of cash when he sold the house. He finally realized his dream of owning a liveaboard boat and had found moorage on a dock in Gig Harbor within biking distance of Allie's home. The idea of leaving government service for good and spending his free time with his granddaughters while messing about on his boat sounded ideal to Colt, and he was convinced that his late wife would have approved.

"Colt, did you bring the plans of that boat of yours with you?

And what did you eventually decide to name her?"

Colt took another sip of bourbon and closed his eyes. "Liberty Risk."

## Southbound Interstate 5, Seattle

In 1967, General Motors produced a limited version of the now-iconic Chevrolet Camaro to qualify for the Sports Car Club of America's Trans Am class. The Z/28 featured a 302 cubic inch V-8 engine that generated 290 horsepower. A firmed-up suspension improved handling, and exterior cues included dual hood and trunk stripes and rally wheels on red-stripe tires. Only 600 Z/28s were built that year, making it a desirable car in 1967, when Trevor Steele bought it. Trevor had just won the bull riding championship in the National Finals Rodeo, the "Superbowl of Rodeos." The day after his historic ride, he strutted into the downtown Oklahoma City Chevrolet dealership and paid $6,000 cash for a brand-new Bolero Red Z/28, complete with broad white racing stripes on the hood and trunk. He drove that car back to his parent's small cattle ranch near Whitefish, Montana, where he placed the solid silver NFR Championship belt buckle on the hearth above his parent's stone fireplace for all to see. It would be the last rodeo buckle Trevor would earn because two months later, an angry steer crushed his right leg in a squeeze chute. His broken leg healed, but with the damage to his knee, he'd walk with a pronounced limp for the rest of his life.

After his parents moved into a retirement home in town, Trevor and his new wife, Elsie, moved into the main house with their young son, Wyatt. The boy loved growing up on the ranch and learning what it meant to be a Montana cowboy. The retired rodeo champ worked with his son at every opportunity to help the boy understand the secrets of bull riding. Life was good until the terrible day in September when Trevor unexpectedly showed up at Whitefish Middle School to tell his twelve-year-old son that Elsie had collapsed in the barn of an aneurysm. "Your mom must have been lying there since morning, Wyatt. I came home for lunch and found her next to the door."

Things changed after that. Wyatt spent hours with his dad learning rodeo skills, but with his mother's death, he started having trouble belonging in school. Classes were easy enough, and he managed to letter in four sports in high school, including rodeo. He found success in rodeo and even won the state championship. But interacting with others challenged him, and he developed a reputation for having a bad temper. Run-ins with local law enforcement became common, but luckily, the local rodeo star was never arrested. After one of Montana's senators offered Wyatt an appointment to the US Naval Academy, his father walked him to the ranch vehicle storage barn. He lifted a canvas tarp off an immaculate 1967 Camaro Z/28.

"I want you to know how proud I am of you, son, for getting into the academy. Rodeo is fun, but it's not a career. After you earn your commission, I want you to have this car. I never could work the clutch with this bad knee. A car like this deserves to be driven, son."

Years later, Wyatt downshifted into third gear to pass the silver Prius on the right that had been going under the speed limit in the passing lane. The powerful V8 growled as Wyatt pressed the accelerator and rocketed the Z/28 down the freeway across the Ship Canal Bridge toward Seattle. It had been eleven years since he took the oath of office as a newly minted ensign on a sunny and humid Annapolis day, and he still enjoyed driving the classic red Camaro whenever he could. After a less-than-stellar career as a naval aviator, Lieutenant Commander Wyatt Steele wondered if he'd be allowed to serve the twenty years required to retire with a pension. He needed to be promoted to commander with its silver oak leaves to be assured of getting the twenty years. And he was pretty sure that he'd never see that promotion. Wyatt exited the freeway and followed the frontage road until he saw the sign "Boeing Museum of Flight." He parked the Camaro several spaces from the other cars and entered the museum's entrance.

"Good afternoon, Lieutenant Commander Steele. Welcome to the Museum of Flight. I'm Dave Ryan. We spoke on the phone."

Wyatt shook Dave's outstretched hand. "How did you know it was me?"

Dave chuckled. "Well, son, I saw those gold oak leaves on your collar and the name badge. I didn't go to college, but I got eyes, and the Air Force did teach us how to read."

Wyatt laughed. He forgot that he was still in uniform, having come straight from the University of Washington, where he taught students about aviation. The man behind the counter was in his late sixties, about five foot five, with thinning gray hair, a round, friendly face, and eyes that sparkled when he spoke. Wyatt towered over the older man at a bit over six foot two.

"Right. Of course. Sorry about that, Mr. Ryan."

"We work with first names here at the museum, Wyatt. Call me Dave. Let's walk over to my office."

Wyatt followed Dave around a corner and down a narrow hallway that ended at a door marked "Private." Dave opened the wooden door and led Wyatt inside the small office.

"Have a seat. Can I offer you a cup of coffee?"

While Dave started brewing a pot of coffee, Wyatt scanned the room. The large metal desk was the same as in countless government offices. Wyatt's attention shifted to the wall behind Dave's desk.

"Thirty years in the Air Force, all of it as a flight engineer and maintainer," said Dave as he pushed a switch on the old coffee maker at the back of the room. "Retired as a chief master sergeant, an E-9. That'd be a master chief in your navy."

Dave handed Wyatt a porcelain coffee cup that must have been white at one point, but years of use had stained the mug several shades of brown. The two men sat down, and Dave opened a paper file on his desk.

"I was excited to receive your application to volunteer at the museum. We usually only get relics like me who want to hang out with old airplanes. What brings you here?"

Wyatt thought for a moment. "I'm single. I'm living alone and working as an instructor at the UW. The job isn't very demanding, and I'm looking for volunteer work to keep me busy after work. I have a connection to Boeing airplanes. I was an aircraft commander in my E-6 squadron at Tinker Air Force Base."

"I was based at Tinker, but that was decades before you. And you say you flew the E-6 Mercury? Hell, that's just the Navy's secret squirrel version of a 707! Do you have any maintenance experience?"

Wyatt nodded. "Yep, I was the avionics division officer. When I wasn't flying, I mostly did management stuff, but I also attended a few Boeing maintenance courses to better understand what the sailors were doing."

"Interesting." Dave pressed his fingertips together and smiled. "I think I have something that might interest you!"


**Ministry of State Security Headquarters, Haidian District, Beijing**

Sun Ping gazed across the lush gardens and watched a crimson sun slowly set beyond the Summer Palace. The magnificent structure was the third palace to be built on that site. British and

French soldiers looted and burned the first during the Second Opium War. The Eight-Nation Alliance destroyed the second palace during the Boxer Rebellion around 1900. The structure and gardens Sun could admire through his office windows were constructed within a few years and served as the summer residence for the imperial family after the abdication of Puyi, the Last Emperor. The Beijing city government decided to convert the Summer Palace into a public park, and it continued to attract between 70,000 and 100,000 visitors each day. The Summer Palace is a UNESCO World Heritage Site, one of the most well-preserved imperial gardens.

Minister Sun Ping returned to his desk and smiled, wondering how many of the Summer Palace's visitors knew that the building on the edge of the gardens housed perhaps the most secretive intelligence organizations in the world. The Ministry of State Security, or MSS, is China's security, intelligence, and secret police agency. Some have described the agency as a combination of the CIA and FBI, with a stated mission of "the security of the country through effective measures against enemy agents, spies, and counter-revolutionary activities designed to sabotage, destabilize or overthrow China's socialist system." With elements at the city, provincial, and township levels throughout China, the MSS and Minister Sun Ping were respected and feared throughout the land.

Minister Sun also served as general secretary of the Central Political and Legal Affairs Commission of the Communist Party of China (CCP). In this role, Sun represented the CCP in overseeing China's judicial, law enforcement, and intelligence systems. In essence, Sun was responsible for overseeing himself. He was in the perfect position to conspire with the Russians against the Americans without the interference or knowledge of anyone else in China.

Sun opened the thick binder on his desk and began making notes, pen on paper. For obvious reasons, no record of his actions regarding the Shanghai Protocol would be committed to any electronic format. More than anyone, Sun knew that nothing saved in an electronic device could be completely protected from those determined to break into the system. Besides, Sun considered himself an experienced practitioner of intelligence tradecraft and often thought the old ways were the most secure.

The meetings with the Russians in Shanghai had gone better than expected. He was pleased to discover they were as convinced that the American president needed to be removed and replaced with someone more sympathetic to Chinese and Russian interests. The president's plan to visit Seattle before flying to San Francisco was fortunate because his agency had invested many years of money and resources in that city. Sun had consistently considered the significant expenditure a long-term investment that now appeared to be paying off in the coming days. He made several notes before returning to the binder in a section marked "Assets." He smiled when he turned to the dossier for an agent he recognized as an old classmate from his days at university. They had shared many cups of tea—and occasionally something a bit stronger—when debating the causes and impacts of the Chinese Communist Revolution. Sun thought his quiet and studious friend would be perfect for intelligence work. He personally managed the recruitment process to make sure the agency's bureaucracy didn't miss the opportunity to add his friend to their stable of intelligence operatives. Sun made several more notes before turning to the next dossier in the section. He wasn't familiar with this agent, but considering the number of agents based in Seattle, it wasn't surprising. He closed the binder and locked it into his safe. All the plan's elements were coming together, and the necessary resources and personnel were positioned and prepared to act. He felt confident that, given just a bit of luck, the shared goal of removing the American president could be achieved. Now, he began to focus on his contingency plans should something unexpected occur. Things rarely went precisely as planned.

# Day Two

## The LeDroit Society, Washington DC

"I'm going out to meet Congressman Bennett, Sandi. And I have a few things to pick up at the pharmacy. I shouldn't be too long."

"Okay, Becci. Take your time!"

Becci Quinn stepped through the foundation's front door and walked down the stone steps before turning right on 2nd Street. She stopped three times to look at clothing displayed in shop windows before crossing the busy street in the middle of the block and continuing down the opposite sidewalk. She crossed the street to look at the apples at the corner fruit stand. Tuesday morning traffic was light, and it was relatively easy for the experienced Russian intelligence officer to confirm that any of the numerous counterintelligence agencies in town weren't following her. She noticed the four small sedans parked in the shared ride lot in front of St. George's Episcopal Church. Weddings and funerals were good business for Uber and Lyft drivers. She waved to the driver in a white Honda Civic and climbed into the rear seat. "Good morning, Mohammed. I'm Becci."

The driver grunted, "Morning," and pulled the car onto the street. She'd already provided the driver her destination when she ordered the car, so no conversation was necessary as they headed south toward the Navy Yard on the Potomac River. Twenty minutes later, the driver turned into a large and near-vacant parking lot directly across from Nationals Park. He opened the

49

small cooler on the front seat, removed a sandwich from Bub and Pops, and tossed it to his passenger. "A half Philly Special. No mayo. Okay, Becci?"

Becci unwrapped the sandwich and took a bite. "Perfect, Mohammed! You remembered!"

"Nothing but the very best for my very best customer! Of course, I remember your fondness for these sandwiches, which are not good for you. Thank you for meeting me at such short notice!" He carefully scanned the parking lot as Becci joined him in the front seat. The pair had worked together for many years, but not as driver and passenger. Mohammed's real name was Yuri Levitsky, a colonel in the Russian GRU. He was assigned as Becci's controller ever since she entered the United States by crossing the Canadian border under a false identity. That had been many years ago; his young operative had been a quick study. Becci had exceeded all expectations, and his superiors in Moscow remained perennially pleased. And that was an excellent thing. Although he supervised more than a dozen other deep-cover operatives, Becci was his favorite because she was one of his best and reminded him of his niece in St. Petersburg.

"Here, have a bottle of water." Mohammed watched Becci finish the sandwich and handed her a light blue folder. "They're calling it the Shanghai Protocol. God knows why. I've summarized the key elements on the first page. Carefully memorize it because you can't take it with you. I'll send you supporting materials and additional information via the usual method."

Becci paused as three teenage boys on skateboards approached the parked car. They stared at the couple in while they circled the car twice. Suddenly, they broke off and headed across the deserted parking lot. Becci waited for a few minutes to be sure they were gone. She carefully read each sentence individually and then the entire page twice. She placed the operation summary on her lap and closed her eyes for a full minute before opening them and reading the document for a third time. She'd developed the memorization method during her training days at an obscure facility outside of Moscow.

"Okay. I understand the principal elements of the operation, and I also understand that you want me to engage my two assets in town to execute their tasks as indicated here. I must admit I'm impressed by the operation's scope."

Becci was surprised by the audacity of the operation and its potential impact if it succeeded.

"The operation's success depends entirely on both of my assets being willing to step forward at the appropriate time to effect the change in government. You understand there would be no backing out for them if the operation fails. They'll be burned. We could never use them again." She didn't mention to her controller that she would also be at significant personal risk in the event of failure. A botched attack on a head of state would result in an exhaustive investigation with unlimited scope and resources. Even if she were to avoid arrest and safely escape to Russia, her country's security forces would never trust her again.

Mohammed took the folder from Becci's hands and placed it into his backpack. "These two men have much to lose but much more to gain. Great rewards come to those willing to risk a great deal. I don't think you will have a problem convincing them. When do you think you can meet with them?"

"Soon. Perhaps later today. It'll be easier to get to Webb than the vice president. I'll let you know." Becci was concerned that she might not be able to convince her assets to do what the GRU had planned. It was one thing to share secrets with a foreign power, but quite another to conspire to remove a sitting president.

## The Russell-Knox Building, Marine Corps Base Quantico, Virginia

Cal Shipley hated the CBS television series "NCIS" more than anyone could imagine. The popular TV show was now in its twentieth season and had succeeded in making the Navy's investigative organization one of the most visible entities in the federal government. Friends and acquaintances continually asked Cal about the series and how closely it portrayed the actual agency. The subject came up at dinner parties, parent-teacher conferences, and sporting events. People wanted to know if Cal knew the actor Mark Harmon and what he was like. Over the years, Cal answered the questions to the best of his ability and tried to change the subject as soon as possible. Even Cal's wife, Meredith, contributed to the problem, commonly agreeing to her friends' requests for the actors' autographs. It was all because Cal Shipley was the director of the Naval Criminal Investigative Service, the real one.

The NCIS was previously called the Naval Investigative Service. In 1992, the agency was renamed as a part of a reorganization following the wake of the problematic investigation of the Navy's Tailhook scandal. The Department of the Navy changed the director position from an active-duty rear admiral to a civilian appointee who would report to the Secretary of the Navy via the Navy's general counsel. Today, the Navy tasks NCIS with naval security, counterintelligence, and criminal investigations. Regarding maritime security, the NCIS created Protective Service Details to protect the secretary of the navy, visiting dignitaries, and senior military commanders. NCIS counterintelligence responsibilities include antiterrorism and surveillance countermeasures. Most of the agency's efforts are related to criminal investigations, including witness protection, drug-suppression activities, and direct support to afloat unit commanders.

One of the inaccuracies portrayed in the television show was that the NCIS headquarters was located at the Navy Yard on the Potomac River. The agency headquarters resided in the Russell-Knox Building at Quantico, where it shared the building with the Air Force Office of Special Investigations, the Defense Intelligence Agency, the Defense Security Service, and the Army Criminal Investigative Division (CID). The military agencies valued the additional security afforded by having the building on an active Marine Corps base.

"Director Shipley, Special Agent DeSantis is here for your meeting."

Cal looked up from his desk and saw his executive assistant standing next to Anna DeSantis, one of the agents seconded to the Army's CID executive protection detail. The pilot-exchange program placed agents, Army and Navy investigators, in one another's agencies for a tour of duty. The idea was to increase cooperation between the two occasionally competing agencies. Cal didn't believe the program was achieving its purpose and intended to terminate the exchange program after the current group of agents completed their tours. A singular benefit of the exchange program to NCIS was that it placed Anna, one of Cal's best and most promising agents, on the secretary of defense's executive protection detail. There was nothing wrong about having an NCIS agent standing next to SECDEF.

"Anna, please take a seat. What can I do for you? Are you ready for your trip to the West Coast?"

"Yes, Director Shipley. Our CID detail has coordinated with the Secret Service regarding the flights, lodging, and other logistics. They have the lead, obviously, but we have responsibility for SECDEF within their overall protection package for POTUS. We'll be wheels up early tomorrow morning and plan to be in Seattle later in the day. After we land, I'll have more details about the San Francisco event."

"That's fine. How old is that son of yours? He must be keeping Kevin busy."

Anna shifted in her chair. "Oh, thanks for asking, sir. Ollie just turned two, and Kevin just got him potty trained. Kevin thinks it hilarious whenever helicopters fly low by our property. Ollie hears them coming before we do and runs for the window to watch them fly over our house. Kevin's looking forward to returning to work but is already worried about leaving Ollie. They've bonded closely, and we appreciate the agency's support."

Kevin Orr was an NCIS special agent on a two-year extended paternity leave from his duties. This was another program that Cal didn't support. He was concerned that agents being gone for such an extended period would require extensive training to regain their previous levels of effectiveness. Anna and Kevin had met years ago while stationed on the USS Ronald Reagan. During that tour, Anna first met Colt Garrett, and as a result, the new defense secretary created the special agent exchange program. Anna's close relationship with Colt Garrett was always on Cal's mind whenever he spoke with her. One never knew what information Anna might share with the senior cabinet member. There were even rumors of Garrett running for elected office, and Cal wanted to make sure that Anna DeSantis had no reason to complain to Garrett about NCIS.

"I appreciate you keeping me up to speed on the trip. Please let us know if we can do anything to support the event in San Francisco. And make sure to tell Kevin that I know the field operation staff is eager to have him back from his leave. Was there anything else you wanted to discuss?"

Anna brought up the important topic she had been considering for months. "Director, I wanted you to know that I'm seriously considering resigning from NCIS. I realize this is unexpected, but I need to be a better mother to Ollie. I don't want to miss any more special years with him. Sorry for springing this on you, particularly now, but I wanted to keep you informed."

Cal couldn't comprehend how someone would even consider leaving behind such a promising career to focus on their children. He had never considered it, and his children had turned out fine. Perhaps more importantly, if Anna resigned from NCIS, he'd lose his inside connection to the SECDEF's office. Cal carefully considered what he said next.

"Let's not rush things, Anna. Plenty of time to consider all your options. Why don't you think about it for a few weeks, and I can explore how we might be able to make this work for you?"

Anna stood up. "Thank you, Director. I've very much enjoyed my time at the agency. I think it's time to start a new chapter in my life. But I'll definitely think about it."

After Anna left his office, Cal wondered if he should try to find another agent to replace her on the SECDEF detail. She seemed intent on leaving NCIS, had already thought about it.

## Hale Broadcasting, 30 Rockefeller Plaza, New York City

Carissa Curtis looked at the large stack of forms before her, wondering why they weren't available online. An IRS Form W2, publicity release, healthcare insurance enrolment, conflict-of-interest affidavit, liability waiver, and other documents that Hale Broadcasting requires of all new employees. Hale would be a dramatic change for the young but promising television news reporter. Her previous employer, CBS, had merged with Viacom to create Paramount Global, a colossal media and entertainment corporation that operated 170 networks and claimed over 700 million subscribers.

In contrast, Hale Broadcasting Systems was a private business cable firm owned and operated by Spencer Hale. More importantly, Carissa's role at HBS might transition from being a special features correspondent to one of the network's anchor positions. Hale Broadcasting included the Hale News Network, Hale Sports Network, and Hale Business Network. Spencer Hale was born in 1948 and, after a brief period as an analyst with the CIA during the Vietnam War, was one of the early pioneers of the fledgling cable television industry. Hale Broadcast's success had made its founder an extremely wealthy man. Forbes documented his liquid assets, not including his HBS or real estate holdings equity, at over three billion dollars. His only child, Zoey, was the only positive result of a disastrous marriage to an actress and the sole heir of a tobacco tycoon. Zoey was single and 52 years old. She served on the HBS board and would be one of the wealthiest women in the country when her father passed.

Carissa finished with the personnel forms and carried the tall stack of paper to the woman sitting at the desk next to the window. "I think I filled them all out correctly," offered Carissa as the stern older woman carefully examined each piece of paper. After several minutes of silence, the human resources staffer smiled thinly. "These all seem to be in order, Ms. Curtis. The only thing left for you today is to meet Mr. Hale. Please follow me."

The Hale Broadcasting executive suite was ten floors above the human resources offices, providing a spectacular view of the city. Spencer Hale's expansive office faced south, and this morning, he found himself enjoying the view of the Empire State Building. Built during the Great Depression, the Art Deco skyscraper was the world's first building with over 100 floors. Slightly to the left, Spenser could see the Statue of Liberty. Even though both structures were built decades ago, he believed they still uniquely represented Manhattan and the entire country. He watched a ferry cross the harbor when his daughter interrupted his thoughts.

"Dad, you even listening? Now is not the time!"

Spencer enjoyed his daughter Zoey more than anyone he knew, but sometimes he found her to be a pain in the ass.

"Damn it, Zoey. It just makes sense. I don't know why you can't see that! We've been talking about this for years!" Spencer walked over to an oversized leather chair, sat, leaned back, and interlaced his fingers behind his head. Zoey Hale leaned forward in her chair. "Dad, I don't think I'm ready to replace you as CEO, not yet. I'm more than comfortable running the board's finance committee and being involved with the backend business. I'm very good at it. Still, I don't think I'm qualified to run the whole operation, particularly the news, sports, and entertainment operations. Those people have enormous egos. I've watched you work magic with them. That's not my skill set, Dad. And you know it."

Spencer knew that his daughter was a better and more intelligent person than he was. The only thing holding her back was her need to be entirely sure of something before she accepted a new responsibility. He held a different perspective, strongly believing that regardless of the opportunity or challenge, he would conquer it and succeed. It wasn't that he was better at business than his daughter. It was just that he had a higher tolerance for risk.

"Who do you mean by 'those people,' Zoey? Come on."

"You, come on, Dad. You know that I mean the talent, the on-air personalities. They call themselves journalists, but most focus on hair and makeup rather than getting the news right. God knows you hire them for looks, not their brains."

Spencer knew the conversation had progressed precisely as he had planned. He tried to keep a poker face when he pressed a button on the phone console. "Steven, please show Ms. Curtis into my office."

After Carissa sat down at the small conference table, she could feel the tension between the CEO of Hale Broadcasting and his daughter. More than twenty years younger than Zoey Hale, Carissa felt uncomfortable as Zoey stared at her for what seemed like an eternity.

"Carissa, I'm Spencer Hale. Allow me to introduce Zoey Hale, one of our board directors. Zoey, this is Carissa Curtis, our newest hire. Carissa, we want you to know how happy we are that you agreed to join our HBS team. We're excited to provide this opportunity for you as well. I've been impressed with your work at CBS and believe you've made a great career decision."

Zoey was still angry that her father had set her up for this meeting. She grudgingly had to admit the old man, nearly eighty, could still manipulate her like a puppeteer at times. She would have to show him and the newly hired reporter that she could hold her own. And why did this young woman look so familiar?

"Please tell me, Ms. Curtis, why did you decide to leave a major broadcast network for our cable organization?"

Carissa glanced at Spencer and then Zoey, trying to understand what was happening. She decided to answer the question truthfully.

"Ms. Hale, I decided to work in an organization where I can do more than just read a teleprompter with a script written by producers. I want to find the story behind the story, the real issues driving the positions that most news organizations only report. The news cycle is getting so rapid that the media is focused on timeliness much more than accuracy. And I want to dig deeper into what drives our policymakers. My interview with Defense

Secretary Garrett exemplifies trying to understand the person behind the decisions."

Now Zoey realized why Carissa looked so familiar. It was the interview with Garrett. She had to admit that the special was one of the reasons why her father was trying to get the defense secretary to run for Congress. Carissa had succeeded in getting Garrett to show his personality on camera, something others had not been able to do. Carissa's connection to Colt Garrett put things in an entirely different light because Zoey had been spending her time with Garrett for the past few months. She decided to steer the conversation away from Colt before things became uncomfortable. "How do you see yourself fitting in here? Perhaps as an anchor?"

Carissa smiled and said, "Of course, every correspondent hopes to be an anchor someday. But I'd prefer to work on more in-depth pieces first and bring those stories to our audience. People will find value in those stories. That's the best way to differentiate the network from our competition."

After Carissa left the office, Spencer removed his glasses and returned to his desk. "What do you think of young Ms. Curtis? Impressive, right? And smart!"

"Certainly that," Zoey replied while she stood to return to her office. "I admit that she surprised me with her answers. You probably made the right decision to hire her."

"Thank you, dear. And it does appear that you can interact with our broadcast staff. Let's continue our discussions regarding your future tomorrow. I have another appointment I need to get to."

Curiosity made Zoey ask her father's assistant who his next appointment was.

"I don't know, Ms. Hale," said Steven. "The calendar just indicates 'private.'"

SHANGHAI PROTOCOL

## The Royal Café, Washington DC

Becci Quinn placed the menu on the small round table. "Tell me about the breakfast special."

"No problem! This morning, we feature our avocado sandwich with a fried egg, Royal cheese spread, heirloom tomatoes, arugula, and pickled shallots on a brioche bun. It's an excellent choice. Can I get you one?"

"That sounds great. Travis, should we make it two?"

National Security Advisor Travis Webb picked up the menu. "Not for me. I want two eggs over medium with a side of sourdough toast. Dry."

The young waiter collected their menus and stopped to speak with a couple at another table to see if they were ready to order.

"I hate it when wait staff say, 'No problem.' I mean, I didn't assume it would be a problem to take my order. And what's with him telling you that you made an excellent choice when you ordered? Did he mean that I didn't?"

Becci sighed and put down her phone. "Oh God, Travis. What's with you this morning? Cut him some slack. The guy was just trying to take our order!"

"Sorry, okay? I just got back from Maryland, and the traffic was abysmal. I thought we were going to have a full breakfast. What a piece of crap menu. Why do you even like this place?"

Becci immediately realized that Travis was in one of his moods. That happened from time to time. Anything that she might say would only make things worse. And she wanted him to keep his voice down. One of the keys to managing agents in the field was making them feel like they were in charge.

"Sorry about that. I just wanted to talk with you immediately; this place is close to the foundation. Let's eat our breakfast first

60

and then get some coffee to go. I want to stretch my legs a bit."

Twenty minutes later, the pair strolled down Florida Avenue with two cups of the house blend coffee. The morning rush hour traffic had subsided, and few pedestrians were on their side of the street. "Travis, I need to brief you on a new operation. This is going to take about an hour, okay?"

Travis had been a paid agent of Russian military intelligence for two years, and Becci was his covert operations officer. His relationship with the Russians started after he found himself in deep debt from his gambling addiction, and the GRU saved him from financial ruin. They'd also taken compromising photos of Travis accepting payments from them, photos that could be proof of his treason.

Travis agreed to provide low-level and mundane government information in return for the debt relief and a promise from the Russians not to publicize the images. That was only at first. Gradually, the Russians increased their demands for more sensitive information with higher security classification levels. Travis was bothered by his acts initially, but after a while, his interactions and information sharing with Becci became part of his identity. He had normalized and rationalized his new life as a traitor as the only way to cope with the reality of his situation. And besides, it had rewards beyond the generous payments to a secret bank account. The Russians had planned and crafted his succeeding the previous national security advisor, even though he was personally responsible for the old man's death.

"Travis," began Becci, "I need you to arrange a meeting with the vice president as soon as possible. We're in the early stages of a plan to have him succeed as president, and there are some specific actions he will need to take when directed." She paused. Looked hard at him. "You don't look shocked. I'm surprised."

"It isn't exactly earth-shattering news that you'd like to see

Carlisle replace Hernández. Unfortunately, the election is still two years away, and the president is determined to reaffirm US support for the QUAD next week in San Francisco. Carlisle and I tried to change her mind at Camp David yesterday, and we even convinced the State Department and most of the intelligence community to support our view. But she's listening to Garrett and the Joint Chiefs. Nothing more we can do."

Becci took the coffee cup from Travis's hand and placed it into a trash can. She paused and causally looked up and down the street. She noticed two women with strollers walking toward them. "Travis, let's cross here."

Satisfied they could not be overheard, she continued. "Yes, I know you both have worked to help us change White House policy regarding the Pacific, which is well appreciated at the highest levels. But what we have in mind is more immediate than the next election."

"What do you mean by more immediate, Becci? Not even an impeachment, which would take months, would prevent her from attending the celebration in San Francisco. Unless . . ."

Travis was beginning to understand what Becci and her superiors were planning but couldn't bring himself to say the words aloud. He and the vice president had been working for Moscow for some time, with different motivations, but neither he nor Carlisle had even contemplated what Becci seemed to be intimating. Was she about to ask them to assassinate President Hernández?

"Travis, are you okay? You need to breathe!"


## Defense Secretary's Office, The Pentagon

Lieutenant Commander Dan Garrett sat quietly while his

father, the secretary of defense, sat across from him, engaged in what Dan observed to be a very heated discussion with a defense contractor. "Damn it, Raymond, we can't take another delay! I realize it's costing you performance awards, but it's costing the Air Force a vital tool for our continental air defense. And the Canadians are very pissed. Your lobbyists won't be able to control what their defence minister will say about this mess to the press. This isn't over by a long shot, Raymond!" Colt slammed the handset into the console so hard that a piece of the phone broke off and flew across the room. He stared at the phone and shook his head.

"Contractors! I hate dealing with them. I know they're making tons of money despite what they say. It's the worst part of this job. And just once, I'd like to see a major weapons system come online within budget and on schedule. Now, what can I do for you, son?"

When the office door swung open, Dan was about to say something, and Lenny Wilson, Garretts's executive assistant, stormed in.

"Sorry, boss. Oh, hi Dan, I didn't know you were here! Boss, it looks like you'll have to testify in front of the Senate Armed Services Committee next Friday. I know you'll be just returning from San Francisco. Still, Senator Shelton insisted that you and the Joint Chiefs chairman appear before his committee to answer their questions about the Hermes system and why Fawthrop is pressing for a change order. They're concerned about another cost overrun. Hey, Dan, what's new?"

"Next Friday, Lenny? Why do they always want to meet on Fridays? We'll be exhausted after the UN event. Call Shelton back and tell him I'll visit Fawthrop Industries this week when we stop in Seattle. I'll call Senator Shelton from Air Force One on the way to San Francisco and update him on Hermes from the air. That should satisfy him. Try to get him to delay our testimony until the following week. We might have better news then."

"Yes, sir," Lenny answered. "Nice seeing you, Dan!" he said as he left Colt's office.

"What's the Hermes system, Dad?"

Colt Garrett was scribbling on a pad. "Hermes? Oh yes. It's a kind of virtual aiming technology that uses a completely new type of energy generation design. Tom Fawthrop is a legitimate genius and owns many patents regarding the technology. I hadn't planned to see him on this trip, but now I'll have to. I don't completely understand the specifics, but I understand that Hermes is behind schedule, and the costs are increasing. I can get you a brief if you're interested. Sorry, give me just another minute, Dan. I need to take this call."

Dan watched his father work for another thirty minutes before deciding to find a better time to talk with him, maybe after the man returned the following week. He stood to leave but heard his father say, "Wait, Dan. I'm sorry. Things are crazy today." He pushed a button in the intercom. "Lenny, please hold my calls until I let you know. Have a seat, Dan. What's up?"

Dan took a breath. "Dad, I discovered I had a detached retina in my left eye last month. Two weeks ago, I had a procedure called a pneumatic retinopexy at Walter Reed to repair it. They injected an air bubble into my eye to push the retina back into place while the doctor used a laser to repair two tears in the eye. I know it sounds horrible, but it wasn't that bad. Looking back, I wish they had given me a Valium. I was out of the clinic in only two hours."

Colt sat silently as his son described the procedure. The thought of someone inserting a needle into his eye made him sick. And why was he just telling him this?

"Valium? I would have needed a general anesthetic! What

happens next? I need to know these things when they happen, son."

"I have another appointment next week to ensure the eye is healing correctly. I should be fine after that. Didn't want to bug you." Dan felt tears form in his eyes. "Except for flying, Dad. The Bureau of Medicine has permanently downed me. I'll never fly for the Navy again."

Dan wiped his eyes. The highly decorated naval aviator and test pilot could not continue to do what made him most happy. He had put off talking with his father until he received the final news from the Navy.

Colt waited until Dan composed himself. "What will you do now?"

The Navy offered me a change of designator to human resources or cryptology. At least I'd be able to finish my twenty years and retire. But I've decided against that, Dad. I can't see myself just marking time for another eight years. I'm not even sure I'd make commander."

Colt knew his son well enough to know that he wasn't looking for guidance—he'd already developed a plan. "So, what have you decided? "

"I'm going to resign my commission, which should take about six months to work its way through the system. The FAA doesn't have a problem with my medical condition. I have my commercial pilot certificate with a multi-engine land rating and more than 2,000 hours of pilot-in-command time. I will have my airline transport pilot certificate in a few months and can start the airline interview process. Ideally, I'd love to work for FedEx of course, but would take a job at UPS as a second choice."

Lenny opened the door. "Sir, sorry to interrupt, but Senator Shelton is holding for you. I think you should take this."

Dan nodded. "No prob, Dad. I have some errands to run at

Crystal City. I'll come over tonight and bring pizza and beer."

Colt watched his son leave his office. He knew Dan was heartbroken, and it killed him that he could do nothing for his only son."

"Okay, Lenny. Put the call through."


## Creighton Farms Golf Club, Virginia

Just twenty minutes from Dulles International Airport and Tysons Corner and less than an hour from downtown Washington, Creighton Farms is close to everything, including great shopping, health care services, vineyards, and the charming historic towns of Middleburg and Leesburg. The exclusive gated community residents enjoy the quiet lifestyle of a luxury club community with all the conveniences of city life just a short drive away. It offers the perfect blend of both worlds. This late afternoon, the sun settled over Mt. Weather, and a cool wind had just started to blow. The vice president and the national security advisor sat next to one another in a golf cart just off the tee box of the eighth hole, patiently waiting for the foursome in front of them to complete their drives. Two other golf carts carrying four of the vice president's protection detail were parked behind them. Instead of the typical golf equipment, alcoholic beverages, and snacks, the Secret Service golf carts held communications gear, emergency medical equipment, and automatic weapons. All for a pleasant afternoon on the links. After the foursome drove their carts toward their balls laying on the meticulously maintained fairway, Joe Carlisle and Travis Webb selected drivers from their golf bags and stepped up to the tee box.

"It looks like a 450-yard, par four, Mr. Vice President. You'll need at least 200 to clear the creek, maybe more. Tough with this wind. I think I'll lay up and play it safe."

Travis Webb traded his driver for a five iron and watched with satisfaction as his ball flew straight for the small creek, landing twenty feet from the creek bed.

"Nicely done!" praised Joe Carlisle as he pressed a white wooden tee into the turf. He looked down the fairway and then back at Travis. "With this wind, I think I will take a mulligan. Okay with you?"

Travis smiled to himself. "Sure, Mr. Vice President." He knew a mulligan was an informal golf term that was a second shot—a do-over. Joe Carlisle was the only golfer Travis knew who defined a mulligan as a shot played by his protection detail.

One of the Secret Service agents stepped up, swung Carlisle's driver, and drove his ball across the creek and up the slope on the other side.

"Thanks for the hand, Rod. Appreciate it."

The agent stepped back behind Carlisle. "Yes, sir. Anytime."

"Mr. Vice President, would you mind strolling down to my ball? I want to discuss something with you."

"Sure, Travis. Boys, I'm going for a walk with Mr. Webb. Just follow us in the carts."

The two men started down the slope toward a creek that divided the fairway in half as three golf carts followed discreetly behind. "Okay, Travis. What did you want to talk about?"

Travis decided it would be best to begin by ensuring that Joe Carlisle understood his position with the Hernández presidency. "Sir, I don't know if you've heard the rumors, but I know that Hernández plans to replace you on the ticket for her reelection campaign. She's been meeting with some influential donors and PACs to test the waters regarding her short list of candidates. She hasn't made a final choice, but it definitely won't be you."

Joe Carlisle had suspected the president wouldn't include him on the ticket, but he hadn't heard the level of rumors that Travis had just shared. He had hoped to start his campaign for the presidency after María's second term, but that was obviously off the table with Travis's latest news.

"Of course, it's disappointing to have my suspicions confirmed. I always realized the Oval Office was a long shot, but I would have made a damn good president. But you didn't need to stroll the fairway to tell me this, Travis."

"No, sir. I didn't." He stopped walking as they approached a sand trap and turned to Carlisle. "I had breakfast with our . . . mutual friend. It seems that important elements remain convinced that a change in US national defense policy is required, and they are unwilling to wait for the results of the next election." He paused, but there was no evident reaction from the vice president. "I can't share more details now. It would be better for you if you remained in the dark. Her associates are highly confident that something may happen to the president such that you will need to assume her office very shortly."

Now, something changed in Carlisle's demeanor.

The vice president wasn't a lawyer, but he had paid enough for their services over the years to understand that Travis had just described treason and conspiracy. The former admiral knew what happened to people convicted of those crimes, not to mention the public disgrace that would ultimately befall his family and friends. And yet, the thought of at least a chance of becoming president was intoxicating. Carlisle had agreed to assist the mutual friend Travis mentioned several years earlier. The money wasn't as important as the feeling of control his activities gave him. And sitting in the Oval Office would be the definition of control.

"Travis, thank you for inviting me out today. I'm really enjoying myself."

68

## Maintenance Hanger, Museum of Flight, Seattle

Wyatt Steele parked his red Camaro beside the museum maintenance hangar in a vast parking lot. He locked the car and walked over to the entrance, where he saw Dave Ryan standing next to an attractive woman in an olive drab flight suit.

"Good evening, Lieutenant Commander Steele! I'd like you to meet my daughter, Chloe. She's on ninety days of temporary duty here at the Boeing Military Delivery Center."

The US Air Force captain extended her hand. "Hi, Commander! Chloe Ryan. Dad told me you'd be helping him with one of his special projects. He asked me to come over after work and see if I might be interested. He's been tight-lipped about his project, and I'm curious to know what it is."

"Nice to meet you, Chloe. Call me Wyatt, please." He noticed the squadron patch on her flight suit. "You're with the 962nd? That's a Sentry air control squadron, right?"

"That's right. After training at Tinker Air Force Base, I've been flying the E-3A out of Joint Base Elmendorf. Anchorage isn't the most exciting place to live, but the NORAD mission is the closest thing we can get to real-world operations during peacetime."

The Sentry, more commonly known as the AWACS or Airborne Warning and Control System, provided operational commanders with an accurate, real-time picture of the battlespace. A highly modified version of Boeing's iconic 707/300, the Sentry's most identifying feature was the 30-foot radar dome mounted above the plane's fuselage. The six-foot thick, frisbee-shaped antenna array could generate a radar picture of more than 250 miles and the ability to provide the information needed for interdiction, reconnaissance, and close-air support for friendly forces. Wyatt had seen several E-3s parked on the tarmac when he drove his car along Interstate 5. But now, he was more interested in discovering more about the cute, auburn-haired, blue-eyed woman in the well-tailored flight suit.

"What brings you to the delivery center?" he said.

"The Air Force wanted one of their operational pilots to conduct the functional test flights before accepting the refurbished birds back into the inventory. I'll be here for another two months before returning to Alaska. Dad said that you're an E-6 pilot. That's a 707 derivative, too?"

"Yep. We flew airborne command post missions and communicated with our subs at sea. Not particularly challenging flying, but I got lots of hours. I'm now an ROTC instructor at the UW in Seattle."

Dave cleared his throat. "Okay, how about we head on in, and I'll introduce you to my special girl, Queenie?"

Dave Ryan led the two officers through a metal door into a dark, cavernous hangar. He toggled several switches, and the hanger was immediately bathed in brilliant light, illuminating a Boeing 707 with the words UNITED STATES OF AMERICA painted on the light blue and white aircraft.

"Dad," Chloe said as he grabbed her father's sleeve. "Your project is Air Force One?"

Dave smiled. "Well, to be precise, you're looking at Special Air Mission, or SAM, 970. It would adopt the callsign Air Force One only if the president were on board."

Wyatt whistled. "Wow. Is this the Kennedy plane? The one that brought home his body from Dallas after he was assassinated?"

"Nope. But that's what everyone thinks when they first see this plane. Here's how I keep the presidential planes straight. Think of them in terms of four generations."

Dave picked up brochures from the display next to the plane and handed them to Chloe and Wyatt.

"The first generation of presidential jets were three model 707-153s, with the military model designation of VC-137B. They carried tail numbers of 58-6970, 971, and 972. They were called Special Air Mission 970, 971, and 972. This bird is SAM 970, nicknamed Queenie, and was delivered in 1959. Queenie replaced President Eisenhower's Super Constellation and served Presidents Eisenhower, Kennedy, Johnson, and Nixon. She even flew Nikita Khrushchev and Henry Kissinger. SAM 971 and SAM 972 were backups to 970 and were used to fly other high-ranking officials. Our museum received SAM 970 on loan from the Air Force, and SAM 971 is on display at the Pima Air & Space Museum in Tucson; 972 was scrapped in 1996."

"The second generation of presidential jets was designated VC-137C. SAM 26000 and 27000 were based on the Boeing 707-353B jet and were the first to be painted with the blue and white Jackie Kennedy paint scheme. SAM 26000 carried John F. Kennedy to Dallas on November 22, 1963. Later that day, 26000 flew him home in a casket to Andrews. SAM 26000, codenamed Angel, is at the National Museum of the Air Force in Dayton. Her twin sister, SAM 27000, was known as the Nixon and Reagan plane and is in the Ronald Reagan Presidential Library in Simi, California."

"What about the newer planes, Dad? The 747s."

"The third and current generation of presidential planes are based on the 747-200B models and are designated VC-25As. The Air Force accepted SAMs 28000 and 29000 in 1990, probably the most recognized symbols of the American presidency. There are many movies about them, too, although I'm not sure about that escape pod in the movie Air Force One."

Wyatt turned to Dave. "Didn't I read that the 747s are being replaced soon? Thirty years in service is a long time." Wyatt patted Dave on his back.

"I'll let that crack about thirty years of service slide, wise guy. But you're right. The fourth generation of presidential aircraft, the 747-8 Intercontinental, is in production and should be in the fleet in 2027 or 2028. The Air Force is calling it VC-25B. The two planes are getting a new paint job, a major communication capability upgrade and a complete passenger cabin remodel. I hope I get a chance to see one."

"Dave," Wyatt asked. "Why's the cowling off engine number four? Don't tell me you're doing engine maintenance!"

"That's exactly what we're doing. Our refurbishment team is going over every inch of Queenie and restoring her to the same condition as when she was in service. The number four engine is only our latest challenge. It's shot, and we definitely need a replacement. The Air Force has been sitting on our request for a new, or more accurately, rebuilt, Pratt & Whitney JT3 engine. I'm not sure they'll approve it. Ever. And what's killing me is that Boeing has a dozen of them on carts just across the runway in depot storage. But enough whining from me. How would you two pilots like a tour of the cockpit?"

Dave led Chloe and Wyatt up the boarding ladder to the forward cabin door. Wyatt placed his left hand on the door's presidential seal and wondered how often John Kennedy had done the same thing. Once inside the plane, they turned left and forward into the ancient cockpit. The flight engineer's panel was on the immediate right, with dozens of analog gauges, lights, buttons, and toggle switches for engine status, fuel system, electrical power, and cabin pressurization. On the left bulkhead was the navigator's station. Here, the navigator used a variety of instruments to determine the plane's current position and calculate the proper heading and speed to reach a destination on schedule.

"Wyatt, since you're senior, why don't you sit in the left seat while Chloe can sit in the copilot seat?"

Wyatt eased himself into the fleece-covered pilot's seat and placed his left hand on the control wheel and his right on the four engine throttles in the center console. He was shocked to feel Chloe put her left hand on his, smile, and say, "Just backing you up, sir."

Wyatt nervously looked forward at the mass of gauges directly before him. "I know the E-6 is a 707, too, but our cockpits had been upgraded to a full glass display. What a mess!"

"I know, right?" Chloe replied. We still have some analog E-3s in the inventory, but I was trained on the new Dragon digital cockpit. I wouldn't even know how to initiate the startup sequence on this old relic."

"I guess it's good I didn't ask you two to fly this thing. I do need your help with some of the system diagrams. Let's go into the project office in the hangar, and I can show you what I have."

### Fauntleroy Park, Seattle

Fauntleroy Park was nestled on the side of a hill and provided West Seattle residents with a lush green escape from everyday life. A small creek meandered through the middle of the park and eventually emptied into Fauntleroy Cove on Puget Sound. West Seattle, now a neighborhood of Seattle, was settled by the Denny Party at Alki Beach in 1851. Some thought the site was so promising that they referred to the location as New York. Sometime later, the settlers named the landing site Alki, which in Chinook jargon means "by and by." The Denny party eventually explored the large deep-water bay around the point and founded Seattle. In 1907, West Seattle residents voted overwhelmingly for joining the City of Seattle. To this day, residents still refer to the area as West Seattle.

The park was adjacent to a local church and youth center with an associated parking lot. After dark year-round, the parking lot was popular with teenagers seeking privacy for age-related activities. A network of unpaved dirt trails crisscrossed natural ravines through the park, occasionally interrupted by wooden boardwalks over swampy areas and rustic bridges over Fauntleroy Creek. Fir trees were everywhere, creating a dense evergreen canopy overhead. Deciduous maple and alder trees completed the forest scenery and created a biodiverse landscape. The sun had set already, and dusk would soon give way to darkness. Professor Sheng Genji preferred walking her small Pekingese dog through the park during these hours because the park typically was void of visitors. The fifty-year-old Chinese national lived alone and taught the Chinese language at the Duwamish International High School, about two miles away.

"Come on, Huangdi. Stop rolling in the mud. You know it means a bath for you when we return home!"

Genji had adopted the small dog three years earlier from a well-respected breeder. She had always wanted a Pekingese, probably because, in ancient times, the breed was owned as companion pets to royalty in her homeland. According to Chinese folklore, Pekingese were created when Buddha reduced a lion to the size of a toy. Some even considered the dogs sacred, a symbol of the lion that was Buddha's guard. Suddenly, Huangdi, which means emperor in Chinese, sniffed the damp air and started barking loudly. He struggled against the leash and pulled the diminutive but stocky woman down the muddy trail.

"Stop. We've been through this before. There's no skunk!"

Genji first heard laughter and then saw two teenage girls walking toward her hand in hand, smoking a cannabis cigarette.

After they had passed and she could no longer hear them, she bent down and petted her dog. "That's okay, Huangdi. Just those awful cigarettes. There are cannabis butts everywhere on this trail. We must not eat them! Now, let's move on."

The woman and her small dog continued down the trail onto a section of raised boardwalk. Wild birds soared overhead and added a symphony of sound that only added to the forest experience. She laughed out loud as she watched her tiny dog jump over each seam between the boardwalk's gray, weathered cedar planks. The walkway transitioned into a gentle curve to the left and then raised slightly into the air to cross the creek below, where three young boys played in the shallow water.

"Excuse me, young men," proclaimed Genji as she walked up the boardwalk. "I seem to have dropped my flashlight. It probably happened when I got out of my car. Would you be so kind as to run for me to the parking lot to see if I dropped it there? Here's some money for your trouble."

She handed the tallest boy a twenty-dollar bill and watched the boys run back the way she had come. She had no illusions they would find her flashlight, which was still in her coat pocket.

"All right, Huangdi. Just wait here while I go to work."

She tied the dog leash to a guard railing, rubbed off the single horizontal white chalk mark on the wooden fence, and carefully eased her way down the steep creek bank. She reached under the wooden bridge and slowly felt along the top of the nearest support beams with outstretched fingers. At last, she found what she was looking for.

She placed the small fir cone into her coat pocket, climbed up the bank, and back onto the boardwalk. Genji nonchalantly checked the trail in both directions. She made a small vertical mark on the railing with a piece of blue chalk she had brought. "Yes, yes, I know it is nearing dinner time, my good puppy. We're going back right now. I'm getting hungry as well!"

## 13 Coins Restaurant, Seattle

Wyatt scanned the menu while waiting for Chloe to return from the restroom. After a couple of hours working at the museum, Chloe suggested they meet for dinner at the trendy International Boulevard restaurant directly across the street from Seattle-Tacoma International Airport. She changed out of her flight suit at her father's house and then ride-shared to the restaurant. Wyatt was shocked when she had walked in ten minutes ago. He was amazed at the transformation from a professional Air Force officer in a flight suit into a stunning woman with shoulder-length auburn hair and an elegant A-line dark blue dress. He wished he had worn something other than his work outfit: a short-sleeved khaki shirt and trousers, with three rows of service ribbons and his gold naval aviator wings above his left pocket and a black nametag above his right. A gold-oakleaf insignia on each collar indicated his rank as a lieutenant commander.

"I hope you like this place," said Chloe as she slid into the booth across from him. "Dad said this is where the museum's big shots take potential patrons. The food should be great, but sometimes the band in the corner can be a little loud."

This evening's entertainment was a solo performer with an acoustic guitar and a keyboard for accompaniment. He was setting up when Wyatt and Chloe first arrived.

After the couple ordered a bottle of wine and dinner, Chloe asked, "So, why did you want to be an ROTC instructor? Are you thinking of teaching after you retire from the Navy?"

Wyatt paused for a moment and took a sip of wine. "No, not exactly. Everything started well enough. Graduation from the academy, then basic at Corpus Christi in the T-34. I couldn't handle the yanking and banking; that's where I got my callsign, EARP."

"You mean as in Wyatt Earp? That's a cool callsign."

"Well, I'm pretty sure I'm called EARP because I got physically sick during high-g maneuvers."

Chloe laughed and asked, "Where did you go after basic?"

"I figured jets weren't in my future, so I requested the maritime pipeline. I stayed at Corpus for the T-44 multi-engine syllabus. After getting my wings, I transferred to Vance to learn to fly the T-1A Jayhawk jet with the 32nd. I finally ended up at Tinker, where I learned to fly the E-6B Mercury. My operational tour was with VQ-4, where I punched my aircraft commander ticket." He stopped, hoping it didn't sound like he was tooting his horn too much.

"Sounds like you were on a great career track. What was your next tour of duty?"

"For the next 30 months, I flew a Cessna Citation for the Customs and Border Patrol. I had some interesting missions and a few hairy experiences."

"I was wondering about the Distinguished Flying Cross you're wearing. It's pretty rare for a 707 driver. How did you earn that?"

Wyatt was about to answer when the servers delivered their dinners. Chloe summarized her flying career, and they ordered the Classic Coins Cheesecake with a pineapple graham crust and raspberry sauce. They were finishing their dessert when Chloe asked, "Is this a full-service date or what?"

Wyatt stared at Chloe. He had no clue how to respond.

"Oh, my God!" Chloe exclaimed. "I was asking you to dance with me. Don't you recognize this song? It's from the movie The Bodyguard. Come on, dummy!"

She led Wyatt onto the small dancefloor, and the couple began slow dancing to a country rendition of I Will Always Love You.

Wyatt's first reaction was relief when he understood what Chloe meant about a full-service date. His second reaction was interest in Chloe calling the dinner a date. But his third and most important reaction was the pleasure at how close she held him as they slowly danced across the floor.

## Genji's House, Seattle

The modest Cape Cod with the brown roof and the immaculately maintained front lawn sat on a tree-lined street. Children rode bikes and skateboarded past her house every day it wasn't raining. Genji had bought the home soon after accepting the teaching position at the local high school. The location was perfect for two reasons. First, a large city park was just down the road where Huangdi could run free. Second, the house was a ten-minute walk from the high school. Genji preferred walking rather than driving, even on cold, rainy days. She knew from her training that surveillance was much easier to detect when walking. Perhaps it was because street surveillance was considered a lost art. Moreover, at her age, she felt she needed the exercise.

"Here you go. Enjoy your dinner while I get to work." The dog ate from a silver-colored metal bowl as Genji removed her coat and hung it in the closet. The two-bedroom house was only 750 square feet but provided all the space the deep-cover Chinese operative needed to perform her duties. Her hobby was instructing Tai Chi at the YWCA, but her primary after-hours activity was serving China's Ministry of State Security as a covert intelligence officer.

"Have you finished with dinner already? Very well. Take this treat and lay down on your rug. This was an exciting day, wasn't it? First, the unexpected directive tasked me to visit the dead drop location in the park immediately. Second, I needed to find a special fir cone under the bridge. Let's see what message awaits us."

Huangdi finished the dog biscuit and lay motionless on the floor. His eyes followed Genji as she walked into the guest bedroom that served as her home office. She closed the room's curtains and sat at the small desk. Placing the fir cone she found on the table's surface, she twisted it to reveal a hidden compartment holding a Micro SD card.

"What do we have here?" Genji carefully inserted the SD card into a slot on the side of her laptop. She typed a long series of keystrokes, and an application window opened on the laptop's screen that listed a single file on the card. She placed her index finger on the laptop's security panel, and an unencrypted message appeared. After reading the message several times and committing the contents to memory, she ejected the SD card from the slot and rebooted the computer. In the small detached garage in her backyard, she found a steel plate and placed it on the cement floor. With the SD card on the steel plate, she pounded it with a small sledgehammer, shattering it into small pieces. Genji set the tiny bits of card into a plastic bowl filled with dilute hydrochloric acid and returned to her living room.

"Sweet Huangdi. It appears that I have much to do. It has been quite a while since I visited city hall. And perhaps I should check on dear Lillian to see how her recovery is going."

# Day Three

## Prince George's County, Maryland

Harold Higgins started the six-cylinder diesel engine and patiently waited for the vehicle to warm up. Although the tractor would be ready to operate in just a few minutes, the regulations were clear that, unless it was an emergency, he was required to wait ten minutes before moving the vehicle. He glanced at his watch and reflected on his six years in the Air Force. Who would have thought that after all that time and training, his primary responsibility would be to warm up a tractor? But it was not just any tractor. This vehicle, a Trepel Challenger 430, could tow the largest airplanes in the world with ease. Costing nearly half a million dollars, the Challenger 430 could work all day long pulling and pushing planes to and from airport gates. The odd-looking tractor was like those seen at any major airport, but it was painted a light shade of blue to match the only plane it would ever tow: Air Force One. To be accurate, the massive, highly modified Boeing 747-200B hooked up behind Harold's aircraft tractor was US Air Force Special Air Mission 28000. It would only be called Air Force One once the president stepped aboard.

Staff Sergeant Higgins released the tractor's parking brake and gently pressed the accelerator. The more than 4,000-ton SAM 28000 dutifully followed behind Harold's tractor as it eased out of the hangar, or what many described as the most secure military facility in the world. SAM 28000 glistened as the sun reflected off the plane's fuselage—not surprising, given that the maintenance crew spent hours hand-polishing every inch of the enormous airplane. Nothing was overlooked to ensure the plane's near-perfect condition was maintained. The aircraft had never experienced a mechanical delay in more than twenty-five years of service. Most credited the three-hundred-person maintenance team with such an outstanding service record. It was widely known that only the Air Force's very best people were selected for the prestigious duty.

The air was cold this morning at Joint Base Andrews—uncomfortably cold for people but perfect for aircraft operations. Cold air is denser than warm air. Engines operate better due to increased oxygen molecules, and the wings become more efficient because more air molecules flow over the surfaces, dramatically increasing takeoff and climb performance. All Harold knew was that cold weather was supposed to be good for flying, and that meant SAM 28000 would be airborne in a few hours, and he could get back to his spy novel at the barracks. With the two orange batons, the marshal directed Harold and SAM 28000 to their assigned spot on the tarmac. When the marshal raised the batons into the air until they touched, Harold stopped the tow and waited until the marshal signaled that SAM 28000's brakes were set and the wheel chocks placed. He disconnected the tow bar and drove the tractor back to the hangar.

Fifteen minutes later, Secretary of Defense Colt Garrett and his assigned personal security team lead, NCIS Special Agent Anna DeSantis, walked up the steps to the upper boarding door of SAM 28000. They were greeted by an Air Force command chief master sergeant in a crisply ironed blue uniform.

"Good morning, Mr. Secretary! Welcome aboard SAM 28000. President Hernández will arrive in approximately thirty minutes, and we'll be airborne as soon as she's safely aboard. I'll show you the way to the VIP section. I know the aircraft commander, Colonel Kirkbride, is eager to meet you."

Colt and Anna soon found themselves sitting in oversized first-class-type leather chairs in the forward section of the plane.

"Mr. Secretary, why isn't Mr. Wilson joining us for the trip? He was listed on the manifest."

"He called me this morning to let me know he just tested positive for COVID. He's feeling fine with no symptoms but still needs to isolate. His wife has banished him to their basement, just like Chris Cuomo in the early days of COVID-19. I hope his kids don't get infected."

"That's too bad, sir. Please let him know the detail will be thinking of him."

"Will do. Speaking of Mr. Wilson, he mentioned you might be leaving NCIS soon. I hope everything's okay."

"I just think it's time to concentrate on being a mom. I like my job, but I've concluded it's better suited for single people. I know you spearheaded the program to have NCIS agents work on your protection detail. Kevin and I both appreciated you looking out for us after the incident on the Reagan."

Colt shuddered when he thought back to the attempts on his life when he was acting secretary. That seemed ages ago now. "Please don't worry about that. You're doing what's best for you and your family." Colt paused and asked, "How are things with NCIS? I'm curious to get an insider's perspective."

Anna was about to respond when a tall Air Force colonel approached their seats.

"Parden me, Secretary Garrett. I'm Frank Kirkbride. I'll be flying you to Seattle this morning. I wonder if you'd be interested in meeting with my crew. They get to know the president fairly well, but having SECDEF aboard is a real treat."

Colt always enjoyed meeting the men and women who served in the Department of Defense. From his service as a naval officer, he knew that an essential responsibility of those in command was personally meeting with the troops. It was important to show that he cared for and appreciated their contribution to the defense team.

He followed Kirkbride.

"Sir, this is the medical suite. Doctor Franklin is checking on his supplies in the aft storage area. We can convert this litter into an operating table and perform many airborne emergency procedures."

Colt wondered how many presidents had spent time on that table during the airplane's twenty-five years of service.

"This, of course, is the communications center where we can communicate with anyone worldwide. During the September 11th attacks, we discovered the president needed the ability to speak directly with the American public during the flight. The next Air Force One will have that capability."

They walked forward into the cockpit. Colonel Kirkbride motioned Colt into the pilot's seat. Colt scanned the mass of dials and switches. "I didn't realize you were still operating with an analog flight deck. Does that impact your operations?"

"Somewhat, sir. I guess the bottom line is that the analog cockpit requires more people. This is another area that will be upgraded with the new aircraft. Probably more significantly, the VC-25B will give us another thousand more miles range and one hundred fifty thousand additional pounds of payload. It's faster as well."

"Will the new plane also have midair refueling capability?"

"I'm not certain, Mr. Secretary. With the increased range, it may not be worth the trade-off for the additional weight of such a system."

Colt made a mental note to review the VC-25B acquisition with his staff when he returned to the Pentagon.

Colonel Kirkbride's earpiece crackled. "Excuse me, Mr.

Secretary. Marine One is on final approach. It might be a good time to return to your seat. I'll be taxiing about five minutes after the president boards."

Colt walked directly back to his seat and buckled the safety belt. He watched the big Sikorsky Sea King taxi slowly and then stopped near SAM 28000. Within a minute of Marine One's blades stopping, he watched President María Hernández walk down five steps onto the tarmac. She was met by an Air Force colonel who escorted her directly to the SAM 28000 boarding stairs. Colt heard Colonel Kirkbride greet the president as she entered the plane. Simultaneously, he listened to the copilot announce that SAM 28000 had just changed its callsign to Air Force One.

They were soon airborne.

"I probably shouldn't admit it, but a shiver still goes up my spine when I hear the callsign change to Air Force One as I step aboard. It's like how I feel whenever I hear Hail to the Chief. Silly, right Colt?"

María Hernández had asked Colt to join her in her private office after Colonel Kirkbride announced Air Force One reached cruising altitude. She had removed her tailored suitcoat and had exchanged it for a black leather flight jacket embroidered with the presidential seal and her name. She leaned back in an oversized leather swivel chair and pushed back from her desk.

"Not in the least, Madam President. I remember the first time I received side honors as a junior officer. I was still in the training pipeline when we were invited aboard a visiting Royal Canadian Navy ship in San Diego. We had more than enough to drink when we stumbled to the ship's quarterdeck to leave. I saluted the officer of the deck and started down the gangway when I heard the ship's loudspeaker blare, 'Ensign, United States Navy, Departing.' We were so delighted in the ceremony that we boarded the other two Canadian ships to receive the same honors. We were stupid and drunk, but it's a good story."

"It's a great story." María moved her chair closer to the desk. "I'd like to continue the conversation we started at Camp David before the Cessna pilot decided to do a low pass over the compound. I know you share my opinion regarding the vice president. Eric Paynter had briefed me on your experience with Carlisle when he was an admiral under your command. I've been thinking about finding someone to replace him for my next term. What's your reaction?"

Colt swived his chair so that he could directly face the president. "I don't think you should be asking me that question. I don't respect the man, and more importantly, I don't think his motivations are aligned with the national interests or the objectives of this administration. We have a past, though, so my views of his capabilities are likely skewed."

"So it sounds like you wouldn't be heartbroken if I selected another running mate. I know that Carlisle has been plotting with Travis Webb to get me to change my mind regarding QUAD and other national security issues. I can't and won't say more about that now, but there's no way that Carlisle will serve as vice president for my second term. Eric is very high on you, and several influential members of Congress feel the same way. Are you interested in the position?"

Colt Garrett was stunned. María had just paid him the highest compliment of his life by asking him to consider joining her campaign for reelection. He was thinking of that when he realized she was staring at him and expecting a reply.

"Madam President, I mean—" His thoughts stumbled. "I . . . thank you for considering me your running mate, but I respectfully cannot accept. My heart wouldn't be in it. I have already decided to resign as SECDEF upon the expiration of your first term. It's time for me to leave this Washington and return to the other."

María looked into his eyes and knew he would not change his mind. After he left the office, she wondered about a man who would refuse an offer to serve as vice president to retire to a quiet personal life. She found the sentiment bewildering and just a tiny bit admirable.

"A strange man, that Colt Garrett," she said aloud as she perused through a stack of documents. "Singular, even."

## The United States Naval Observatory, Washington DC

The Naval Observatory, an operational center for tracking celestial objects and a residence for the vice president, boasts a storied history that mirrors the development of the nation's military and scientific capabilities. Established in 1830 as the Depot of Charts and Instruments, the Naval Observatory focused initially on providing charts, maps, and navigation equipment to the United States Navy. In 1844, the institution relocated to its current site in Washington, DC, where it became a vital part of the nation's efforts to explore and understand the vast, uncharted frontiers of the high seas and the cosmos.

The observatory's architecture is a stunning reflection of its scientific and military functions. The main building, completed in 1893, features an imposing neoclassical façade, a nod to the grandiosity of its mission. However, the observatory's most distinctive feature is the imposing 12-inch Zeiss refracting telescope housed in a dome atop the structure, a symbol of America's determination to gaze further into the heavens and unlock the secrets of the universe.

Among its many achievements, the observatory creates and

maintains the United States Master Clock, a timekeeping device of unparalleled precision that synchronizes global positioning systems, military operations, and various civilian services. It is said that the ticking of the Master Clock is a constant reminder to the vice president of the immense responsibility and gravity of their role in the nation's affairs.

During the height of the Cold War, as tensions between the United States and the Soviet Union reached a fever pitch, the observatory served as a critical link in the global network of radar stations that monitored Soviet missile launches. Its state-of-the-art systems enabled American forces to respond with lightning speed, minimizing the risk of nuclear catastrophe.

In 1974, the observatory underwent a significant transformation when it became the official residence of the US vice president. The decision to house the second-in-command at the observatory was strategic; its location on a sprawling, 72-acre wooded compound offered security and privacy, vital assets in a growing geopolitical uncertainty.

Today, the vice president's residence, the "Admiral's House," is a beautiful 33-room mansion combining Queen Anne and Victorian architectural styles. Built in 1893, the residence features an elegant wrap-around porch, a distinctive turret, and a rich history that spans three centuries. Though the building has been updated and expanded, it retains its original charm, providing a fitting home for the nation's vice president.

The Naval Observatory, with its unique blend of science, technology, and military prowess, is an institution that is steeped in the spirit of American ingenuity and determination. As the vice president's residence, it symbolizes the enduring partnership between the military and the civilian government. But Vice President Carlisle didn't care about any of that. He didn't want to live at the Naval Observatory any longer. He wanted to live at the

White House. And so did his wife, Robin.

"Could it be true? What exactly did Travis say?"

Carlisle knew that Robin would be excited about the prospect of him becoming president, maybe even more than he was. Robin yearned to step up from her relatively insignificant role as the vice president's spouse into the limelight cast upon the first lady. The publicity, travel, and notoriety of being the president's spouse was something she had considered unlikely until her husband shared the golf course conversation with Travis. She'd known for some time that Joe was somehow involved with international intrigue, and she wasn't phased in the least that an outside force may bring the couple to the White House.

"I think the less we say at this point, the better, Robin. We need to be prepared to act should the opportunity present itself. I think I'll take a walk around the grounds before lunch."

Carlisle couldn't quite believe his good fortune. The only son of Senator Emmett Carlisle, Joe Carlisle spent the first twenty years of his professional life as a naval officer. His career quickly progressed until he reached the rank of rear admiral, commanding a carrier battle group in the Pacific. Unfortunately for him, then Assistant Secretary of Defense Colt Garrett was making a routine visit to the flagship when the secretary of defense unexpectedly died. The president appointed Colt as secretary of defense, and conflict between him and Carlisle led to Carlisle's removal from his command. Carlisle was subsequently elected to the US House of Representatives and then finally as vice president under María Hernández. His disdain for Colt Garrett continued to grow over the years, and the two men couldn't stand to be in the same room as one another.

Carlisle slowly walked through the rose garden behind the observatory while his protection detail trailed close behind. He became excited with the prospect of replacing María Hernández, and he began to work out what he would say if he were informed that something terrible had happened to the woman.

## Mayor's Office, Seattle WA

Ron Gin picked up his favorite Star Trek memorabilia, one of the six walking tribbles created for the episode *The Trouble with Tribbles.* The TV prop was constructed of faux, reddish-brown fur mounted over a battery-powered dog toy. Ron paid over ten thousand dollars for the tribble via an online auction. Next to the tribble sat Ron's prized possession, the first phaser used by Captain James T. Kirk. Ron would never confide to anyone he had paid more than $600,000 for the small object because he could not afford such extravagance on his city salary.

Ron looked out of the windows of his seventh-floor corner office at the Seattle skyline. He marveled that a grandson of Chinese immigrants from Guangzhou could be elected mayor of one of the most progressive cities in the world, home to Boeing, Microsoft, and Amazon. Ron's grandparents had started a small construction company in the 1920s before the Great Depression, capitalizing on the abundance of inexpensive immigrant labor. The company's profits paid for Ron's father to be educated as an architect, providing a beautiful home for the family in Seattle's Wallingford district. Ron decided he didn't want to pursue a career in the family business, opting instead for a future in public service. He earned a master's degree in public administration from Seattle University and found a staff position on a city councilman's staff. Ron loved the challenges of crafting public policy and, before long, successfully ran for an open position in the state legislature. Working in Olympia taught Ron the art and science of lawmaking. He learned how to exchange votes for favors and that political alliances can shift with public sentiment in a moment.

When he decided to run for mayor, Ron asked his father for financial support. That's when things grew more complicated. Ron's father explained that he wouldn't continue to fund his son's political aspirations and that he'd have to find support elsewhere. Ron wasn't sure where to turn and asked his grandfather for guidance. The following week, Ron visited him at a local retirement care center.

"Perhaps this person may be of some assistance, Ronald. I know she has helped others in our community to accomplish their goals. You should call her."

Ron looked at the crumpled business card the old man had handed him. He doubted it would help, but he had no other options.

A week later, he met with the person suggested by his grandfather and was surprised to learn that she was willing to provide political advice and financial support for his campaign. She hired political strategists and campaign staff to jump-start his mayoral campaign. The woman seemed to know everyone in the Seattle Chinese community, and soon, Ron's campaign fundraising goals were exceeded. His family celebrated the election returns with the campaign staff, and Ron's father beamed with pride as his son made his acceptance speech in the hotel ballroom.

Ron's first term as mayor was challenging because he had much to learn about running a major metropolitan city. Electrical power, roads, infrastructure, law enforcement, and fire protection were all new to him. He methodically worked through each issue and usually found a way to succeed. The difficulties came in his second term during the summer of 2020. Protestors took over a six-block area of Seattle and proclaimed it a sovereign nation. The Capitol Hill Autonomous Zone, or CHAZ, gained national attention as private property was damaged and people were injured. The Black Lives Matter movement quickly gained national attention, and the insurgency threatened to spread to other Seattle communities. Ron was about to order the police to remove the protestors when he received a phone call from the woman who had funded his two campaigns.

"Ron, dear. Do you recognize my voice?"

He stared at the number on his phone. "Yes, I do recognize your voice. How can I help?"

"I'd very much prefer that you let the protestors on Capitol Hill remain as they are. You are to vacate the police station there and let the protest continue. Do you understand what I am saying?"

At that moment, Ron Gin understood that the support and substantial funds he had received came with a catch. And that catch was to do precisely what he was being told.

That had been almost three years ago, and even though the mysterious amounts of money were deposited into his bank account, he often wondered if he would ever hear from that woman again. He was sitting at his desk when his assistant knocked and entered his office.

"Mr. Mayor, Ms. Sheng is here to see you. May I show her in?"


## Air Force One, Boeing Field, Seattle

Boeing Field, officially known as King County International Airport, was founded in 1928 by William Boeing, the founder of Boeing Aircraft Company, as a private airfield to test and showcase his company's airplanes. Over the years, Boeing Field played a significant role in aviation history. In the 1930s, Boeing Field became a hub for commercial aviation in the Pacific

Northwest. The airport served as the main base for United Airlines and several other regional carriers. During World War II, the United States Army Air Corps used the airport as a military base. It was an important center for manufacturing and testing the Boeing B-17 Flying Fortress.

In the post-war years, Boeing Field played an important role in aviation. The airport was the site of several significant aircraft developments, including the Boeing 707, the world's first successful commercial jet airliner. In the 1960s, Boeing Field also served as the primary hub for the supersonic transport program, which aimed to create a commercial aircraft capable of supersonic flight. In the 1990s, new runways and taxiways were built, and the airport's terminal was modernized. Today, Boeing Field is one of the busiest general aviation airports in the country, with more than 200,000 aircraft operations annually. The airport is a hub for various aviation activities, including flight training, corporate and business aviation, and air cargo operations.

Colonel Kirkbride had lined up the big 747 on runway 32L with the gear and control flaps down. As he neared the end of the runway, Kirkbride reduced the throttles and pulled back on the controls to flare the airplane. The main wheels squeaked as they touched the pavement, and the nose gently lowered until its wheels also touched down. Kirkbride applied the brakes and reverse thrust to slow the massive airplane as it continued down the 10,000-foot runway.

"Whoa, big fella!" exclaimed the experienced pilot as he brought Air Force One to a slow roll and then onto the taxiway leading to the military ramp. All the major broadcast and cable news channels transmitted images of the most famous airplane in the world as it slowed and then stopped on the tarmac. After Kirkbride shut down the four turbofan engines, a set of movable stairs was positioned at the forward passenger door within a few minutes. Air Force One never used a boarding gate because the airplane needed to be able to depart at a moment's notice. The members of the press and assembled local dignitaries watched the passenger door open. President María Hernández walked through the door and paused at the top of the stairs as she waved to the crowd. As she descended the stairs, Colt followed behind, and they were met on the tarmac by Washington State Governor Marcus Gadman and Seattle Mayor Ron Gin.

"Madam President, welcome to Washington State. I understand you'll only be here for a few days, but I'd like to meet with you to discuss my environmental initiatives. We have developed some innovative policies that might have national relevance."

María was about to respond when her chief of staff interrupted. "That sounds great, Governor. Can you get me a briefing paper on the subject? Our trip agenda is extremely tight, with the visit to Fawthrop Industries tomorrow and the gala at the Museum of Flight on Friday. I'll see if I can find an opportunity to work something in."

"Thanks, Eric. We'll get the paper to you later today."

Colt chuckled. The chief of staff had diplomatically told the governor he wouldn't get a meeting with the president by ambushing her in a receiving line. He should know better. After meeting with the Fawthrop executives tomorrow, Colt planned to visit Joint Base Lewis McChord near Tacoma in the early afternoon. The side trip was primarily for personal reasons, but he also wanted to avoid being near the governor.

María offered her hand to Ron Gin. "Mr. Mayor, thank you for welcoming us to your city. I'm looking forward to getting a better understanding of your homeless problem. I saw the news program *Seattle is Dying*, and I think it's terrible how this beautiful city has changed since I first visited it years ago. I hope you can help me understand what needs to be done."

Ron nodded. "I look forward to our conversation, President Hernández. I remain convinced that the solution does not involve increased law enforcement; these are social problems, and we need those trained to deal with them."

María wasn't sure that increased police shouldn't be part of the solution to Seattle's homelessness crisis. The defund-the-police policies of other major cities had been a recipe for disaster. She also noticed that Mayor Gin seemed on edge, but she dismissed her concern when she considered he was probably just nervous about meeting the president.

Eric Paynter whispered into María's ear. "President Hernández, please come this way to the motorcade. We're heading to your suite at the Four Seasons downtown. You'll have a chance to rest before this evening's fundraiser at the Miller's estate in Madison Park. It will probably be a late night."

Jeri and Philip Miller owned an impressive mansion on the shores of Lake Washington. In addition to owning several Seattle professional sports franchises, they had long supported María and her campaigns. María wasn't looking forward to another long evening of meeting supporters and feigning interest in their personal lives. But considering that each guest made a $25,000 campaign contribution just for the privilege of meeting her, she knew it was where she needed to be.

Colt and Anna DeSantis entered a black armored Suburban in the president's motorcade.

"Mr. Garrett," began Anna, "we should be at the hotel in about fifteen minutes. Your suite is on the tenth floor. The Secret Service has taken over that entire floor. You'll need this badge to access that floor. Your luggage will already be in your room. Do you plan on going out this evening? It won't be a problem, but we'll need to coordinate with the president's protection detail if you do."

Colt looked out the SUV's darkened window as the motorcade
sped north on a deserted Interstate 5. "I bet there's a bunch of
voters wishing the president didn't arrive during rush hour—
something to think about as the election gets closer. No, Anna. I
have no plans for the evening. I'll probably order something from
room service and return to that latest Tom Carroll novel."

Anna was glad to hear the secretary wasn't planning to go
anywhere this evening. It meant she could go off-shift and let
the Secret Service assume responsibility for his protection. She
looked forward to taking a long, hot shower and having a video
call with Kevin and the kids.

## Shanghai, People's Republic of China

Minister of State Security Sun Ping always considered
Shanghai two different cities each time he visited the ancient
metropolis—one new and the other old. In the heart of Shanghai
lies the Financial District, a dazzling showcase of the city's might.
A place where towering skyscrapers reach toward the sky, covered
in thousands of glass windows that gleam in the sun like a million
glittering diamonds. The Jin Mao Tower and the Shanghai World
Financial Center dominate the skyline, like giants standing tall
amongst the clouds. These buildings are home to some of the
biggest companies in the world, their logos displayed like badges
of honor across their steel and glass bodies. In this part of town,
the air is filled with the scent of high-grade coffee brewing in chic
cafés mingled with the faint trace of polished metal and glass. The
streets echo with the sound of clicking high-heels, busy phone
conversations in a dozen different languages, and the soft hum of
electric cars zipping by. It's a place of power and money, where

people rush around in designer suits, always looking at their high-tech watches because every second counts.

However, Sun Ping thought, not all that glitters is gold, as he meandered alone down a shaded alley. Away from the financial district, there's a starkly different world. In the shadows of the high-rises are the city's slums, where life is far removed from the hustle and bustle of commerce and luxury. The buildings here are humble, some even makeshift, built with whatever materials could be found or afforded. There's a stark contrast between the steel and glass towers of the financial district and the bricks, wood, and rusted metal of these neighborhoods. Streets are narrower, and the air is heavy with the smell of cheap street food, mixed with a hint of grime and the tangy scent of the nearby Huangpu River. The sounds Sun Ping heard were different, too. Instead of the rhythmic hum of electric cars, the slums echo the clamor of a bustling open-air market. He listened to the haggling voices of vendors selling everything from fruits to second-hand clothes, mixed with the cries of street children playing and the occasional barking of a stray dog.

In the financial district, life is fast-paced, always on the move, and always looking ahead. In the slums, it's about survival, about making it through another day. Yet, Minister Sun perceived a sense of community here, a shared struggle typically absent in the cold, impersonal skyscrapers. In all its glory and grime, Shanghai is a city of contrasts, a city that blends the traditional with the modern, the affluent with the impoverished, and the triumphant with the struggling. And just like the Yangtze River that flows through it, the city moves forward, ever-changing, ever-adapting, and holding within it stories of a thousand lives lived in the shadow of its towers.

Sun Ping entered the door of a small tea shop and walked past a dozen small tables with customers sipping their favorite concoctions. Worn and weathered wooden floorboards creaked under his feet as he eased down a narrow, dimly lit hall. Minister Sun turned to ensure he was alone and opened the only door in the hall.

"Good morning, General," he said as he closed and locked the door behind him. Sun pulled out a wooden chair and sat at the only table in the tiny space. Another man sat quietly across from him, enjoying a cup of tea. He silently poured tea into a second cup and pushed it toward Sun.

"Good morning, Minister. I trust your flight from Beijing was pleasant. As I get older, I find I dislike air travel increasingly with each flight. Perhaps someday, I will not travel by air at all."

Minister Sun couldn't quite imagine how the vice chairman of China's Central Military Commission could perform his vast duties without air travel. Still, he decided to forgo the topic and use the little time he had to discuss more pressing concerns.

"As you know, General, our plan to effect a change in the American government leadership is moving forward. Our resources in the Pacific Northwest are quickly executing their assigned tasks, and our Russian friends tell me that they have received assurances from their assets in the capital that they will be ready to assume their new responsibilities afterward. I must stress that your continued support and discretion are essential to this operation. Should the chairman become aware of our activities, we both would be in regrettable situations."

"If the chairman were to learn what we are doing, our families would never see us again. Treason would be the charge, and the punishment would be immediate. No doubt there."

Sun refilled the two teacups and set the porcelain kettle on the table. "You knew what was at stake when we reached out to the Russians without authority. And as we have discussed on many occasions, once the operation is successful, the chairman will be pleased with the result and perhaps even take credit for himself. If we should fail, I expect he will still approve of our actions and be eternally thankful that he was not involved."

The general finished his cup of tea and stood to leave. "I do not feel better knowing that in the event of our failure, the chairman will appreciate our efforts as he orders our executions!"

Sun waited an hour after the general departed before leaving the small shop. As he retraced his path through the crowded slum, he considered what the general had said. He supposed that in a few days, he would know if his plan would succeed and his life would continue.

## Lillian's Apartment, Seattle

Lillian's apartment was a tiny, one-bedroom dwelling nestled in the heart of a run-down Seattle neighborhood. As Genji followed Lillian through the creaking door, a wave of pungent stench immediately assaulted her senses, overpowering any hope of finding a breath of fresh air. The room was cloaked in a thick haze of cigarette smoke, its acrid stench mingling with the unmistakable stink of urine that permeated the air.

The apartment itself reflected the chaotic life Lillian led—a disheveled battlefield of filth and despair. Once a faded shade of cream, the walls were now stained and grimy as if they had absorbed the essence of Lillian's squalid existence. The tattered remnants of peeling wallpaper clung desperately to the walls like a faded memory of better days. A single, besmirched window offered a feeble attempt at illumination, its thin, tattered curtains barely capable of keeping out the prying eyes of the outside world. Dust particles danced in the slivers of sunlight that penetrated the dirty glass, casting a somber, ethereal glow on the disarray within.

The living room, cluttered and chaotic, was a minefield of discarded objects. Piles of crumpled, stained clothing lay haphazardly strewn across the threadbare couch. Empty food containers littered the worn-out carpet, attracting a swarm of insects that feasted upon the forgotten remnants of meals past. In one corner of the room, an unsteady tower of unwashed dishes teetered precariously on the edge of the kitchen sink, defying gravity. The miasma of decay clung to the air, mingling with the musty odor of dampness that hung heavily in the room. Flies buzzed lazily around, their incessant humming providing a constant, unsettling soundtrack.

As Genji moved further into the apartment, she couldn't help but notice the unmistakable signs of drug use. Vials of murky liquid, needles strewn carelessly on the floor, and scorched spoons with blackened residue—a tableau of addiction. The remnants of Lillian's desperate attempts to escape reality lay scattered across every surface, a stark reminder of the toll her addiction had taken.

And then, the dogs. Two emaciated, neglected creatures wandered through the apartment, their matted fur mottled with grime. Their mournful howls echoed through the air, a pitiful chorus of abandoned souls. Their presence only added to the pervasive sense of desolation that saturated the apartment. Every inch of the woman's home screamed of neglect and decay. It was a place where hope had long since withered away, leaving behind only the remnants of a once vibrant soul drowning in a sea of addiction and broken dreams. Genji cringed as she made herself sit on the disgusting couch.

"Genji, can I make you a cup of tea?"

Before waiting for an answer, Lillian began hunting for her teapot. Minutes later, she handed Genji a stained ceramic mug.

"I don't know if the tea's any good, but at least it's hot!"

Genji attempted to remember when she had her last hepatitis vaccine and then realized that Lillian's apartment likely contained all five types of the disease. Nevertheless, she took a fake sip from the cup and placed it on the table. "I think I will let this cool a bit. Tell me, are you enjoying Tai Chi?"

Lillian had been taking Genji's beginner-level class at the community center for the past four weeks. She felt the exercise was good for her, and there were always free snacks available.

"I do like the class. Sort of like exercising and letting your mind wander at once."

"I am glad you find it enjoyable. And thank you for inviting me to your home after class. You live here alone?"

Lillian petted one of the dogs. "Yes, mostly. Like I mentioned last week, sometimes I need to earn a little extra money to pay my bills and occasionally bring a guy over here. They usually don't stay very long."

Genji knew about Lillian's drug and alcohol dependency, but she was surprised last week when Lillian casually mentioned her sex work. Genji knew that people living on the edge were easy targets for manipulation, so she suggested they meet after class.

"Genji, is Tai Chi really Kung Fu? One of my friends says it's basically the same."

Genji was about to take a sip of tea but then placed the mug back on the table. "My teacher in China said that Tai Chi is one of the most famous Chinese martial arts of the internal style. Many of my American students think of Chinese martial arts as the styles typically displayed in action movies. These styles, such as Kung Fu, concentrate on the external form, featuring rapid body movements and violent punching motions—the internal styles, such as tai chi, stress breathing, and the mental component. Movement is usually soft, aqueous, gentle, and almost elegant. Haven't you noticed that? The student's breathing deepens and slows, improving visual and mental concentration, relaxing the body, and allowing the life force to flow unimpeded throughout the body. These techniques help integrate the mind and body and allow the student to achieve total harmony of the inner and outer self."

"Wow. Very cool. I always feel better when I hear you speak. I can't wait to learn more."

Genji considered her following words very carefully. "Lillian, how is work going? Do you like your new job?"

Lillian was a night janitor for the Strudel Haus, a small neighborhood bakery. She had been laid off from her old janitorial position at Fawthrop Industries for reporting late to work too many times and for her belligerent behavior toward other employees. After leaving Fawthrop Industries, she was arrested for throwing a brick through the company's main entrance. Because the brick injured an employee, Lillian was convicted of assault and served a thirty-day sentence in the King County jail.

"The new job's okay, I guess, but it certainly doesn't pay as much as the old one. And I get no benefits because I'm only working part-time."

"That's terrible. It sounds like Fawthrop messed things up for you. It just doesn't seem fair."

## Genji's House, Seattle

"Hello, Huangdi! Such a good boy! I've missed you as well! How about a treat!"

Genji placed her purse and leather briefcase on the kitchen table and opened a plastic container filled with bacon-flavored dog snacks.

"I've had a very busy day and cannot wait to tell you all about it. I'll get your dinner, and then we can throw the ball in the backyard. I even have a special surprise for you this evening!"

Genji poured a cup of kibble into Huangdi's bowl. She changed out of her black silk Tai Chi clothing into a more comfortable set of sweatpants and a cotton top. After an hour of backyard play, Genji started to prepare her dinner of wonton soup, chow mein, and steamed rice.

"Mayor Gin was more reluctant to participate in our plans than I had anticipated, Huangdi. He attempted to convince me that he was more useful to us as a policy influencer rather than as someone who would take direct action in support of our cause. Imagine that." She liked talking out her issues with Huangdi, and it often helped her find solutions to the thorniest conflicts simply by verbalizing the situations to her adored Pekingese. "He cited his actions during several highly publicized social justice protests as more vital than what I asked him to do today. I needed to recalibrate his thinking such that he realized that his role was to do whatever I asked. Isn't that right, baby boy? I suspect he now regrets accepting our support of his political career over the years, but that is no matter. He now fully understands his situation and has accepted his assignment."

Genji watched the evening television news as she enjoyed her dinner. The small dog closely watched her chew each mouthful, ever hopeful for something else to eat. After the news broadcast ended, Genji hand-washed the few dishes in her kitchen sink.

"Seeing Lillian's apartment was quite a shock, though, Huangdi. So much worse than I had imagined. Such filth and squalor in the home of such an intelligent woman! During training, we were taught that intelligent people often have many psychological issues, which can make them attractive recruits for our work. I suppose their intellect sets them apart from most people, making it difficult for them to fit into the rest of society. Isn't that interesting?"

The experienced covert agent found the topic fascinating. It was why she initially cultivated a relationship with Lillian.

"These people with high IQs can have many problems. They cannot relate to the opposite sex, tend to be loners, and have trouble shutting down their brains at night. This often leads to substance abuse, a very bad thing for the health, which probably explains Lillian's addictive behavior. And they lie, Huangdi. Oh, how they lie. It's relatively easy for them to categorize information and keep it all straight. They lie to fit in, and sometimes it works. You would think these smart people would be difficult to fool, but the opposite is actually true. Perhaps it is their ego or even greed. Regardless, all these things combine to make my dear friend Lillian perfect for what I have planned for her. Tomorrow evening, I will be meeting with her again. That is when I'll set the hook."

Huangdi started to bark, and then Genji's doorbell rang. She opened the door and saw a young man standing on her porch with a small cardboard box.

"I have four more for you, Ms. Sheng. Five bucks, okay?"

Genji handed the teenager a crumpled five-dollar bill. "Thank you, Jeffery. Have a nice evening."

She carried the cardboard box through the house and out into the backyard. "I told you I had a surprise for you, Huangdi!"

She placed the box on the grass and opened it. Four baby rabbits jumped out and scattered throughout the large yard. Huangdi yelped with delight as he tore across the turf after the small animals. After the horrifying carnage, Genji returned to her house and sat down to finish the novel she had started the night before.

# TOM CARROLL

## MV Orion, North of Los Angeles

It was a calm, moonlit night as the massive ocean-going container ship glided north along the Southern California coast. A gentle breeze whispered through the air, carrying the scent of saltwater and distant seaweed. Motor Vessel Orion, a state-owned enterprise of the People's Republic of China, was transporting precious cargo. The captain, a seasoned sailor named Shao Gang, guided the massive ship safely. From the navigation bridge, high above the main deck, Captain Shao surveyed the dark horizon with his senses attuned to signs of danger. The bridge was a marvel of technology, filled with instruments and screens that provided crucial information about the ship's position, speed, and course. Some screens displayed charts of the coastal waters, while others showed radar images that revealed nearby vessels or obstacles. The soft glow of the instruments bathed the bridge in a bluish light, casting eerie shadows on the walls. Despite all the ship's technology, Shao trusted one piece of equipment more than any other. His binoculars.

To the west, the vast expanse of the Pacific Ocean stretched out before Shao, the moonlight dancing on the waves like a galaxy of tiny silver stars. Far to the east, the silhouette of the California coastline appeared as a jagged ribbon of darkness against the night sky. Occasionally, the distant twinkle of a shore-side city would break the monotony of the black landscape. As Shao adjusted the ship's course to avoid a group of fishing boats, he listened intently to the sounds around him. The engine's hum, a low and constant drone, filled the background. It was a reassuring sound, evidence that the ship's heart continued to beat with steady power. Outside, the wind whispered through the rigging, and the ship's bow sliced through the water, leaving a foamy white trail in its wake. These were the sounds of the sea, the familiar chorus that accompanied Shao on every voyage.

Despite the peaceful scene, Shao was alert and focused. He knew that even on the calmest nights, danger could lurk beneath the waves or in the shadows of the coastline. Rogue waves, hidden reefs, and other vessels could all threaten the ship and its cargo. In the back of his mind, he was always aware of the terrible storms that could rise up without warning, turning the tranquil ocean into a vortex of wind and water. Shao breathed deeply, savoring the salty sea air filling his lungs. It was a unique aroma, a mixture of ocean spray, diesel exhaust, and the faint hint of rust from the ship's aging hull. The scent was as familiar to him as the smell of his own home, a constant reminder of the life he had chosen decades ago. The four-to-eight watch was his favorite because he was typically alone on the bridge, free to practice his craft without interruption. Soon, the night would gradually give way to daylight, and his relief would arrive with fresh coffee.

"Good morning, Captain Shao. I brought you some tea."

Shao was disappointed to see that instead of his watch relief, one of his special passengers, Major Tang, had joined him on the bridge bearing a small Styrofoam cup of tea.

"I drink black coffee when we are underway, Major. I believe I mentioned this previously."

Major Tang was the commanding officer of a 30-person special detachment onboard the Orion. Outwardly, the MV Orion appeared to be one of the hundreds of merchant container ships transporting cargo along the Pacific coast of North America. Her covert mission was to gather intelligence of interest to the PRC wherever and whenever it might exist. Orion's current mission was to loiter near Naval Base Ventura County, about an hour's drive north of Los Angeles. The US Navy operated three major installations on the base: Point Magu, Port Hueneme, and San

Nicolas Island. Those facilities' multiple warfare, weapons, and engineering commands provided abundant intelligence collection opportunities for foreign powers. It was the perfect assignment for the MV Orion and her crew of intelligence collection specialists operating deep within the ship's hull. From time to time, Orion would find itself in the company of US Coast Guard cutters, US Navy combatants, and a wide variety of US military aircraft. It was evident to Captain Shao that the US government knew what Orion was doing in their coastal waters and wanted to ensure the Chinese knew they knew it.

Major Tang looked forward through the bridge windows. "My, the ship's nose sure is bouncing in these seas. My technicians are becoming seasick. Is there nothing that can be done to reduce the motion?"

Captain Shao sighed. "Not nose, Major. Bow. You are not in an airplane. You are aboard a ship at sea. And no, as long as we remain in this area, we must endure the roiling seas. I can't change that. You may plan on a better ride once we conclude our mission here and sail to the Pacific Northwest."

Major Tang laughed. He constantly amused himself by infuriating the elderly mariner by purposely not using nautical expressions while on the Orion. "Right, Captain. Sorry about that. And as long as we are being precise in our language, please remember that I fly helicopters, not airplanes!"

# Day Four

## The West Wing, Washington DC

Joe Carlisle, vice president, former congressman, and admiral, lounged in his office, an impressive room in the West Wing of the White House. Sunlight poured in from the west-facing window, casting a warm glow on the fine-textured carpet, a shade of rich navy. The walls, painted a dignified gray, echoed the solemnity of his position. His gaze fell upon the Treasury Building, a symbol of financial might, basking in the morning light.

Prominently displayed in his office were two reminders of his past—a Civil War-era US Navy boarding cutlass and a wooden A-6E Intruder aircraft model. The cutlass, a gift from his influential senator father when he joined the Navy, gleamed under the overhead lights. Next to it, the aircraft model was a tiny testament to a time he'd rather forget: an error leading to an emergency ejection over the Mediterranean, saved only by his father's intervention.

Lulled by the peaceful rhythm of the air conditioning, Joe slipped into introspection. Conversations on the golf course on Tuesday with Travis detonated thoughts of an unexpected promotion. The presidency. He smiled, the power of the Oval Office tantalizing. But a twinge of doubt rippled beneath his confidence. Did he, a man who had ascended the ranks through charm and luck, genuinely have the mettle for the highest office in the land? Or were his past roles just stepping stones, a fortunate sequence of events, on his path to power?

A soft sound interrupted his thoughts. He turned, and his

cheeks flushed as he found Travis patiently waiting. He had quietly entered his office and sat down while Joe was lost in thought. An immediate wave of embarrassment washed over him as he realized he was not alone. He cleared his throat, steadied his voice, and, with a forced smile, said, "Travis, let's get to work."

National Security Advisor Travis Webb momentarily looked at the vice president, turned, and closed the heavy oak door. "Are you all right, Joe? You seemed concerned about something. Shall I come back later?"

Carlisle laughed. "Not to worry, Travis. I was thinking of how proud Robin will be to serve as first lady. I think she's more excited about it than I am."

Travis wasn't confident that Joe was sincere, but they had more important issues to discuss. "I spoke with our mutual friend again yesterday, and she gave me some additional background on the plan. The bottom line is that we will go about our normal routines for the next few days—nothing unusual. Don't cancel or reschedule any recurring meetings. If you're scheduled to meet with a sports team or a youth group, attend the meetings. That way, our reaction to the news will be genuine and unscripted. The staff and the press will scrutinize everything we say and do. Make sure you speak with Robin about this. It goes without saying to tell no one else, Joe."

"Okay, I get it, sure. And I'll speak with Robin as well." He made several notes on a pad of paper. "Anything else?"

"Just this. Our friend shared that our first indication that the plan is moving forward will be something in the national news. Remember, all your conversations could be subject to discovery in the event of legal action. Don't say anything on the phone." Carlisle continued to write on the pad. "And stop writing any of this down."

Carlisle threw aside the pad. "Legal action? By whom?"

"Assuming this all goes according to the plan, and you become president, your succession could face legal challenges. I'm just saying you need to be very careful. Don't take any chances."

Carlisle rested his elbows on his desk and pressed his fingertips together. He hadn't considered that his succession to the presidency could be challenged, and he wanted to understand the basis for such an action.

"But I thought the vice president automatically becomes president if something happens to POTUS. What are you talking about?"

Travis sighed. "The Presidential Succession Act of 1947 determines who becomes president in the event of a vacancy mid-term. The sequence is vice president, House speaker, and Senate president pro tempore. After that, the sequence is secretary of state, secretary of the treasury, secretary of defense, and the attorney general."

"Yes, yes. I know all that. My question is about the basis of a challenge to the vice president becoming president."

"The key issue is who becomes acting president in the absence of the president. The 25th Amendment of the US Constitution addresses that issue. And there are other laws as well. Article I of the Constitution, the 12th and the 20th Amendments also are relevant. We must follow all the laws to ensure no legal challenge is valid."

"Okay, okay. I'm no lawyer. We'll need to work with White House counsel to ensure we follow the process. I'll leave that to you."

Travis made a few notes on his notepad. "One last thing. Our friend also mentioned that the Russians aren't the only people involved. She said that Moscow has been working with the Chinese Communist Party to ensure the plan is successful. She didn't get into details regarding the CCP's role, but she led me to believe they have crucial resources in place."

"It's hard to imagine the Russians working cooperatively with the Chinese. I wonder what brought them together?"

Travis stood, walked toward the door, and turned to face the vice president. "I'm not certain. But I got the idea that the Russians had no other options."

After Travis left his office, Carlisle looked out his office window. As he was standing there, a small bird crashed into the glass and fell to the grass lawn below.

"I hope I have a better future than that," Joe said aloud as he looked at his agenda for the remaining day.

## Four Seasons Hotel, Seattle, Washington

The dawning cast a serene glow over the awakening city, prepared to welcome the first light of a spring sunrise. On the 14th floor of the four-star hotel, Colt stood by the suite's window, his gaze fixed on the world outside. He was born and raised in Seattle, a place that held the key to his fondest memories. As he looked out, his eyes were drawn to Elliott Bay, where he had learned to sail as a young boy. The water sparkled with the dawn of daylight, reflecting the early hues of orange and pink. He could almost hear the gentle lapping of the waves against the hull of his first boat, a sloop he had named "Spindrift." Those were the days when worries were few, and the sea was his playground. He made a mental note to check on his new boat.

A smile tugged at the corners of his mouth as he recalled another memory, one that still made his heart ache a bit. It was the memory of his first date with Joanna, a girl who'd captured his adolescent heart. It was on a warm summer day, just like this one, that they had shared their first kiss. The sweet taste of nostalgia filled his mind as he remembered the warmth of her lips against his. But decades had passed, and he had grown older. He had worked as a deckhand on a harbor tour boat, ferrying tourists along the breathtaking waterfront. The memory of those days overwhelmed him with a painful nostalgia for the carefree youth he once had. Now, standing in this hotel room, he returned to the city that held his youth but with a heaviness he hadn't anticipated. High cholesterol and recent weight gain had forced him to change his eating habits. The tantalizing aroma of room service breakfast meals wafted through the air, teasing his senses. But he knew he had to resist. His health came first, even if it meant sacrificing the simple pleasure of indulgence.

As he continued to gaze outside, his eyes shifted to the ferries gliding across the bay. They were like graceful giants, their white hulls contrasting against the deep blue waters. Each ferry carried its own story, connecting people and places in a dance of constant movement. Beyond the bay, the sun continued to ascend, casting a golden glow over the Olympic Mountains to the west. The jagged peaks were slowly illuminated, unveiling their majestic beauty. It was a sight that never failed to awe him, a reminder of the vastness of nature and the world beyond his worries. At that moment, as he stood by the window, Colt felt a mixture of emotions. Nostalgia continued to stir within him, that bittersweet longing for days gone by. But he also felt a sense of gratitude for the memories he had made and the beauty that still surrounded him. He was more confident than ever that he was making the right decision to end his government career and retire to the Pacific Northwest. And so, with a final glance at the scene outside, he turned away and sat to enjoy his breakfast of oatmeal and whole wheat toast. And then his laptop chimed, announcing an incoming video call.

"Good morning, Steve. How are things at the Pentagon?"

Steve Holmes's grinning face filled Colt's laptop screen. "Just great, boss. It's amazing how well things run when you're out of the office!"

Steve and Colt were good friends, a relationship that had started when they served as undersecretaries of defense in the Harrison administration. Steve ran the intelligence functions while Colt coordinated defense policy. When Colt was appointed defense secretary, he knew he wanted Steve as his deputy. Competence was a common enough trait within the Beltway; trust and loyalty were much rarer. Steve embodied all three.

"That's what I was thinking, Steve. Maybe I should just stay out here. I'll talk with the president about it when I see her later today."

"Don't even think about it. Just a senior moment you're having. And if you do it, know this. My resignation letter will drop moments after yours. I don't have the patience to train another defense secretary!"

The two men enjoyed the banter but realized it wasn't far from the truth. They had grown tired of the constant fights with elected officials and other agencies and were frustrated with fighting the same battles year after year. They each wanted to focus on personal interests and relationships in the final quarter of life. Priorities had shifted.

"Okay. Now that you've made it clear that you're not interested in replacing me, what can I do for you?"

"Mr. Secretary, our investigation into that security matter uncovered information confirming our earlier suspicions. I can brief you more fully when we talk on a secure circuit, but I thought you'd be interested in knowing that the team believes they have sufficient information to bring to the Justice Department and request an indictment."

Colt was more than interested in the news that Steve

just shared. He referred to an ongoing defense department investigation to find the source of a classified information leak within the US intelligence community. The data was passed to Russian intelligence and led to an assassination attempt of Colt during his fact-finding mission to Cambodia. At the time, Colt and Steve strongly suspected the mole was Travis Webb. For obvious reasons, knowledge of the investigation had remained within a select few at the defense department. Steve's news meant that the team had developed solid proof that Travis was the mole, and the next step would be officially handing over the investigation to the attorney general. Colt wanted to ask Steve if there was evidence that the vice president was also complicit, but that conversation would also need to wait until the two men could talk privately.

"Steve, do you still have that other phone for personal use? I'd like to talk with you about you and Trixie coming out to stay on the boat next month."

Steve knew that Colt was referring to the burner phone he kept for off-the-record calls with Colt. "Sure, boss. Call me this weekend, and we can review the details."

Colt ended the video call and then finished the last of his coffee. He decided he needed to talk with President Hernández about the Travis Webb situation as soon as they could find time alone. He knew it would not be a pleasant conversation.

## Mayor's Office, Seattle

Mayor Ron Gin was surprised to hear that Sheng Genji was waiting to see him. It was only yesterday that she had unexpectedly visited him in his office and tasked him with assisting her in bringing shame and embarrassment to President

Hernández and her administration. He reluctantly agreed to help with the plan after Genji clarified that he had no choice. With her years of financial help, he had effectively sold his compliance, which if revealed could land him in federal prison till he was an old man, not to mention the additional threat of physical violence to his family. Ron had initially resigned himself to work for Genji and the CCP but had second thoughts after meeting President Hernández at the airport. He was surprised by her charisma and warmth. He knew he had to comply with his instructions from China but wasn't happy about it. She was his president, after all. It wasn't until he left the airport that he fully comprehended that he was about to commit treason. What would his family say if they knew? Ron pressed a button on his speakerphone. "Sidney, please show in Ms. Sheng."

"You must love coming to work here each day, Mr. Mayor— such a beautiful view of your city—a powerful man in an impressive office. You must be very proud of what you have accomplished in such a short time with the support of some very generous constituents. And your political career is just beginning to move forward. After we conclude our business tomorrow evening, we should plan to meet to discuss a possible run for Congress. An empty seat in the 1$^{st}$ Congressional District is a rare opportunity for you to move to the next step in government service. I have already spoken to my superiors, and I assure you that campaign and financial assistance will not be an issue."

Ron poured two cups of Oolong tea and joined Genji on the leather couch. Even though he'd accepted money from Genji before, he now knew that she and her superiors were trying to push him into positions of more significant influence for their purposes. The thought made him feel sad and helpless.

"I'm surprised to see you today. What can I do for you?"

Genji placed her teacup on the coffee table. "I need to give you your detailed instructions for tomorrow's gala. None of this must be written down. Is that understood?"

Ron nodded.

"As I mentioned yesterday, President Hernández will attend a gala at the Boeing Museum of Flight tomorrow evening. We understand that you have been asked to make some welcoming remarks, and then you will introduce the president. You're scheduled to begin your comments at 6:00 pm, and President Hernández will speak at 6:15. The timing is critical. We have arranged for a small explosive device to detonate at precisely 6:15. A loud sound will be followed by large amounts of a foul-smelling but harmless, orange-colored smoke cloud. A stink bomb, if you prefer. This will cause a great deal of panic and confusion. The Secret Service will immediately evacuate President Hernández according to their security procedures."

"Meanwhile, the press outside the museum will observe a small gathering of dissidents protesting the president's support of the QUAD agreement. Other groups will claim responsibility for the explosion. The news media will become obsessed and saturated with attempts to identify the persons responsible and related stories about the event and the protestors. We believe the result will be a heightened awareness of the QUAD and why it should be dissolved."

Ron was relieved to learn that President Hernández would not be physically harmed, and the entire operation appeared to focus on creating a negative public opinion of the QUAD. This was just dirty politics elevated to a more nefarious level. Not even close to treason. And the thought of becoming a member of Congress was undoubtedly attractive. Although the promotion would mean a $20,000 reduction in salary, it would also substantially reduce his workload. The city employed over 10,000 employees, while a congressional staff was limited to just eighteen. And the opportunities for non-salary compensation were enormous. A member of Congress who sat on important committees was a very powerful person. Also, it was common knowledge that members of Congress dramatically increased their investment portfolios. When he noticed Genji smiling, he even thought about which city staff would transition to his congressional office. He decided to focus on the task at hand.

"So, I just need to ensure the president is onstage at 6:15? That's all?"

"In addition, Ron, we'll need access to the museum. Who is responsible for security there?"

"The airport has its police department, but for an event of this size and importance, the Secret Service has asked the Seattle Police to perform the security vetting function. SPD will provide the personnel and systems to clear everyone at the event, all subject to Secret Service oversight. Why?"

Genji finished her tea and walked over to large windows facing Puget Sound. "I will need six security badges for stagehands and another for a maintenance person—seven badges. I will send you the names and photographs for the stage badges later today. Do you foresee any difficulties obtaining them?"

Ron thought about whom to speak with to get the security badges. It would have to be someone in the information services division he could trust and who would trust him. Perhaps the young technician who frequently helped him with his laptop. The recent hire would likely jump at the chance to impress the mayor. And not ask too many questions.

"No, I don't think it will be a problem. I have someone in mind. When will you need them?" He wanted to ask for more but resisted the urge—perhaps because he didn't want to hear the answers.

"I think tomorrow at noon would work for the stagehands'

badges, but I need the one maintenance badge with this name and photograph when I return after lunch. I need you to deliver the stagehands' badges to this address tomorrow."

She handed Ron a flimsy piece of paper with an address written in pencil. "Memorize this address. I need you to take the stagehand badges there no later than 2:00 pm. Knock on the main door and ask for Song. He will give you further instructions."

After Ron handed the paper back to Genji, she placed it into an empty cup, poured tea over the piece of paper, and watched it quickly dissolve.

Moments later, Genji pressed the elevator button, and the doors silently closed. As she descended to the ground floor, she considered how much she would miss working with Ron Gin. Such a talented and resourceful young man. But she had her orders.

### Fawthrop Industries, Military Systems Division, Seattle

Fawthrop Industries is a multi-national corporation headquartered in Seattle. Initially founded in 1932 by Arthur Fawthrop, an emigrant from Portsmouth, England, the company started as an explosives manufacturing plant. Arthur successfully competed with other explosives contractors for US government contracts. He was well positioned to provide gunpowder and other weapons components as America became the allies' arsenal in the opening days of the Second World War. After the Japanese attack on Pearl Harbor in 1941, global demand for Fawthrop products increased exponentially. Arthur reinvested the resulting windfall profits into his research and development department and, in 1946, hired scientists and engineers who sought post-war employment. Arthur's foresight led to his company's position as a pioneer in computer science and electronic engineering.

Edward Fawthrop followed his father as the company's CEO in 1965 and continued to grow and diversify the firm. Because of his education as an electrical engineer, Ed continued to move the company away from simply explosives manufacturing and retooled the entire business into electronics weapons design and manufacturing. He created Fawthrop Industries Military Systems, one of six Fawthrop Industries business units. The military systems division developed and manufactured advanced combat, missile, rocket, manned, and unmanned systems for military customers, including the US Navy, NASA, Air Force, Marine Corps, and other nations. Its most recent contract with the Air Force was the Hermes system, a state-of-the-art virtual aiming subsystem.

Ed retired in 1990 due to a heart disease diagnosis and passed company leadership and management to his son, Thomas. Ever since, Tom had dutifully run the family business, more of an empire now. And while he continued to expand the firm's market share in defense systems, his heart wasn't in it. He struggled with the ethics of leading one of the world's most successful defense contracts until he realized that he could use the corporation's profits to fund his philanthropic interests. The result became the Fawthrop Foundation, one of North America's most generous and impactful non-profit organizations. And it was because of the foundation's work that President María Hernández stood in front of more than five hundred Fawthrop employees today.

"Thank you, Secretary Garrett, for that introduction. And thank you, the people of Fawthrop Industries. Your work has allowed this country's citizens to live safely for decades. When Secretary Garrett asked if I would be willing to stop in Seattle and meet this amazing company's scientists, engineers, and technicians, I jumped at the opportunity."

Colt watched as the crowd cheered for María. She was a well-practiced politician. He was privately pleased that he typically wasn't required to make these types of speeches. He saw María pause for the applause before she continued.

"I do have a surprise for you today. Tom, will you join me on stage?"

Tom Fawthrop was surprised at being asked to join President Hernández at the podium. He paused momentarily, then used a wooden cane to stand from his seat in the front row and slowly walked to the front of the auditorium.

"The Presidential Medal of Freedom is our nation's highest civilian honor. It is presented to those individuals who have contributed to the prosperity, values, or security of the United States, world peace, or other significant societal, public, or private endeavors. I think that our country can be defined by one word: perseverance. Thomas Fawthrop has demonstrated perseverance and good old-fashioned hard work for decades. He has overcome challenges and has had the tenacity to succeed despite them. His foundation benefits millions of deserving people worldwide, and we enjoy a better tomorrow because of him. Thomas Fawthrop, it is my high honor and extreme privilege to bestow the Presidential Medal of Freedom with distinction upon you."

An aide handed María the award, a golden star with white enamel and a red enamel pentagon behind it, suspended from a dark blue ribbon. She fastened the ribbon and medal around Tom's neck, stood back, and joined the audience as they applauded and yelled their approval. An embarrassed and grateful Tom Fawthrop beamed at the crowd and raised his arm in appreciation. After a brief reception, President Hernández and her security detail made their way out of the complex and on to her next appointment. Colt Garrett and his protection detail remained for a follow-up meeting with Fawthrop and his executive team.

"Congratulations again, Mr. Fawthrop, on your award. Most deserving. I wonder if we might spend a few minutes to discuss the challenges you're experiencing with the Hermes project and the rumors circulating of a pending change order?"

Tom Fawthrop placed his medal and the accompanying blue shoulder sash on the conference table and smiled. "So, Mr. Secretary. The award from the president was intended to soften me up for this meeting? Good cop, bad cop on the presidential level?"

Colt was about to respond when he noticed the twinkle in the old man's eye. "You got that right, Mr. Fawthrop. Nothing at all to do with the work of your foundation."

"Ha!" exclaimed Tom Fawthrop as he grabbed Colt's arm. "How about you and I take a little stroll?"

Outside of the headquarters, the two men walked arm-in-arm. "I know the change order was unexpected, Mr. Secretary. But we have run into unforeseen delays. Delays that cost money. The government always wants fixed-price contracts, but those costs shouldn't come from my profit margin when the Air Force changes the project scope. If you get your staff to look closer at the specifications we bid and the changes the Air Force has requested, you'll understand why we are behind schedule and why costs are increasing. I'm not trying to cheat the government. I just want to be treated fairly."

Later, Colt thought about what Fawthrop had said while he sat in the car on the way to Joint Base Lewis McChord. He decided to give the man the benefit of the doubt. He'd ask the staff to conduct a complete project review and get the Air Force to explain the change order. The results might prove interesting.

## Joint Base Lewis McChord, Washington

Joint Base Lewis-McChord, or JBLM, is home to the US Army First Corps and the US Air Force 62nd Airlift Wing. Located in the heart of the Pacific Northwest's Puget Sound region, JBLM is the Department of Defense's premier military installation on the West Coast. The joint base, which began operation in 2010 from the consolidation of Fort Lewis and McChord Air Force Base, is one of twelve joint bases created by the 2005 Base Realignment and Closure Commission. JBLM celebrated its centennial anniversary in 2017, making it the oldest military installation in the Pacific Northwest. Fort Lewis was established in 1917, and McChord Air Force base was established in 1947, the same year the US Air Force became a separate armed forces branch.

JBLM is a training and mobilization center for all services and is the only Army power-projection platform west of the Rockies. Its critical geographic location provides rapid access to the deep-water ports of Tacoma, Olympia, and Seattle for deploying equipment. Unit personnel can be deployed from McChord Field, and individuals and small groups can also use nearby Sea-Tac Airport. JBLM's strategic location allows Air Force units to conduct combat humanitarian airlifts to any place in the world with the C-17A Globemaster, the most flexible cargo aircraft in the airlift force.

The Western Air Defense Sector (WADS) building at JBLM is an imposing structure, a fortress built to last. Standing tall amidst the lush green fir trees of Washington State, its gray concrete walls are North America's first line of defense against any airborne threats from the Pacific Ocean.

From a distance, the building looks like it is made of giant concrete blocks stacked on each other, with sharp corners and edges that cut through the sky. Somewhat like St. Peter's Basilica at the Vatican, its sheer size is enough to make anyone feel small and insignificant in comparison. The walls are thick and impenetrable, and stern-looking security force personnel constantly guard the heavy iron gates at the entrance.

Upon entering the WADS building, visitors are greeted by a large, brightly lit lobby. The floors are polished to a mirror-like shine, reflecting the light from overhead fluorescent lights. The walls are covered with maps and charts, and several flags proudly display the Western Air Defense Sector emblem. In the middle of the room stands a tall, glass trophy case filled with medals and awards that showcase the unit's accomplishments and dedication to protecting the nation.

The atmosphere inside the building is portentous and purposeful—men and women in uniform hustle about, carrying out their duties with precision and efficiency. Their boots clicking against the floor echo through the hallways, punctuated by the occasional sharp salute or the low hum of conversation. The air is thick with the smell of strong coffee, a must-have for those working long shifts in the nerve center of the continent's western air defense.

At the heart of the WADS building lies its operations center, a massive room filled with advanced technology and the brains that operate it. Rows of computer stations line the walls, each operated by a dedicated technician, either Canadian or American, whose eyes remain glued to their screens, monitoring the skies for any potential threats. Above them, large screens display real-time data from radar systems and satellite feeds, keeping the command informed and ready to act at a second's notice. In the center of the operations room is a raised platform, where the Western Air Defense Sector commander oversees the entire operation. With a clear view of every station and screen, she can quickly assess any situation and give orders to her team.

Colt Garrett stood in the center of the large room and turned to the WADS commander, Colonel Kari Hunter of the Washington Air National Guard. "Why don't you give me the same unclassified brief you'd give to the local chamber of commerce? It's probably more concise and interesting than what you planned to present to me."

"Mr. Secretary, the Western Air Defense Sector is one of two sectors responsible to the Continental US North American Aerospace Defense Command Region and the North American Aerospace Defense Command. Our missions are peacetime air sovereignty, strategic air defense, and airborne counterdrug operations in the continental US. This is a Washington Air National Guard unit, but I directly report to First Air Force at Tyndall Air Force Base in Florida."

Colt looked around the control center. Scores of intelligent, dedicated, and motivated young people. "Lots of different uniforms here, Colonel."

"Yes, sir, Mr. Secretary. We're a bi-national command. We have people from the Air Guard, Army, Navy, civilians, and the Royal Canadian Air Force. We exercise operational control of Air Guard fighter aircraft, primarily F-15s and F-16s. These citizen airmen are on continuous alert. We use radar data and the radio capabilities of sites throughout the western United States. We also use radar data from tethered aerostats and other radars to improve our low-level coverage of the southwestern border. We feed radar data from all these sources into our computers here, where my team correlates and identifies all airborne targets. They scramble our alert fighters to identify those whose origin is unknown. And they are fully armed if they need to go kinetic."

Colt knew the military used the term "kinetic" to refer to missiles or other traditional types of weapon systems that physically engage targets, as opposed to non-kinetic tools, which can include cyber, electronic warfare, and other means of attack. He also knew that military officers loved to use the term at every opportunity.

"Impressive, Colonel. But I have a good idea of how our air defense systems work. I must confess that I didn't come to learn about your command today. I want to ask you a personal question about your older brother."

Colonel Hunter didn't know what to say. The defense secretary wanted her to share personal information about her brother, Aaron, the Secretary of the Air Force. She needed to tread carefully.

"What is it you want to know, Secretary Garrett? I'll help . . . if I can."

"Excellent! I've known Aaron for decades and know most of his friends. I even recommended him for his job. But no matter whom I ask or how many unofficial investigations I authorize, I cannot determine what Aaron's callsign means. I know it's COOTS because it's embroidered on his flight jacket. Please tell me what it means."

Colonel Hunter smiled, relieved. "I believe that I can help you with that, sir. But I'd like something from you in return."

Colt was excited that he was moments away from discovering the meaning of his friend's callsign. "What can I do for you? Your pick of assignments?"

"No, Mr. Secretary. Not an assignment. I want your challenge coin."

Whenever military members find themselves in a bar, they occasionally challenge one another to see who has the best coin. The coin of the defense secretary is considered rare, sure to avoid paying for a round of drinks. Colt reached into his pocket, removed his personalized coin, and placed it in Colonel Hunter's hand.

"Deal!" he said. "And now, what does COOTS mean?"

Colonel Hunter looked at Colt's coin. "It's an acronym. It stands for Constantly Overemphasizing Own Tactical Significance."

Colt clapped his hands together. "Excellent, Colonel! Outstanding!"

## Boeing Museum of Flight, Seattle

Wyatt Steele tightened a bolt on the side cowling panel of engine number three, the inboard turbofan suspended from SAM 970's starboard wing. He knew to be careful to prevent stripping the expensive bolt, but soon, he found himself thinking about the students in his Navy ROTC class discussing the upcoming designation announcement, the Navy's four-digit code for what they would do after receiving their commissions. The midshipmen with good eyesight invariably dreamed of becoming naval aviators and embarking on a two-year-long path to earning the coveted wings of gold. Because Wyatt wore that insignia on his uniform, the unit's commanding officer had asked him to mentor the young men and women regarding the selection process and criteria for the major training pipelines. Earlier in the day, he had met with a classroom filled with eager young midshipmen, each wanting to know the key to being selected to become a fighter pilot. He smiled when he remembered how nearly everyone in the room raised a hand when he'd ask them who wanted to fly jets. It was always the same. Everyone wanted to turn and burn and feel the need for speed, that is, until they experienced it for the first time. He remembered his first flight in a T-34 trainer and hated how the high-speed maneuvers crushed him down and back into his ejection seat. And then he lost consciousness as the blood drained from his brain and flowed into his lower body. And his large frame wasn't made for the tight confines of a tactical aircraft. It was why he selected the maritime pipeline. Flying the P-3C Orion turboprop from a shore-based airfield seemed preferable to living on an aircraft carrier. But instead of learning to fly the Orion, the Navy selected Wyatt to fly the E-6B Mercury reconnaissance aircraft, outwardly much like the old 707 he was working on that evening.

"Easy, Wyatt! You're going to overstress that bolt!" shouted Dave Ryan from the hangar floor below Wyatt's ladder. "You need to use the torque wrench I gave you to tighten the bolt to specs. I thought you said you knew how to do this work."

Wyatt stopped daydreaming and concentrated on the task at hand. When the wrench made a clicking sound, he knew that the bolt was correctly torqued. "Sorry, Dave. Was thinking about work. The cowling is now secure." Wyatt placed his tools into a canvas bag and climbed down the ladder.

"Are we going to start working on engine number four next? It looks like it could use it!"

Dave placed the tool bag onto the maintenance cart. "Nothing you or anybody can do about that engine. Totally shot. We gave up on refurbishing it years ago when we first got the plane from the Air Force. We'll just put the cowling back on and clean it up. You can give me a hand with that if you have some time before you go home."

The two men repositioned the ladder and attached the cowling panels to the damaged engine. "What would it cost to replace it? Assuming you could find one."

Dave smiled at the younger man. "Oh, we can find one, all right. The Air Force has a dozen across the runway at the military ramp. Boeing lets the Air Force store them there to be available if they're needed for any of the military planes. I suppose I could get one if the museum had an extra three million sitting around. I even submitted a request to the Air Force for a replacement, given that they own the plane. But no joy. I guess we're pretty low on the priority list. And besides, it's not as if it's required. I mean, the plane will sit in the museum while people take selfies in front of it."

"You're probably right. It's a shame, though. Nothing prevents this bird from flying except that one busted engine. That'd be something!"

Dave laughed and then looked at the ancient aircraft. "Yes. That would indeed be something!" He paused and looked intently at Wyatt.

"I have something I've been meaning to say to you, and I guess now's as good a time as any."

Wyatt sensed a change in Dave's demeanor and turned to face the older man.

"Sure."

Dave wiped his hands with a cotton towel. "I'm certain this is none of my business, but it's been on my mind. I know you've been seeing Chloe this week, and she said you two are going out again tonight. She's a grown woman. God knows she can make her own decisions. But I've been around, you know. I can tell you're the type of man women like. Maybe too easily. Not the family type. Don't get me wrong. You're a nice enough guy. But I don't think you're right for my daughter. She's just starting her career, and I'd hate for her to get involved with you and then get hurt. Or abandon her dreams. I'm just saying. No offense, of course. Like I said."

Wyatt silently collapsed the aluminum ladder and leaned it against the hangar wall. He grabbed his jacket and was leaving when Dave said, "I suppose you won't be dropping by here anymore? Can't say I'd blame you."

Wyatt stopped at the door and turned to face Dave. "Have you mentioned any of this to Chloe? About your concern for her?"

"No. I guess I thought we should talk first."

"I'll speak with Chloe about this. And Dave, I'll keep working on the plane."

## Genji's House, Seattle

Lillian approached the tiny home and knocked twice on the solid front door. She could hear a dog barking and then a muffled voice before the door opened, and she saw Genji's smiling face.

"Good evening, Lillian. Please, please come in!"

Lillian followed the woman through a small entryway into a modest living room arranged with tastefully selected furniture. The room reminded her of her grandmother's home in Tacoma, where her mother often sent her when the woman entertained a new friend. The room temperature, smell, sights, and sounds combined to take her back to a time when she was happiest. She noticed that everything seemed clean and orderly, unlike her place. It occurred to Lillian that Genji must have been shocked to find out how she lived.

"Huangdi, stop that!" The small dog was sniffing Lillian's clothes, and Genji was concerned he might find something harmful.

"I am sorry, Lillian. That's how he greets everyone. I'll put him outside." Genji picked up the dog and carried him through the kitchen and out the back door. When she returned to her living room, she found Lillian sitting on the sofa. She sat next to Lillian and took her hand.

"Thank you for coming over to visit. I wanted you to see my

130

home; dinner will be ready in about half an hour. Can I get you anything to drink? Tea? Water? Perhaps a glass of wine?"

Lillian was just a few days into her latest attempt at sobriety. The thought of a glass of wine made her heart quicken. "Well, one glass wouldn't hurt."

Genji returned with a bottle of chardonnay and two wine glasses. She filled the glasses and handed one to Lillian. "Here is to a new friendship!" She took a sip, placed her wineglass on the end table, and turned to face Lillian.

"Now, dear, I need to tell you about something I've been working on. I think you might find it interesting. Can you keep a secret?"

Lillian took another sip of wine and nodded her head.

"I am working with a group of activists who see the need for a more peaceful world. We believe multinational corporations working with governments are responsible for the world's pain and suffering. These companies hold powerful influence over elected officials and have successfully influenced them to purchase massive quantities of weapons of war. They profit from the resulting conflicts and wars, and there appears to be nothing to stop them. My friends and I have an idea of how to bring the world's attention to these despicable corporations and the people who run them."

Lillian had heard Genji talk about her peace and conflict resolution concerns. But now, she noticed that Genji spoke with a degree of conviction and force she hadn't revealed earlier.

"What are you planning to do?"

"Lillian," Genji began, "President Hernández will attend a black-tie gala at the Museum of Flight at Boeing Field tomorrow evening. The president will be making some comments about defense treaties. I don't understand the details, but all the area's defense contractors, including Tom Fawthrop, will be there. I

**131**

know how badly his company treated you. Earlier today, the president even gave him a medal. Can you imagine?"

Lillian still harbored a deep sense of resentment toward Fawthrop and his corporation. She blamed the company and the Fawthrop family personally for her summary firing from the firm.

"I do hate the man, Genji. He's what's wrong with the country."

"I am glad you feel that way. I want to ask for your help at the gala."

Lillian finished her glass of wine. "Sure. What do you want me to do?"

Genji refilled Lillian's glass and poured a small amount into her own. She'd long mastered the art of appearing to drink at the same rate as others while consuming only a few ounces.

"I would like you to visit the museum about an hour before closing. Buy a regular admission ticket and remain in the restroom stall until the building clears. Just keep quiet and don't talk with anyone. Here's some cash for the ticket and a security badge." She handed Lillian an old twenty-dollar bill and the badge.

"You should wear a black top, slacks, and working shoes. At exactly 6:10, you will leave the restroom and walk over to the engine display case. You may take the map with you."

She pointed to a location on a museum map on the coffee table. "On the top right edge of the display cabinet, you will find a small panel. It is about two inches square. You will slide the panel to the side, and you will be able to feel a small toggle switch inside. Please watch the stage for the moment the president ascends. When that happens, flip the toggle switch, and walk immediately toward the door."

Lillian was shocked at what she was hearing. "Are you asking me to set off a bomb?"

Genji laughed. "Heavens no, Lillian. We don't want to hurt

132

anyone. We want to embarrass them. Inside the display support is a small incendiary device. Five minutes after you flip that switch, the support box will emit large billows of smelly, colored smoke into the main exhibit display hall. The event will be ruined, and the press will be there to share it with the world. Our organization will claim responsibility, and maybe we can gain enough attention to make a difference." She poured Lillian another glass of wine.

"You want to make a difference, do you not, Lillian?"

## MV Liberty Risk, Gig Harbor, Washington

The retired Coast Guard chief carefully checked each mooring line to ensure the yacht was securely snug against the floating dock. The red-headed man had spent most of his career as a maritime law enforcement specialist working on anti-terrorist and force protection issues, but he had started as a deckhand and still knew a thing or two about small boats. Colin Flynn took his job as the yacht's caretaker very seriously, beginning and ending each day with a thorough safety check of each space and system of the motor yacht. He worked as a fast rescue boat instructor at the nearby maritime academy, where mariners from the oil and gas, commercial, and cruise industries came to learn their trade. A messy divorce left him with only half of his retirement. The instructor's job helped him to make ends meet. He jumped at the chance when he saw the notice on the academy's bulletin board for a liveaboard caretaker on a luxury yacht. On the rare occurrence when the yacht's owner came aboard, he'd bunk out with his sister in her Tacoma condo.

The Liberty Risk was a newly built, 70-foot Hampton pilothouse motor cruiser with four staterooms, three forward on the lower deck for the owner and his guests. Next was the engine room with its two CAT 1,000 horsepower diesel engines, and aft of that was the crew's quarters in the lazarette. That's where Colin slept when the owner was away. The yacht's living spaces were located on the main deck. The pilothouse was forward with a swath of navigation and systems monitoring screens. The galley was just aft of the pilothouse and was in an open design, allowing views forward to the pilothouse and aft to the main salon. The salon was a large open room with plush, living room-style furniture. Big side windows and a door accessed the aft deck lounging area. Above the main deck was the covered flying bridge, a secondary control station where the yacht could be conned in good weather. Colin knew he could never afford to live in such luxury, and he appreciated being able to live there rent-free. But tonight, he began packing a bag because the owner had called to notify him that he'd be coming down to the marina and spending the night onboard.

"Permission to come aboard?" asked Colt Garrett as he stood at the yacht's gangway with two Secret Service agents.

"Permission granted, Skipper," replied Colin, "although I keep telling you that you don't need to ask permission to board your boat, Colt! I even hoisted your flag!"

Colt looked up at the boat's mast and saw the defense secretary's flag flying—blue with a colored bald eagle in the center and white stars in each corner. The two friends shook hands and entered the yacht's main salon.

"So, you're only here for one night? It's a shame you won't be taking her out. The weather's going to be great for a few days."

Colt sighed. "Yep, one night. I flew in yesterday with the president and stayed last night in Seattle. We have an event tomorrow evening and more meetings on Saturday. We'll be in San Francisco for the weekend and attend the UN celebration before returning to DC."

"I watched Air Force One land on the news last night. People have been complaining about I-5 being shut down during rush hour. I think the president might have lost a few votes."

"I'll mention that to her when I see her tomorrow. Is there anything I need to know about the boat before you go for the evening? I assume there's food and wine onboard?"

"Yes, sir, Mr. Secretary. I'm sure you will find everything you will need."

He stood, gave Colt a sloppy salute, and stopped to speak with one of the protection agents while Colt responded to a text. After grabbing his duffel bag, Colin waved goodbye to Colt and stepped off the yacht.

After the Secret Service agents left the yacht to assume their posts on the marina float, Colt stepped down the stairs from the pilothouse to the master stateroom on the lower deck to change out of his suit into what he referred to as his boat attire: blue jeans and a Hawaiian shirt. He had just undressed when he heard a noise behind him. He turned and was surprised to see a partially clothed Zoey Hale standing in the passageway.

"You might want to stop putting on clothes, Colt," she purred. Zoey draped her arms around his neck and whispered, "It will make things much easier for me."

Two hours later, Colt and Zoey found themselves in the galley preparing dinner.

"You surprised me. I had no idea that you were flying out here." Colt set the dinner plates on the salon table, and they sat down to eat. "Are you going to attend tomorrow's gala with your father?"

Zoey cut into the ribeye steak and glanced at her watch. "You mean this evening's gala, don't you? It's well past midnight!"

Colt slightly blushed. "I guess I must have been distracted or something."

"Or something? I suppose I should take that as a compliment, Mr. Secretary. I do want to compliment you on this little toy of yours. It appears that government jobs pay more than I expected."

"They don't. After Linda died, I sold our home and bought it with the proceeds. I found this moorage in Gig Harbor so that I could be close to my grandchildren after I retire. I'm looking forward to leaving all the political drama behind and spending my days messing about in boats."

Zoey smiled. "Isn't that a line from *Wind in the Willows*? You are a grandfather!"

Colt nodded his head. "Finish your dinner, and I'll read you a bedtime story, Zoey!"

# Day Five

## Abandoned Warehouse, Seattle

The late afternoon sun could not pierce the stubborn cloud
cover over Seattle's industrial area. Ron squinted at the gloom,
navigating his sleek late-model Mercedes sedan down a street
scarred with cracks and potholes. The addresses on the industrial
buildings were faded, forcing Ron to slow down. At last, he
spotted the address Genji had given him, the digits barely visible
on a grime-covered wall. He parked the car, unease prickling
behind his ears. This was no place for a vehicle like his. Too
gleaming, too conspicuous in the run-down surroundings.

He surveyed the neglected warehouse before him. Darkened
windows stared back, shattered panes offering shadowy glimpses
into the dark interior. Piles of forgotten trash lay strewn around
the perimeter, adding to the eerie desolation. An aura of
decay hung heavy in the air, a silent testament to the building's
abandonment. Pushing down his trepidation with a surge of
adrenaline, Ron made his way toward a door bearing a faded
"Office Manager" sign. Each step felt weighted, as if the broken
pavement was trying to hold him back. He could taste the grit of
fear and anticipation on his tongue as he reached the weather-
beaten door.

He knocked hesitantly on the rusty surface, the hollow sound
echoing around him. His mind swirled with questions. Song, the
man he was about to meet, was probably a Chinese operative.
Ron had no idea what to expect, but he knew one thing: he was
about to cross a line he had never thought he would. The chill of

the metal door seeped through his knuckles, the tangible reality of his impending actions. His pulse echoed in his ears, marking the seconds that seemed to stretch into infinity. In the silence that followed, the enormity of his situation sank in, an ominous shadow on his fear- and excitement-laced anticipation. The door creaked open to reveal a young, tall, dark-haired Asian man wearing navy blue coveralls with "Roberts" embroidered in white above the left pocket.

Ron stared at the man's face, and it occurred to him that he could have been a relative. He glanced again at the embroidered name and said, "I'm supposed to meet a Song or a Mr. Song."

The man silently stared at Ron and shifted his gaze to the area outside of the door behind Ron. Seemingly satisfied, he held the door open and motioned Ron inside. Ron was surprised to find his legs propelling him forward and into whatever danger awaited him.

Once inside the old warehouse, his eyes adjusted to the dimly lit space. He followed this "Mr. Roberts" into the center of the warehouse, where a small group of men gathered around an oblong box about eight feet long and three feet wide. Eight bright work lights mounted on tall yellow stanchions bathed the box in an eerie glow of LED-projected light. Several wooden pallets were stacked next to the box, providing a temporary work bench arranged with different types of electronic test equipment in black Pelican boxes and an assortment of hand tools and electrical wires. Just beyond the lighted area, Ron saw two small tan-colored pickup trucks parked inside the warehouse. As Ron approached the open oblong box, one of the men quickly closed the top panel. He felt apprehensive as the men stared at him. Why didn't they speak? What was he supposed to do? Ron was about to say something when he smelled the strong scent of road tar. Or was it motor oil? Something familiar he recognized from the city's road maintenance building. Where was that coming from? Was this the smoke-generating device Genji had mentioned? He decided that he needed to focus on his task and get back to his office.

"Is one of you Mr. Song?" asked Ron, quickly looking from one face to another.

The man with the name "Roberts" embroidered on his coveralls stepped forward and held his hand out to Ron. "Badges," he said, looking at Ron directly.

Ron decided that this must be Mr. Song. He slowly reached into his suitcoat pocket and removed six plastic security badges, each with a photo on the front. He placed the stack of badges and lanyards into Song's outstretched hand. He watched as Song looked at the image on each badge and handed one to each team member. Song looked at Ron and said, "Leave."

Ron quickly walked away from the small group of men and headed straight to the warehouse door. Without looking back, he exited the building and almost ran once outside to reach the relative safety of his German sedan. Driving back the same way he had come, he felt relieved as he put distance between himself and the warehouse. He didn't like the look of the serious-looking men in that building and was eager to have this whole incident behind him. Thinking back to Genji's instructions, all that remained for him to do was to introduce the president at the gala this evening and act surprised when the smoke bomb was detonated. He would have to speak with the police investigators afterward, of course. And he would need to remain at the museum for the necessary press conference. The major news outlets would send their most seasoned reporters, and he smiled at the prospect of national media attention. His mind drifted to the promise of the congressional campaign that Genji offered to sponsor. It would be good to leave Seattle's problems behind, even though many claimed his decisions and policies had caused many of them. He'd need to find a new residence in the nation's capital. Something convenient to his new congressional office. And then, an unassociated but terrifying thought suddenly occurred to him. He had seen the faces of the men in the warehouse. They had not attempted to conceal their identities. He could identify them. And they didn't seem at all concerned.

## The Museum of Flight, Seattle

Stepping through the Boeing Museum of Flight's doors, Colt instantly sensed its purpose's grandeur: preserving and showcasing the wonders of aviation history. He entered the T.A. Wilson Great Gallery, named after one of the pioneers of the Boeing Company. The Great Gallery was a three million-cubic-foot, six-story, glass-and-steel exhibit hall containing more than forty full-size historic aircraft, including the nine-ton Douglas DC-3 hanging from the space-frame ceiling in flight attitude. T.A. Wilson gained notoriety within Boeing when he successfully led the Minuteman intercontinental ballistic missile program. He became company president in 1968 and chief executive officer a year later. As CEO, he developed the 757 and 767 jetliners, and he was president of the company until 1972, when he was appointed chairman of the board. Wilson died in 1999, responsible for Boeing's leadership in the aviation and space industries.

Colt took a moment to appreciate the gallery's architecture, the high walls and soaring ceilings designed to inspire awe through its display of some of the most significant aircraft in history.

As the evening sun filtered through the gallery's vast glass facade, his gaze was drawn irresistibly toward the center of the Great Hall, the SR-71 Blackbird. A colossal bird of titanium and polymer composites, standing testament to the zenith of human ingenuity. Its sharp edges cut a striking silhouette against the setting sun, its midnight black surface absorbing the dying light like an ethereal shadow.

It was not just the imposing size or the unique color that filled Colt with awe, but the Blackbird's legacy. This legendary aircraft could reach altitudes of over 85,000 feet and speeds greater than Mach 3, numbers that would seem unbelievable to the uninitiated. But it was real, as accurate as the chilling story of Gary Powers, who was shot down in a U-2 during a high-altitude reconnaissance mission over the Soviet Union. Walking through the gallery, Colt imagined what it might have been like for Powers, isolated at that incredible altitude, surrounded by the chill of the stratosphere, all alone with the whine of the engine. Then, to successfully survive after he was shot down and tried as a spy in the communist country. The thought was both terrifying and exhilarating. As the glow of the setting sun dwindled into twilight, a profound sense of gratitude settled in Colt's heart. Gratitude for the brave pilots such as Powers who risked, and sometimes lost, their lives in the service of their country during the perilous Cold War years.

"I said, it's good to see you again, Mr. Secretary. Are you okay?" Spencer Hale had one hand on Colt's shoulder, and with the other, he held Colt's hand firmly. "And I believe you know my daughter, Zoey? I think you met one another at the Kennedy Center Honors last summer, where Billy Crystal and Dionne Warwick were recognized. What an evening!"

Colt shook Zoey's outstretched hand and tried to remain professional as embarrassment swept over him. "Yes. Of course. Very nice to see you again, Ms. Hale. Your dress is stunning. Has Spencer made any progress in his plan to have you take his seat? He mentioned it to me when we shared a golf cart last month."

Zoey took some glee in Colt's discomfort at pretending in front of her father that they hadn't been sleeping with one another for the last six months. She liked seeing the man flustered and decided to continue the conversation to see how long she could extend his discomfort.

"We shouldn't be publicly discussing HBS corporate business, Mr. Secretary. We wouldn't want to give our shareholders a reason to panic. But speaking of people's careers, my dad says you may be considering a run for elected office."

Colt was about to reply when Spencer said, "Madam President! I'm looking forward to hearing your comments this evening!"

President Hernández had stepped up behind Colt and joined the conversation. "Good evening, Mr. Hale. Thank you. I hope you won't be disappointed. Did I overhear someone say that my defense secretary is considering running for office? I hope not mine!"

María turned to face Zoey. "I'm María Hernández. And you must be Zoey! Heard great things about you. You're much younger than I expected for someone with such an impressive resume." An aide had just whispered into the president's ear the identity and background of the woman speaking with Spencer and Colt. More than once, María wondered how she would ever make it through a significant social event without the assistance of her know-it-all aides.

Spencer coughed. "President Hernández, it's all my fault. I've been pushing Colt for months to throw his hat into the ring for Congress, even promising to help back his campaign. I assure you I'd never support a candidate against you!" All four laughed while a server offered a tray of appetizers and refilled their champagne glasses.

María turned to Zoey. "Tell me, Ms. Hale. Do you share your father's views of Mr. Garrett's skills? Do you think I should be worried?"

María was joking about the prospect of Colt challenging her in the primary, but she noticed a momentary reaction on Zoey's face. Discomfort? Embarrassment? What could that mean? Did Zoey think that Colt would run for president? No, it was something else. Interesting.

"I believe you'll be reelected regardless of who might enter the race, President Hernández," Zoey replied, "but I'll leave any political speculation to my father. And I do need to apologize, but I must leave before your remarks. I have a business meeting early tomorrow morning in New York. Our corporate plane is waiting for me."

"Not to worry, Ms. Hale. My chief of staff is on his way back to Washington. I suppose it's because he's already heard the speech!"

The group laughed at the president's self-deprecating joke. Zoey shook hands with everyone and walked to the exit.

María turned to Spencer. "An interesting and capable woman, Mr. Hale. You must be proud."

"I am, Madam President. She has a great future at HBS!"

The museum's director stepped forward. "Excuse me, President Hernández. I want to introduce one of our museum's most valuable team members, Dave Ryan, who maintains all our exhibits."

Dave was nervous as he shook President Hernández's hand. "An honor to meet you, Madam President," he stammered. "Is there anything, in particular, you'd like to see while you are here?"

"Now that you mention it, Mr. Garrett spent much of the flight out here talking with me about a retired Air Force One." She glanced around the immense space. "But I don't see it here. Do you have it in another building?"

Dave started to feel more at ease as he began talking about

his airplanes. "All large airplanes are displayed across the street in our aviation pavilion. We have the world's only presentation of the first Boeing 727, 737, and 747 jets, the rare Boeing 247D and Douglas DC-2 airliners from the 1930s, the only Concorde on the West Coast, and the new Boeing 787 Dreamliner. Unfortunately, the retired Air Force One, or SAM 970, is undergoing refurbishment in our maintenance hangar on the other side of the runway."

Dave smiled as a thought occurred to him. "You know, there might be a way for me to show you SAM 970. I'll need a few minutes to see if I can make this happen."

## The Boeing Field Tunnels

President María Hernández carefully descended the worn-out steel steps with her hand firmly clamped onto the chilled railing. The long tunnel deep beneath the busy runway yawned into darkness, its dim lighting casting ghostly echoes on the wet concrete walls. The small group clustered closely as they ventured into the artery of steel and concrete.

When Dave Ryan suggested that María and a small group could use an old tunnel under the runway to get to the maintenance hangar and see the old Air Force One, her security detail lead immediately refused. But after a few minutes of conversation, the Secret Service agent finally agreed if he and at least one other agent could accompany the group. María, Colt, Special Agent Anna DeSantis, and her protection team lead, Special Agent Cade Blanton, followed Dave as he slowly made his way through the decades-old tunnel.

"You see, Madam President, this tunnel is just one of a network of utility tunnels and trenches that were required to build Boeing airplanes over the years. A massive maze that snakes underground throughout the plant. Altogether, Boeing dug miles of tunnels to accommodate utility mains, emergency evacuation, and miles of trenches for branch utility lines. Most of these tunnels are no longer used because of water mains flooding, but this one is still functional, so we can get to the maintenance hangar without driving completely around the plant and airfield."

The tunnel seemed to swallow the roar of a jet landing overhead, reducing the loud sound to a muffled thunder. It echoed eerily, bouncing off the damp walls and intertwining with the subdued whisper of the vigilant protection agents. María's heart thumped in time with their careful steps, each footfall reverberating in the eerie stillness.

Their flashlight beams danced on the ceiling, illuminating a dazzling tapestry of spiderwebs. They glistened like dew-kissed cobwebs in the morning sun, a strange beauty contrasting the austere surroundings. María could not suppress a shudder as her gaze caught the occasional scurry of a rat, some mere skeletal remains and others alive, fleeting shadows in the underbelly of the complex.

The air was thick with the musty scent of damp earth and old machinery. A perfume mingled with the acrid trace of jet fuel filtering from the runway above. It filled María's nostrils, a tangible testament to the tunnel's age and its inherent history, as tangible as the rusted rivets on the tunnel walls.

Guided by the steady beam from Dave's flashlight, their journey through the labyrinth paused momentarily. A rusted steel door emerged from the darkness, embellished with a faded Cold War-era Civil Defense fallout shelter sign. María placed her hand on the sign, touching the

black circle against a yellow rectangular background. Inside the circle, she could barely make out three yellow triangles with the apexes of the triangles pointing down.

"Mr. Ryan," asked María, "why is there a fallout shelter under Boeing Field? It seems like a strange place for one. I mean, under a runway. Whom would it be for?"

"Interesting story, President Hernández." Dave shined his flashlight on the old sign. "It goes back to the 1960s and the early days of the Cold War. Boeing rationalized at the time that a shelter was needed to protect the senior military and defense civilians working at the plant in the event of a nuclear strike. It was assumed that Seattle would be a primary target if the Cold War should escalate into a shooting war. The region was home to many military bases. Boeing probably just wanted a shelter to protect the company's executives and families. I remember being in school during air raid drills. Duck and cover. People were even building bomb shelters in their backyards."

María wondered about the influence that the company might wield as a principal defense contractor and didn't doubt Ryan's suggestion that the shelter was built to alleviate the personal concerns of company executives. Almost anything was possible with the assistance of powerful senators who served on influential committees. This would have happened during the Kennedy administration when Warren Magnusson and Henry Jackson represented the state of Washington in the Senate. If they supported the idea of a fallout shelter under the local defense contractor's plant, the defense department would no doubt have played along. She was still thinking about the fallout shelter as the group climbed another flight of metal stairs and through a heavy steel door.

## Museum Maintenance Hangar

Wyatt Steele was greasing one of SAM 970's main landing gear's wheel axles when he heard Dave shout, "Hello. Anyone here?"

Wyatt hadn't spoken with Dave since last night when he'd been asked to stop seeing the man's daughter. Wyatt and Chloe had talked later that evening over drinks about what Dave had said. Wyatt wasn't surprised at her reaction to her father's interference in her social life.

"None of his business," Chloe said. "End of story. He still thinks I'm a child and that he needs to make decisions for me. I'm an Air Force officer and can more than take care of myself."

Despite Dave's concern, they agreed to continue to see one another but decided to conceal their developing relationship from Dave. Wyatt knew that Dave was planning on attending the gala at the museum and assumed he would have until Monday to continue the discussion with him. But now the man was in the hangar. Wyatt set down the grease gun and stepped out from under the wing. After wiping his hands on a rag, he saw Dave walking toward him, leading a small group.

"Madam President, Secretary Garrett, this is Lieutenant Commander Wyatt Steele of the US Navy. Wyatt is one of the museum's volunteers, helping us refurbish SAM 970."

Wyatt immediately forgot that he had planned to tell Dave about his conversation with Chloe. He stammered, "President Hernández. I'm honored to meet you!" Before he knew it, María was shaking his grease-covered hand. He cringed as she tried to clean her hand with a handkerchief she kept ready for that purpose.

"Oh, my God!" exclaimed Wyatt. "I'm so sorry, Madam President!"

María laughed. "Not to worry, commander. I grew up in the oil and gas business. My father calls this liquid gold. Please don't give it another thought. Mr. Ryan said you're a volunteer here?"

"Yes, ma'am," replied Wyatt, stiffening to the position of attention as he remembered he was speaking to his commander-in-chief. I have a background in the 707-type aircraft, and I'm helping Mr. Ryan get this aircraft ready to move back on display in the aviation pavilion; mostly, I just do the grunt work."

Colt offered his hand. "Colt Garrett, Commander. A pleasure to meet you."

The two men shook hands, and Wyatt couldn't believe he was meeting the other member of the National Command Authority. "Nice meeting you too, Mr. Secretary! You have a great reputation with the troops, sir. It's good to have someone at the Pentagon looking out for them."

Colt was embarrassed at the unexpected compliment in front of the president and wanted to change the subject quickly. "Tell me, Commander, where are you stationed? And did I hear you say you have experience with the Boeing 707?"

"I'm an ROTC instructor at the UW in Seattle, sir. And yes, I'm type-rated in the 707. My last tour was flying the E-6B Mercury out of Tinker Air Force Base. A completely different mission from the one that 970 flew, but of course, the airplanes fly pretty much the same, sir."

Colt liked talking with young naval aviators. They reminded him of his son. Like Wyatt, they were more focused on discussing airplanes than impressing senior officers—even the defense secretary.

Dave patted the stair railing leading to the airplane's rear entry. "President Hernández, if you would follow me, I'll give you a quick tour of 970."

Then Special Agent Blanton moved forward. "Mr. Ryan,

before you start the tour, I'll need to do a quick security sweep of the airplane. Agent DeSantis will remain with the president and SECDEF until I return."

The severe and tall Secret Service agent briskly climbed the stairs and disappeared into the fuselage. Moments later, he descended the stairs and announced, "All clear. You're good to go, Mr. Ryan."

Dave led the president, Special Agent Blanton, Colt, and Special Agent DeSantis up the stairs and into the fuselage. His decades as a museum docent guiding tourists through the famous airplane were evident as he started the tour.

"Welcome to Special Air Mission 58-6970, or as we call her, SAM 970. This modified Boeing 707 was delivered in 1959 and was the first jet-powered Air Force One. This plane was the primary aircraft for Presidents Eisenhower and Kennedy and remained in the Air Force VIP fleet until 1996."

Dave motioned to his right. "At the extreme rear of the plane are restrooms and the aft galley, where food for the staff and press was prepared. And just ahead is the section where the junior staff and journalists would be seated. When the airplane is displayed, visitors are blocked from sitting in the seats by large plexiglass panels. They've been removed for the restoration, so feel free to sit for a moment."

Dave waited while the president and her party settled into the large blue seats. "Pretty comfortable, right? One of the questions we often get is regarding the plane's paint scheme. Until 1961, this aircraft was painted white, silver, and red Air Force colors. First Lady Jackie Kennedy and designer Raymond Lowry created a blue, silver, and white color scheme that President Jimmy Carter modified. SAM 970 wears the newer paint scheme, which continues to this day on the current presidential fleet, including SAM 28000, the airplane you flew in on."

While the others in the group looked at the plane's interior, Cade Blanton looked at his watch. He didn't like the president being away from the museum, but she had strongly insisted. He hoped the tour would end quickly and he could get President Hernández back to the gala. "Thank you, Mr. Ryan," Cade said. "I think we need to move on."

Dave nodded. "Yes. Of course. Please follow me through this bulkhead where the senior staff would sit and work."

The group followed Dave into the next compartment, where they could see a small table on each side of the aisle surrounded by eight airline seats. A secretary's station was positioned behind one of the table groups, and a set of metal file cabinets were secured to the floor on the other side of the airplane. Dave noticed as the stern Secret Service agent looked at his watch again. "Moving further forward," he said, "you can see the president's office on the right."

María looked into the office where her predecessors had worked while in flight. She was awed when she touched the desk and thought about them but was thankful that the current Air Force One was much more expansive. "It's too bad Eric had to fly back to DC earlier today. He's constantly complaining about the lack of working space on our Air Force One."

"And here is the president's conference room. You'll notice a temperature control knob on the conference table. It's fake! Lyndon Johnson preferred to keep the cabin hot, much to the annoyance of everyone else. The fake temperature control knob would signal the flight deck so the crew could raise the temperature slightly. Johnson would still think it was getting warmer but not too warm for everyone else."

Maria noticed a small, hinged panel on the door's bottom. "What is this for? Ventilation?"

Dave laughed. "Madam President, that's a doggie door that

President Johnson had installed so that his beagles, named Him and Her, could join him in the conference room when the door was closed." Maria could only imagine the cost of even the small alteration to an Air Force aircraft, all at the public's expense. It was another reminder of her obligation to not waste taxpayer money.

Dave motioned to his left. "Next is the presidential toilet. We'll keep walking forward to see more seats. The compartment on the right is a communication station where the president could contact the ground to send coded messages. Across the aisle are Air Force One's safes, where the classified codes to initiate a nuclear strike were stored. I understand it's called the football?"

Dave led the group forward into the cockpit. "The flight crew consisted of four people, with a navigator sitting on your extreme left, and the captain in front of the navigator. To the captain's right was the co-pilot, and behind the co-pilot was the flight engineer. The navigator and flight engineer roles are computerized in more modern aircraft. Most now fly with just two flight crew."

Dave walked out of the front left door and down the stairs, followed by María and the others. "Thank you, Mr. Ryan, for showing us your airplane. It was quite an experience!"

Dave beamed. "I'm glad we could make this happen, Madam President!" Glancing at Cade Blanton, he continued, "I think I better get you folks back to the gala."

María touched his left arm. "Would it be possible to stop and visit that fallout shelter we passed in the tunnel? I'd love to see a relic from the Cold War."

Cade Blanton cleared his throat. "Unfortunately, Madam President, I must return you to the gala as soon as possible. We're behind schedule already, ma'am."

María Hernández sighed and shrugged her shoulders. "You

heard the man, Mr. Ryan. Back to the museum!"

After the VIPs left the hangar, Wyatt decided to call it an evening and drive back to his apartment. He didn't want to run into Dave again that night, and besides, it was a good night for a drive along Lake Washington with the windows open, the wind in his hair, and some George Strait music blasting from his speakers. As he walked to his car, he was glad he hadn't been invited to return to the museum with the president and her group. He guessed it might have had something to do with his greasy overalls.

### Fallout Shelter beneath Boeing Field, Seattle

Except they didn't go directly back to the museum. Dave led the group back through the old tunnel when President Hernández insisted they stop briefly to see the old fallout shelter. "I just want to see inside, and then we can be on our way," announced María as Dave unlocked the rusty door. When Dave switched on the overhead lights, he stepped into a large, dark room suddenly bathed in an eerie and yellowish glow.

"It's amazing that the electricity still works after all these years," Dave murmured as the small group followed him and gathered in the center of the room. The two agents conducted a quick security scan of the shelter before returning to María's side.

"It's all clear, Madam President," announced Special Agent Blanton as he rechecked his watch. "We need to get back to the museum to keep on schedule. I've not communicated with the main detail since we entered the tunnel, so I've broken security protocol."

"Yes, Cade. I understand. Mr. Ryan, would you mind giving us the Reader's Digest version of why this shelter is here and how it came to be?"

Dave stepped into the center of the group. "President Hernández, Secretary Garrett, you'll remember the conflict between the United States and the Soviets at the end of the Second World War. The space race, a period of tension, and low-level conflict without outright war."

Colt nodded. He'd served in the Navy during the Cold War and remembered several instances where he wouldn't define the conflict as low-level, but he remained silent as Dave continued his comments.

"Deeply concerned with the spread of communism and the potential of a Russian nuclear attack, the US government organized and promoted a nationwide civil defense program. The Kennedy administration spearheaded a $200 million initiative to fund fallout shelters, and the Seattle Civilian Defense Corps built more than 850 civilian shelters throughout the city. Residents were to be warned of an emergency with a three-ton siren mounted on the roof of the Seattle Police garage downtown. If you follow me to this wall, I'll show you something unsettling."

Dave waited until the group had joined him in front of a faded map mounted on the room's wall. "This is a map of the entire shelter system, codenamed Operation Northwest Passage. You can see that it's a hand-drawn diagram on top of a blueprint boundary map of Seattle."

María touched the map and one of the inked markings. "What do these rings signify, Mr. Ryan?"

"Madam President, those are concentric rings detailing the expected severity of destruction in the city, ranging from utter destruction at the center to minor damage at the outermost rings. You can see the position of this shelter at the outer ring, as well as a point of embarkation at the Seattle waterfront."

Colt raised his hand. "Mr. Ryan, was there a shelter beneath

Interstate 5?" Colt pointed to a shelter symbol on the map just north of Seattle.

"Not was there a shelter underneath I-5, Mr. Secretary; there is one. It's the only fallout shelter in the country built under the interstate highway system. In 1960, they broke ground on the shelter, and the door opened onto Ravenna Street. You can still see the entrance door as you drive through the underpass."

"That's amazing. I'd love to see that the next time I'm in Seattle." He stepped closer to the map. "What made the planners select the center of the target? Presumably, this was not based on knowledge of Russian war plans."

"Good, Mr. Secretary. Remember, this planning was done by men who had served in the war. They assumed an enemy would target a crucial facility to achieve the greatest disruption for follow-up strikes. You'll notice that the center of this target map is the switching area for the railyard south of Seattle."

Colt recalled his past when, as an intelligence officer, he developed potential targets in the event of war. It all made sense to him, and he chilled at the thought of the damage a nuclear weapon would have inflicted on the city.

"Really, Madam President. We must leave now. I need to insist."

María looked at her exasperated security detail head. "You're right, Cade. But one last question, Mr. Ryan. Earlier, you mentioned a rumor about Boeing wanting to protect the company's executives. Are there any other rumors you want to share with us?"

Dave smiled at María. "There are always stories circulating, Madam President. If forced to choose, my money would be on the self-protection angle. It just seems plausible to me. People were looking out for their own families. I don't know if it's true, but I suspect it is."

## Boeing Museum of Flight

Seattle Mayor Ron Gin checked his watch and leaned closer to the Secret Service agent beside him. He clearly remembered his instructions from Genji, and he knew the timing was crucial. "Where are they? I'm supposed to introduce the president for her remarks right now!"

The agent looked at Ron and then softly spoke into his shirtsleeve microphone. He repeated the words into the microphone and then silently waited for a response in his earphone. Several seconds later, he turned back to Ron. "Sorry, Mr. Mayor. I haven't had comms with the detail yet. We'll get underway as soon as the president returns."

The exasperated and nervous mayor rechecked his watch, stepped onto the stage, adjusted the microphone, and addressed the audience. "Good evening, everyone. Welcome to Seattle and the Boeing Museum of Flight. This is one of my favorite venues in our beautiful city, and I want to thank the Boeing Company for hosting us this evening. And could I get a hand for the Emerald String Quartet? I first heard them perform at McCaw Hall last year, and I was delighted that the museum could book them for this event. Thank you, ladies!" The four women stood and bowed while the audience showed their appreciation.

"Before I introduce President Hernández, I'd like to recognize some honored guests in the audience. First, the governor of the State of Washington, the Honorable Marcus Gadman."

The career politician shook Ron's hand and addressed the crowd. "Thank you, ladies and gentlemen. Rebecca and I are pleased to be here this evening to celebrate with you. I've known Tom Fawthrop for years and sincerely appreciate his counsel and support." He motioned to Tom, who was standing close to the stage.

Tom turned to the lobbyist standing next to him. "And by support, I think he means my substantial contributions to his political action committee. Of course, I get nothing in return except great satisfaction from knowing I'm supporting a good cause. It warms my generous heart."

The lobbyist laughed at the older man's sarcasm while carefully looking around to see if anyone had overheard Tom.

After the applause died down, the governor continued. "And I need to recognize our lieutenant governor and secretary of state who drove up from Olympia with Rebecca and me. It was my idea to share the ride so that we could use the freeway's carpool lane!"

The guests laughed, knowing he and his state patrol escort would use any lane they pleased. "With the top three state officials in the room, I wonder if anyone's still working in the state capital?"

The audience once more politely laughed, many of them thinking the state would run much better when the politicians were absent.

"I want to share with you that President Hernández and I were able to spend some time discussing my ideas to increase trade with China. We agreed to continue the conversation after she gets a chance to review my proposal. Thank you, Mr. Mayor, for the invitation to this gala. We're looking forward to the rest of the evening and meeting everyone here." During an election year, the governor wanted to meet and greet as many voters as possible personally. And he calculated that he could get away with referring to a fictional meeting with the president because she wasn't in the room. Politics is a game of such maneuvers. The governor patted Ron on the shoulder and joined his wife near the enormous hors d'oeuvres table.

Ron looked at the clock on the wall near him and sighed. He stepped up to the microphone and smiled at the audience. "Well folks, President Hernández will be with us momentarily. Why not take the opportunity to check out some of the amazing airplanes on display? There's a lot of aviation history in this room. And please enjoy the excellent champagne and appetizers. We'll get started shortly."

On the opposite side of the immense room, Lillian waited nervously beside a large display platform with a jet engine mounted above. The wall clock indicated it was 6:35, well after Genji said the president would be speaking. She didn't know what to do. Perhaps the president wasn't coming? She saw Tom Fawthrop talking with the governor, and she made her decision. Lillian found the small panel on the back of the cabinet. She slid it open, found the toggle switch with her hand, and flipped it to the right. Without taking her eyes off Fawthrop, she calmly walked across the museum's floor and out through the main entrance. She crossed East Marginal Way and was about to get into a city bus when a bright light was followed immediately by the thunder of a tremendous explosion. The bus shielded Lillian from the torrent of debris that cascaded everywhere. Lillian immediately realized that the switch she flipped had destroyed the museum and everyone in it.

## National Military Command Center, The Pentagon

Brigadier General Jerome McClune stood at the heart of the National Military Command Center, an underground sanctuary within the Pentagon. The NMCC, an epitome of American military might, served as the nerve center for operations and decision-making. From this hallowed bunker, strategic responses were coordinated and the nation's security safeguarded.

McClune, a one-star general in the United States Marine Corps, assumed the deputy director of operations role and led the NMCC watch team during their twelve-hour shift. A proud graduate of the Citadel, he had received his commission as a second lieutenant, carrying the bravery of his alma mater with him. Standing 5'6" with a stocky build, he exuded an abrupt, task-focused demeanor. However, beneath the hardened exterior, McClune was a compassionate leader who deeply cared for the welfare of his troops, serving as a fatherly figure to them. He enjoyed mentoring junior officers on how best to navigate career pitfalls.

Though highly pleased with his recent promotion to brigadier general, McClune couldn't help but yearn for his previous role as a commander of the 31st Marine Expeditionary Unit in Okinawa, Japan. He was a combat leader at heart and wanted to receive another command assignment eventually. He pondered the possibility of securing a more career-enhancing position within the Pentagon, perhaps serving on the Joint Chiefs of Staff policy team.

As the watch team settled into their duties, a calm and slightly mundane atmosphere pervaded the watch floor. Computer screens flickered with data, messages were meticulously read, and defense system readiness levels were diligently checked. Amid this tranquil backdrop, a voice with a heavy Long Island accent cut through the silence, offering the general another cup of coffee. Nearby, an Army sergeant vacuumed stray popcorn kernels left behind by the previous watch.

McClune's attention was momentarily diverted by the lively conversation of two nearby Marines. The young men animatedly discussed their plans for the upcoming weekend, eagerly sharing their excitement about attending the Morgan Wallen concert at

RFK Stadium. The Marines engaged in playful banter, discussing whom they would bring as their dates, their enthusiasm filling the room with youthful energy. Watching them, McClune momentarily thought back to his days as a Citadel cadet, planning for an upcoming weekend with his friends. On one of those weekends in Charleston, he had first met Terri, his wife of twenty-two years. Terri and the kids were happy not to be limited to Okinawa's seventy miles, not to mention the luxury of shopping somewhere other than the base exchange. He was thinking of what he would get Terri for their anniversary when his desk phone rang, and he reached for the receiver.

"NMCC Watch Commander. Go!"

"NMCC, this is Air Force One. Flash Traffic. PINNACLE OPREP 3. I say again, PINNACLE OPREP 3, over."

A PINNACLE OPREP 3 describes an event of such importance that it needs to be brought to the immediate attention of the National Command Authority, Joint Chiefs of Staff, the NMCC, and other national-level leadership. A phone notification of the event must be made within five minutes, immediately followed by a message report.

General McClune covered the phone's receiver, raised his right fist, and yelled, "Quiet!" Every eye in the NMCC turned to the watch commander as he spoke calmly into the phone. "This is the NMCC watch commander, Brigadier General McClune, US Marines. I copy your PINNACLE, Air Force One. Go with voice report, over."

"This is Colonel Kirkbride, General. I'm in an Air Force maintenance facility at Boeing Field in Seattle. I just witnessed the destruction of the Boeing Museum, where POTUS and SECDEF were attending a gala with the Washington State governor and about 300 others. It was some explosion, General. Horrific, the building in complete ruins. The Secret Service team here has lost contact with the POTUS protection detail, and they're racing to the museum, or what's left of it. I'll head to Air Force One and prepare to depart, assuming we can find POTUS. My hands are going to be full getting that done. Can you handle sending the PINNACLE message out, sir?"

"Roger that, Colonel. And Godspeed!"

While General McClune was on the phone with Colonel Kirkbride, the NMCC came alive as every system, sensor, and communication device in the command center began transmitting initial disaster reports. The center transformed from a quiet work environment into an efficient war room. McClune's deputy, Captain Scott Ibarra, joined the general at his desk while he attempted to locate the Joint Chiefs of Staff chairman on leave in Maine. McClune finally located Admiral Simmons at a vacation rental cottage and made a voice report regarding the potential death of President Hernández and Secretary Garrett. The chairman ordered that the country's defense condition be increased to DEFCON 4, immediately placing the military on heightened alert and increasing surveillance and intelligence-gathering activities.

On another phone line, Captain Ibarra spoke with the deputy defense secretary, Steve Holmes. Holmes would become acting defense secretary until his boss could be found. McClune grabbed a thick white binder with the letters COG on the spine and initiated a predetermined set of continuity of government actions to ensure the country had a leadership team in place. He notified the White House Situation Room and the Secret Service command center that President Hernández may have been killed. He then focused on defense department readiness while other government agencies implemented emergency plans. Duty officers throughout the nation's capital initiated emergency procedures. Deployed US forces throughout the world prepared for worst-case scenarios. No one in the national security apparatus was getting to bed tonight.

## The US Naval Observatory, Washington DC

Joe and Robin Carlisle had no intention of going to bed early tonight because Travis had told them that the event that would propel Joe into the presidency would occur within the hour. Joe was downstairs watching cable news to learn if something had happened to President Hernández yet. The couple had briefly considered dressing in casual clothes when the expected announcement came, not to arouse suspicion, but Robin was insistent that the first images of her as first lady would not show her in blue jeans. That was why she sat in her second-floor bedroom doing her hair and makeup. Ever since Wednesday, when Joe told her he'd soon be president, she could think of nothing else. Not of him becoming president but of her becoming the first lady.

The job of the first lady has always been important to the history of the United States. Edith Roosevelt, Teddy's wife, hired a social secretary in 1901. Eleanor Roosevelt was the first to broaden the office outside administrative and social secretaries when she hired a personal secretary. But it was Jackie Kennedy who elevated the role of first lady to that of actual celebrity by hiring a press secretary. Jackie became famous for setting a high style, fashion, and charm standard. Today, the Office of the First Lady or First Gentleman, in the case of male spouses, employs more than a dozen staffers dedicated to supporting the president's spouse. Although the office's role has expanded over the decades, its principal function is to assist the first lady in promoting the president's agenda and initiatives. But in Robin's mind, the office was there to support her agenda, priorities, and the particular causes she planned to identify and publicize soon after Joe was sworn in as president. The last forty-eight hours had been exciting, and Robin was eager to start her new life. There was only one problem that troubled her as she brushed her hair.

Yesterday, Robin visited her longtime hairdresser at a local day spa to get her hair cut. It had been only two weeks since her last cut, but she knew that she would be in the public eye, and like her attire, she wanted everything else about her appearance to be perfect. Toni had been cutting Robin's hair since Joe had been a congressman, and the two women had become close friends. She was curious about why Robin needed a cut so soon and had pressed the issue while cutting her hair. Robin hadn't been prepared for her questioning and did a poor job of coming up with a reason.

"Oh," she had said to Toni, "it's just that you do such a great job, and I'm anticipating that I'll be in the press now more than ever."

Toni seemed satisfied with her explanation and changed the subject. "My God, I didn't tell you. Remember that break-in we had last month? It turned out that somebody was targeting hair stylists and day spas and reselling the stolen supplies and equipment online. The owner, Melony, was distraught. She installed new locks on the doors and light fixtures outside to make us feel safer walking to our cars. That parking lot gets spooky during the winter evenings. I appreciate that she's looking out for the staff."

Toni was finishing up her work when she asked, "So, we'll be seeing you again next week? You're getting a facial with Andrea on Wednesday."

Robin was checking out her reflection in the mirror when she responded, "Oh, about that facial appointment. I need to cancel that. And this probably will be the last time I get my haircut here, dear."

Toni had experienced customers changing hairdressers before, but Robin and she were close friends, and she was hurt at the thought of someone replacing her. Robin saw her painful expression and wanted to reassure her friend that it wasn't a personal decision.

"It's nothing to do with you, Toni. It's just that I'll be living at the White House very soon, and I believe they have their own hairdressers there."

Toni was confused. "But why are you going to live at the White House? You're not the first lady."

Robin Carlisle put her coat on and picked up her purse. "Very soon, Toni. Very soon."

Looking at her watch, Robin noticed it was nearly 10:00 pm. She walked downstairs and found Joe watching the television news. Suddenly, as the news anchor announced breaking news, the study's door flew open, and five Secret Service agents rushed into the room. Two agents gently grabbed Joe's arms and moved him quickly to the door.

"Wait a second. I need this," shouted Joe. He picked up a light blue folder embossed with an Arthur Andersen & Co. logo from a side table and said, "Okay. Now we can go!"

Another pair of agents grabbed Robin, and the Carlisles soon found themselves in the back seat of a black Suburban racing away from the Naval Observatory. One of the agents explained to Joe that something had happened to President Hernández, and they were being taken directly to the White House Situation Room. The agent driving the armored Suburban watched his passengers in the rear-view mirror. He saw the look of concern and worry on Joe Carlisle's face, but he was surprised to see what he thought was the shadow of a smile on his wife's face.

# TOM CARROLL

## O'Blarney's Irish Pub, Olympia, Washington

Alex Cassidy looked up from his favorite meal, fish and chips, and raised his empty glass to get the waitress's attention. "Maggie, when you get a chance, could I get another amber ale, please? And more ketchup while you're at it?"

Maggie had worked at the bar for two years and had grown to like the regular customer. He was always polite and one of her better tippers. "Sure, honey. I'll be right back with it."

Alex looked up to continue watching the Seattle Kraken play the Sharks in San Jose. It was near the end of the NHL's regular season, and beating the Sharks was critical for the Kraken to earn the division's third slot in the Stanley Cup playoffs. The fan base had grown logarithmically since the expansion team was formed in 2021, and Alex had become one of the team's most rabid fans. He certainly had time for sports now that he was single again. His divorce was over a year ago, about the same time he was sworn in as Washington State Treasurer.

The divorce was one of the reasons that he was on a first-name basis with many of the pub's wait staff. He ate dinner here several nights a week. He agreed to let Kelly have the house and, in return, got the three-bedroom condo they had acquired as an investment property. Alex lived there alone and tried to find any excuse to avoid spending time there. His job kept him busy enough, being responsible for the safety and security of the state's money, now and into the future. It was a big job, managing the cash flows of all significant state accounts with deposits, withdrawals, and transfers of more than $300 billion annually. A finance degree from Stanford University and an MBA from UCLA were just the first two achievements on his resume. His first job was with the Washington State Investment

**165**

Board, where he had learned the intricacies of investing for the state's retirement funds. Two terms in the state's House of Representatives gave him insight into state operations and politics. The experience gave him the confidence to run for statewide office successfully.

The pub crowd groaned and jeered when the Sharks scored their third goal and now led the Kraken by two. It wasn't looking good for a Stanley Cup this year. Maggie had just delivered another glass of beer to Alex when the big-screen TV image switched from the hockey game to a news broadcast. Once more, the crowd groaned, thinking someone had changed the channel. But a hush fell over the room as the pub's patrons realized the game had been interrupted by a breaking news broadcast. Customers who, just moments earlier, were cheering for their team now sat transfixed as the screen showed the rubble of what only hours ago had been the Boeing Museum of Flight at Boeing Field. News helicopters transmitted live footage of the still-burning building, with tall, towering columns of black smoke climbing into the clouds. Then, Alex read with horror the news station's banner at the top of the screen. The president and governor had been attending an event in the museum and were presumed to have been killed in the explosion.

Alex watched scores of firefighters attack the burning structure from all sides. Ladder trucks with long extended ladders drenched the building's flaming ruins with water streams from high-capacity nozzles. He worried about his friend, the lieutenant governor, and the challenges he would face assuming the governor's role in such a terrible way. And what about the governor's wife? Did she attend the event as well? The news anchor interviewed a fire battalion chief about the blaze when five tall Washington State Troopers in light blue uniforms entered the pub and walked directly to Alex's table.

"Excuse me, sir. You're State Treasurer Alex Cassidy, correct?"

Alex was stunned for a moment and then collected himself. "That's right, trooper. I'm the state treasurer. What's going on?"

"Sir, I'm Captain Shawn Davis, and I need you to come with us right now. We need to get you to the governor's mansion right away. These troopers will serve as your executive protection detail."

With a sense of foreboding, Alex looked at the TV screen and then back at Captain Davis. "I don't understand, Captain. What's this all about?"

Davis nodded his head. "What this is all about, sir, is that we believe the lieutenant governor and the secretary of state were at that event with the governor and President Hernández. You're next in the line of succession to become Washington's governor."

Alex stared at the police officer in disbelief. He had thousands of questions but said nothing while the news anchor continued to describe the accident scene.

"We need to leave for the mansion immediately. Please, follow me."

Maggie watched as the troopers escorted Alex through the pub's front door and into the back seat of an unmarked police car parked directly outside. A customer touched her on the arm. "Maggie, who was that the troopers left with?"

Maggie was about to tell the customer it was the state treasurer but paused to watch through the window as the black sedan and two white state patrol cars sped away with sirens blaring and blue lights flashing. "Unless I heard it wrong. He's now our new governor!"

The three police cars pulled into the mansion's circular drive and parked directly in front of the impressive, nineteen-room brick structure. Captain Davis escorted Alex past the trooper standing guard at the front entrance and into the mansion's foyer.

A short woman of about fifty stood in the room's center with her arms akimbo, clearly not pleased.

"Mr. Cassidy, this is Mrs. Benson, the Executive Mansion's housekeeper. Mrs. Benson, this is Mr. Alex Cassidy, the state treasurer . . . and acting governor. Thank you for coming in at this hour. I understand the chief of staff has explained what happened to the governor and Mrs. Gadman. Mr. Cassidy will be staying here for the time being until we find Governor Gadman. It's our best option for providing Mr. Cassidy's protection. I've sent a trooper to Mr. Cassidy's home to bring some of his clothing."

Mrs. Benson stepped forward and offered her hand to Alex. "Welcome to the Executive Mansion, Mr. Cassidy. I have a guest room ready for you on the second floor. "

## Hale Broadcasting, 30 Rockefeller Plaza, New York

Carissa Curtis, Hale Broadcasting's newest correspondent, was surprised to be summoned into the office of Zoey Hale at this late hour. She had been watching the breaking news broadcast on the HBS monitors and couldn't believe that President Hernández might have been killed in what was being described as a massive explosion at a Seattle area museum. For the last two hours, all the major news channels had canceled regular programming. They were fervently teaming with local affiliates to broadcast live images and interviews to their audiences. Social media platforms were slammed with posts by live video users and pictures of the scene. The story of the likely death of a president transfixed the entire nation and people throughout the world. Baby boomers drew parallels between their experience with the assassination of JFK and the evening's tragedy. Most could remember precisely where they were and what they did that terrible day in November 1963. Others spoke of September 11.

"Thank you for coming so quickly, Carissa." Zoey briskly walked to her desk and sat down. "I asked to see you tonight because the network would like you to anchor our coverage of the explosion in Seattle. HBS wardrobe, hair, and makeup are waiting for you as soon as we're done here. You go live in fifteen minutes."

Carissa was stunned by Zoey's comments. This was the biggest story of the year, maybe even the decade. She was so absorbed with the impact of what she had just been told that she only now noticed that Zoey's eyes were red, her mascara running down her cheeks.

"Ms. Hale, are you okay? Did you know the president personally?"

Zoey took a moment to wipe her eyes. "I did meet the president earlier today in Seattle before I flew back to New York. But you need to know that my father was in the museum when it exploded. And hasn't been released yet, but I know that Colton Garrett was also at that event in Seattle. This is why we're asking you to lead our coverage. You know Garrett better than any other broadcast journalist. The nation is in shock right now. Please put a personal slant on our coverage. Do you think you can do that, Carissa? Can you channel your feelings and help our audience through this catastrophe?"

Carissa stood and straightened her skirt. "Yes, of course I can." She felt terrible about Zoey losing her father. She couldn't imagine what she was going through.

"I better be getting down to wardrobe. Anything else?"

Zoey looked at Carissa for several seconds. "Yes. One more thing. Colt Garrett and I have been in a personal relationship for several months. Nobody knows about it, but that will all come out now. I don't want you to be blindsided about it."

Carissa quietly excused herself and left the office in a rush. It was a lot to take in in a very short amount of time. The death of a president and defense secretary? Who was responsible? And for what reason? She considered her interviews with Colt Garrett and why she respected and liked the man. It was all very sad. She stepped into the elevator and decided to gather herself and concentrate on telling the story to her viewers. She was sure the next few days would be long and challenging.

# Day Six

## GRU Headquarters, Moscow

Admiral Kornilov sat silently at his office desk, reading the large stack of newspapers his aide had placed there. He carefully read the top few stories of the Wall Street Journal, New York Times, Washington Post, Los Angeles Times, and Sunday Times. Each prestigious newspaper confirmed what Kornilov's massive intelligence agency had already reported. The president of the United States, María Hernández, was missing after a bomb of some type exploded in a Seattle aviation museum she had been visiting. Vice President Joseph Carlisle had assumed his constitutional responsibilities as president pending the rescue of the president or, as the news media was increasingly speculating, the recovery of her remains. The newspaper articles included photos of the building's destruction, and it was difficult to imagine how anyone could have survived the explosion and almost immediate collapse of the structure. Interviews with first responders indicated that the rescue or recovery of survivors or victims would likely take several days to ensure that more would not perish in the effort. In the eight hours since the explosion, more than a dozen bodies had been found in the towering and still smoldering debris pile, but no one had been found alive.

The three-star admiral turned to the four flat-screen television monitors in his office. Each major news network had correspondents on the scene broadcasting live images of the destruction. Even though it was still dark in Seattle, emergency lighting allowed the cameras to capture the hundreds of emergency workers carefully sifting through the rubble. Specially trained canine units were being used to locate victims. At the same time, other specialists placed sophisticated audio sensors at critical locations around the building in an attempt to detect the presence of life. The momentousness of the tragedy moved Kornilov despite being aware that he had approved the series of events that created it. He turned away from the monitors and pushed the stack of newspapers to the side.

"Good morning, Rear Admiral Orlov. Thank you for patiently waiting while I learned what the Western press has been reporting about your operation. Of course, I've read our intelligence assessments and your report, but reviewing what the Western media reports after an incident of this magnitude has long been my practice. I assume you have been in our operations center all night?"

Sofia self-consciously smoothed her hair back with her hand, realizing she must be a sight after the long hours in the stuffy Moscow operations room. "Yes, sir. I wanted to be there as events unfolded. As I stated in my report, it appears that the Chinese assets in Seattle have executed the plan perfectly. The American president has likely been eliminated. Even if she were to be somehow found alive at this point, she would likely be severely injured and, therefore, at a minimum, be prevented from attending the UN celebration in San Francisco. As you have seen from the media reports, most experts question the possibility of finding survivors."

Admiral Kornilov nodded. "You are probably correct. Has our asset in Georgetown been in contact with the new president since the explosion? I think it is important to establish communications as soon as possible so that Mr. Carlisle remembers that he is part of our operation. I am concerned that he may conveniently forget our relationship once in the Oval Office and start acting independently."

"Becci Quinn has spoken with Carlisle twice since he was escorted to the White House. She cannot speak with him while he is in the Situation Room, but the Oval Office has proven to be the best location to communicate with him. It is the one place in the White House where he is unafraid of being overheard."

Kornilov smiled. "It is rather amusing to consider we are speaking directly to him in the Oval Office. It appears this Shanghai Protocol of yours is achieving initial success. Once Carlisle reverses Hernández's plan to reaffirm the Pacific alliance, the net result will be a significant reduction in America's influence and power in the region."

"Yes, Admiral. I understand your concerns regarding Carlisle and Webb, for that matter. But protecting their interests will overcome any newfound feelings of patriotism or even guilt. Nevertheless, I will remain vigilant to detect any change of heart."

"I assume you have had contact with our friends in Shanghai. Any new developments there?'

"I spoke with Minister Sun an hour ago. He shared that the operation was a success, and all that remains is to tie up a few loose ends. He regretted the loss of a compromised local politician, but I suspect he brought up the subject to demonstrate the expense his agency had incurred. I do have some concerns, though."

The senior intelligence professional removed his reading glasses. His experience had told him to listen to a subordinate expressing doubt about an operation.

"Oh? Out with it!"

Sofia momentarily gathered her thoughts. "I am getting the impression that Minister Sun may not be acting on behalf of the CCP. There is a strong possibility that his country's involvement in our plan to replace President Hernández is entirely on his initiative."

"And what makes you think that, Orlov?"

"I hesitate to respond in this way, sir, but it is merely a feeling I have after many hours of interaction with him. His guard was down briefly when he mentioned the risk he took in working with us. After this last call, I realized he specifically said the risk was to himself rather than to China or the CCP. I know we have assumed they are one and the same, but perhaps they are not."

Admiral Kornilov remained expressionless as he carefully listened and considered what Sofia Orlov had said. However, the prospect of being personally responsible for an operation with the Chinese that the CCP may not have officially authorized was frightening. At this point, he could only hope the operation would go as planned.

## Deputy Defense Secretary's Office, The Pentagon

Steve Holmes was quickly rushed to his office just minutes after the news of the tragedy in Seattle reached the Pentagon. With the probable death of Secretary Garrett, Steve immediately became acting secretary and would remain in the role until Colt Garrett was found, alive or dead. Steve would have preferred to think about his friend and begin to process his own grief. But his duty as a principal element of the national command authority during a time when both President Hernández and Secretary Garrett had been the victims of an assassination attempt would have to take precedence. He had a long history with Colt Garrett, both serving as undersecretaries of defense in a previous administration. Steve wasn't surprised when his friend was appointed defense secretary after the unexpected death of Secretary O'Kane. Colt's policy expertise and apolitical reputation made him the better choice. Even Steve's wife, Trixie, thought so and was incredibly proud when Steve was appointed as Colt's deputy. Trixie was overcome with grief when Steve was notified about the explosion in Seattle. After spending a few minutes comforting his wife, Steve was picked up and driven in an armored SUV to the safety of his office. He had slept a few hours on his office sofa and then decided to change into something more appropriate than the blue striped pajamas he wore when the agents arrived at his home. Steve stepped over to his closet, where he always kept a change of clothes for just this occasion. He selected a charcoal gray wool suit, a crisp white shirt, and a change of underwear and placed them on the sofa. At least I'll look like a cabinet member for the press conference. He thought as he walked to the tiny shower at the back of his office restroom.

After the quick shower and shave, Steve let his secretary know he was presentable and could start his day. Moments later, a rumbled and bleary-eyed Lenny Wilson joined him in the office and dropped into a chair. Lenny set a steaming cup on Steve's desktop. "I figured you could use a cup before things get crazy, Mr. Secretary. How are you feeling? Any news about Colt or the president?"

"Let's keep it to 'Steve' while you're in this office, Lenny. And refer to me as 'Mr. Holmes' in front of the staff and the press. Colt's still the defense secretary, and he will be until we can find him." Lenny saw the look on Steve's face and knew the man was hurting as much as he was.

"As to how I'm feeling right now, just between us, I'm in a state of shock that somebody or an organization would attempt to assassinate POTUS on US soil. I realize it's happened before, but somehow, I thought that all of our safeguards and intel would have foreseen and prevented it."

Lenny was well aware that Steve's background in the

intelligence community had led him to have faith in the IC's ability to see and know all. A dangerous and foolhardy assumption, but Lenny decided this wasn't the best moment to offer that opinion.

He pushed the coffee mug closer to Steve. "Yes, sir. It's hard to imagine how they missed it. But you mentioned somebody or an organization. What about a nation-state? Plenty that don't agree with President Hernández's policy decisions."

Steve sipped from the mug and then pressed his fingers together. "Possibly, Lenny, but unlikely. This would be an act of war, and I can't imagine why an adversary would take such a risk. It's just more probable that the bombing was the work of an extremist or terrorist organization. We don't know anything yet, but we will. I've ordered Kurt Shaffer to fly to Seattle to lead the DOD efforts. He should land in Seattle within the hour to assess the situation with the local law enforcement. The FBI and the Secret Service already have agents at the scene. I'm working with Northern Command to get some boots on the ground should Shaffer require some muscle."

Lenny could only imagine the jurisdictional complexity involved with the attempted assassination of a president on US territory. He had read about the infighting between the Kennedy executive protection detail and the Dallas PD in the immediate aftermath of the JFK assassination in 1963. The Secret Service agents physically pushed JFK's casket through a DPD detail to get it to Love Field, onto Air Force One, and then to Washington.

"If anyone can manage through that mess, Admiral Shaffer can. And he had a close relationship with Secretary Garrett. They served together."

Steve slammed the mug on his desk, sending coffee flying. "Damn it, Lenny. Shaffer HAS a close relationship with Colt. We don't know that Colt didn't survive. At least not yet."

Lenny nodded. "Yes, sir. Sorry, sir." He waited as Steve cleaned up the spilled coffee with a paper napkin. Lenny realized that Steve must be struggling with the loss of his friend while being burdened with leading the massive agency. And then Lenny forgot himself momentarily and blurted out, "He was my friend, too."

Both men sat silently, each consumed with their thoughts. Lenny decided to change the subject. "Have you contacted Dan and Allie yet? They must be going crazy with not knowing if their father survived."

Steve shook his head. "Not yet. I didn't know what to say."

Lenny thought for a moment. "I'll do it, sir. It would be best for you to remain focused on running things here until Secretary Garrett returns. I'll tell them you're thinking of them."

Steve looked at Lenny and forced a smile. "Thanks. I think I'll wander down to the NMCC and see if there's been any news."

He walked Lenny to the office door and touched his shoulder. "Take care. I'm just glad that I'm not Joe Carlisle right now!"

## The Oval Office

Joe Carlisle gazed through the windows of the most impressive office in the world and realized he had finally reached his lifelong ambition to become president of the United States. The accomplishment dwarfed everything he had ever achieved in what many would have considered a stellar career. Joe knew he would be forever known to history and looked forward to the power he would yield. He would have fame, fortune, and popularity he'd only half-imagined before. Important and famous people would hang on to his every word, and beautiful women would find him interesting and attractive. He was lingering on that thought when Travis Webb interrupted his daydream.

"Excuse me, Mr. President, but I thought we should discuss an important topic. Our mutual friend has insisted that we resolve the question of your legal status as president before others raise it. And I agree with her."

Joe Carlisle turned from the window, sat at the impressive desk, and pressed his bony fingers together. "Yes, Travis. And just what does our Russian friend insist that we resolve?"

Travis knew the Oval Office was routinely swept for electronic surveillance devices, but he still felt nervous speaking aloud about them working with the Russians. His delay in responding to Carlisle's question only succeeded in irritating the new president.

"Damn it, man. I already told you it was safe to talk here! Out with it!"

Travis paused another moment, looked around the office, and then began. "Yes, sir. As you know, the Constitution explicitly states the vice president assumes the presidency on the death or resignation of the incumbent."

Carlisle drummed his fingers on the desk and stared at Travis. "And?"

"And, with the level of destruction we've observed at the museum, it's reasonable to believe that President Hernández has been killed, and you automatically assume the presidency. The media is already assuming that's the case."

Carlisle was looking intently at Travis. He signaled with his hand for him to continue.

"Well, sir. The Russians, and the Chinese, as well, are advising that we delay invoking the constitutional powers and, instead, invoke the provisions of the 25th Amendment. The 25th allows the vice president to serve as acting president until the president's death has been confirmed. The thinking is that you would be seen as more compassionate and concerned about President Hernández and Secretary Garrett if you delayed assuming the office until the body turns up. Now is the time to assume the role of trusted guardian of the country, even mourner in chief, rather than be seen as too eager to replace President Hernández. Recall how badly Al Haig was depicted for his comments in the aftermath of the Reagan assassination attempt."

Joe Carlisle remembered Secretary of State Haig's ill-timed and incorrect comment, "I'm in control here." But he still wasn't convinced he should wait to assume the presidency. "Get her on the phone now. I want to hear it for myself."

Travis blinked his eyes. "You want me to call her from the Oval Office?" He waited for an answer but watched as Carlisle turned and stared out the window.

The phone call with Becci Quinn went badly. She clarified that Carlisle had no option but to follow her directions explicitly. After the call, Joe Carlisle gathered his thoughts before speaking to Travis. It was becoming increasingly clear that although he would be president, he would also have to take orders from Moscow and Beijing. But there were ways to change the status quo and remove the foreign interference. But that could wait for another day. Now, he decided he would move forward as acting president. He looked up at Travis.

"Okay. Acting president, but just until they find the body. And I've decided to leave Steve Holmes as acting defense secretary. After the bodies have been discovered, I'll appoint you acting SECDEF and then push for Senate confirmation."

Travis left the Oval Office very pleased. The meeting with Carlisle went better than he had expected. He confirmed he could control Joe Carlisle's ego and manipulate the man as Becci directed. He was excited by the prospect of finally rising to secretary of defense and being accorded the respect he long deserved. It was a good day.

## Wyatt Steele's Apartment, Fremont

Wyatt happened upon the old apartment building when out for a morning run shortly after moving to Seattle. The Navy had temporarily put him up in a local hotel for the short term, but he needed to find a more permanent housing solution. A hand-written sign in the window grabbed his attention, and after a brief conversation with the building manager, Wyatt quickly signed a three-year lease. The four-story brick building was in the Gothic and Victorian styles. The manager said it had been built after the Great Seattle Fire in 1989, caused by an overturned glue pot in a carpentry shop. Wyatt didn't mind the noisy and temperamental steam heating system. It reminded him of his grandfather's home.

It was Saturday morning, which was Wyatt's long run day. All active duty and reserve sailors must perform an annual physical readiness test to demonstrate their physical fitness and the ability to execute military tasks. Wyatt wasn't concerned about the upcoming test. He typically ran most days of the week because it was during running that he solved most of his problems. He needed to consider his developing relationship with Chloe and her father's command to stay away from her. He laced up his running shoes, set the security alarm, closed the front door, and headed into the sleepy Fremont neighborhood.

Fremont is situated north of downtown Seattle along the Fremont Cut of the Lake Washington Ship Canal. The canal connects the freshwater body of Lake Washington with the saltwater inland sea of Puget Sound. Some referred to the neighborhood as "The People's Republic of Fremont" because of its past as the center of the area's counterculture. One example of Fremont's left-of-center reputation is the statute of Vladimir Lenin that was brought there from Slovakia after the fall of communism. Wyatt started east on Northlake Way this morning and passed under the Aurora Bridge. Under the bridge's north end was the Fremont Troll, an eighteen-foot-high sculpture of a gigantic troll smashing a Volkswagen Beetle in its hand. Wyatt slowed his run and carefully avoided the tourists crowded around the troll before he increased his pace for the ten-mile run.

As Wyatt settled into his running zone, he let his mind wander to his most recent problem: continuing to see Chloe without alienating her father. He respected the man but realized his feelings for Chloe were growing stronger each day. It had been some time since he had met someone as special as she was. After thinking through several options and scenarios, he ultimately decided that he needed to be forthright with Dave. He looked at his watch and realized he needed to return to his apartment. He was the NROTC duty officer that Saturday and wanted to be on time to assume the watch. It wasn't that anything ever happened at the command that might have required him to do anything. The NROTC unit was just a building on the University of Washington campus. However, the Navy had a long tradition of having a duty officer at each command, necessary or not. He crossed the street and started back to his apartment.

The cold water streamed off Wyatt's back as he stood in the ancient ceramic tub surrounded by an opaque shower curtain that was probably older than he was. Years of rodeo injuries and the resulting surgical scars marked his muscular back. Women often told him they found his back and its scars strangely attractive, but he was self-conscious of the disfigurement and rarely took his shirt off in public. He efficiently toweled off his torso and legs before quickly dressing in his service khaki uniform: long pants and a short-sleeved open-collar shirt adorned with gold oak leaves on each collar, three rows of ribbons, and his Naval Aviator wings. While frying eggs for breakfast, he first heard the news of the museum explosion on the TV. Forgetting breakfast, Wyatt sat transfixed on his sofa and focused on the news broadcast. He saw images of the destroyed museum, a building only days before he had strolled through. But it was when the news anchor announced the likely death of President Hernández and Secretary Garrett that Wyatt felt a state of shock. He had met both only yesterday, and now they were gone. Forever. As a naval aviator, Wyatt had previously experienced the loss of a fellow pilot, but this seemed different. He needed to get to work to determine what the classified message traffic mentioned about the explosion. And he decided to call Chloe to find out what she was hearing. Grabbing the keys to his vintage Camaro, he raced out of his apartment.

## US Navy C37A, Eastern Pacific, Flight Level 410

Admiral Kurt Shaffer, commander, Indo-Pacific Command, tried to rest as the military Gulfstream V business jet approached the west coast of the United States. Flying on the twelve-passenger executive jet was immensely more comfortable than the F/A-18 Super Hornet Kurt had flown for most of his time in the Navy. But at this point in his career, and given his age, the convenience of a bathroom and a galley seemed more important than the ability to fly at twice the speed of sound, even without an ejection seat. Kurt Shaffer was responsible for all Department of Defense forces in an area encompassing about half the earth's surface, stretching from the waters off the West Coast of the US to the western border of India and from Antarctica to the North Pole. He was responsible for 380,000 sailors, soldiers, Marines, airmen, Coast Guardsmen, and DOD civilians in a geography covering thirty-six nations, fourteen time zones, and more than fifty percent of the world's population. He reported directly to the secretary of defense, who reported directly to the president. This morning, the acting secretary of defense had personally ordered him to fly to Seattle and assume federal responsibility for the museum explosion site. He knew navigating the treacherous waters of conflicting federal, state, and local jurisdictions would be difficult, but he had other matters on his mind. Personal matters.

The Navy pilots had pushed the jet's two Rolls-Royce turbofan engines to the limit because the four-star admiral had requested that he "get to Seattle yesterday." Admiral Shaffer's reputation as an exceptional and gifted fighter pilot was legend throughout the fleet, and the two young aviators didn't want to disappoint him. The aircraft commander checked his navigation data and keyed the intercom. "Admiral Shaffer, I just checked in with Seattle Center, and we're about to start our descent. Sir, we should be on the deck at Boeing Field in about twenty minutes. We need to secure the cabin for landing."

Kurt Shaffer pressed a small button on his desk. "Thank you, Commander. Nice job getting here so quickly. Well done, son." He released the button and finished the coffee in his cup. Colt Garrett was dead. That's what Steve Holmes had said. The words had gone like a knife through his heart. He'd known Colt since they had served together in the same air wing. Colt even gave him his call sign, VINCE, when he mistakenly landed on the wrong aircraft carrier, USS Carl Vincent. Kurt smiled when he remembered the incident. For decades, the two men had grown closer. Their families were close friends, and they shared countless celebrations of births, weddings, and even funerals. He would miss Colt Garrett more than anyone would know.

Kurt let his thoughts shift to the loss of a sitting president and the impact the event might have on his responsibilities in the Pacific. Would adversaries take advantage of the leadership change? How quickly might the new president embrace his new domestic and global responsibilities? Kurt was well familiar with Joe Carlisle and his limitations. Joe had reported to Kurt when Joe was a rear admiral before entering politics. Kurt Shaffer relieved Carlisle of his carrier group command for a lack of confidence in his abilities. Now Carlisle would be the commander-in-chief. And no doubt, Joe Carlisle would find a reason to replace Kurt at the earliest opportunity. Kurt pinched his nose and equalized the increasing pressure on his eardrums as the jet descended. Kurt remembered back to his first Navy physical when he was asked to demonstrate clearing his ears. Until that moment, he had no idea that failing that simple test would mean that his career as an officer would have been over.

He next started thinking about his priorities over the next few days. First, he'd need to establish working relationships with the plethora of federal, state, and local officials who, in all probability, believed that they were in primary charge of the rescue and recovery efforts. He knew it would take some convincing for him to assume overall command of the explosion site. He thumbed through several federal documents that would help establish his authority. He was glad Steve Holmes had already ordered special support if required. A thought occurred to him as he finished a second bottle of water and tightened his seat belt in preparation for landing. He pressed the intercom button.

"Commander, would you contact the tower at Boeing Field to get clearance for a low pass before we land? I want to see the damage from the air."

# SHANGHAI PROTOCOL

## Fallout Shelter, Boeing Field

Colt Garrett looked at his watch and noted that more than twelve hours had elapsed since a loud explosion was heard in the ancient shelter, immediately followed by a power outage in the Cold War-era bunker. Despite hours of effort, Special Agents DeSantis and Blanton could not pry open the shelter's steel door. Cade Blanton suspected the entry was blocked or jammed somehow due to the explosion. Dave Ryan's flashlight gave out just a few hours after the explosion, and the group's only light source was their smartphones. The phone batteries eventually drained, and now Colt sat beside President Hernández on an old canvas military cot in total darkness. The smell of her cologne somehow made the mildew of the old shelter bearable.

"I'm sorry for insisting we revisit the shelter, Colt. This is all my fault. No lights. No communication with the outside world. I wonder how long before they find us. And what could have caused that explosion?"

Colt Garrett had been thinking about the explosion for the last several hours. Perhaps a gas leak? Or an aircraft crash? Both were reasonable assumptions. Airfields contained many elements that might cause a massive explosion. The explosion's cause didn't bother Colt as much as the fact they hadn't been rescued yet. He knew that every resource available would be expended to find the president. And yet they had heard nothing. Something was very wrong. Colt turned to María.

"Madam President, your insistence on returning to the shelter probably saved our lives. Whatever caused that explosion and trapped us here likely severely damaged the access tunnel. This shelter was designed to withstand a nuclear event. I think we can survive here until the rescue team finds us." Dave Ryan had been trying to decipher the generator startup procedures he had found

**186**

mounted on the wall, trying to read them by the light of some old matches he found. Colt pointed this out to keep the president distracted.

María touched his arm. "Thanks, Colt. I didn't mean to invite you to my pity party. I'm sure we'll be found soon. My husband is probably worried sick."

Colt heard her words but could tell she didn't quite believe what she was saying. It was common knowledge that her marriage had been maintained for the optics. A divorced president wouldn't poll well. Despite her intelligence and competence, María Hernández didn't strike Colt as a happy person, and he had long suspected that her failed marriage was partly the cause. He was about to respond when the sounds of a diesel motor echoed in the room, and the electric overhead lights flickered and then remained on.

María Hernández stood up from the cot and smiled at the small group. "It appears that Mr. Ryan has been successful with the generator. Perhaps we should inventory this shelter and see what it offers while we can still see."

Colt and the two agents stood and began walking through the shelter again. This time, they searched for items that might contribute to their survival and the prospect of being found.

María gathered the team around a small, gray metal desk an hour later. "Who'd like to go first?" she asked.

Dave Ryan cleared his throat. "It looks like we're good with water and food for some time. I found about forty cases of MREs and several pallets of canned water in the storage room. We can also use the additional military cots and wool blankets we found."

"That's great, Mr. Ryan. How long do you believe the generator will run?"

"Based on how much fuel we've used so far, we have enough diesel to last about four days, assuming we shut down for eight hours each night. The exhaust gas vents out to the surface through a series of ducts."

"That's good news. Anything else?"

"Yes, ma'am. The shelter does have an escape hatch that leads to a secondary tunnel and a path to the surface. It appears the hatch has been welded shut for some reason, and we don't have the gear to cut the welds."

Colt stepped forward. "I guess having an escape path would have been too easy." He looked at the Secret Service agent.

"Mr. Blanton, where are we with weapons?"

"Reasonably good, Mr. Secretary. Special Agent DeSantis and I are armed with our 9mm Glock 19s, and we each have three fifteen-round magazines. No long guns. My radio is still operational, but the shelter is shielding any reception."

President Hernández noticed that Colt had taken over the meeting, but she didn't feel the need to interrupt.

"Anna, what about comms?"

Anna DeSantis referred to her notebook. "I checked each of the landline phones, and none are operational. There are six radio consoles on the far wall, but I couldn't get them to power up. The batteries are probably dead. But there is some good news."

All eyes stared at Anna. "There is a working television in the operations room, with a coaxial cable that must be routed to an antenna on the surface. I got reception to analog broadcast stations, including local affiliates of the major news channels. They're all talking about an explosion at the museum."

Colt Garrett nodded and smiled for the first time since the explosion. "Finally, some good news!"

# TOM CARROLL

## Security Office, Boeing Field

In 1999, the King County Sherriff's Office and the King County Department of Transportation entered a partnership to provide a unique combination of services to Boeing Field. The Sheriff's Department created a special unit that combined law enforcement and fire protection within the same organization. As a result, the deputies were cross-trained to combat aircraft fires. When his mobile phone rang, Sergeant Zach Thomas was working on the duty schedule at his desk. The call was from the commanding office of his Army reserve unit, who had a special request. Zach served as a staff sergeant at Joint Base Lewis McChord one weekend per month and for two weeks a year. He'd served on active duty for eight years and had joined the reserve to complete the twenty years of service required for military retirement. After the brief phone conversation, Zach powered down his workstation and headed for his patrol car. Minutes later, he stopped at Gate 3B and approached the deputy on guard.

"Morning, Derrick! Any issues with the press since you came on duty?"

The local and national press outlets had been attempting to gain airport access. Still, Zach Thomas's deputies were under strict orders to prevent anyone without authorization from getting onto Boeing Field.

"No, quiet here—nothing like the main gates. What's up?"

Zach was about to respond to the deputy's question when a convoy of ten military trucks approached the gate. An armored Humvee led the convoy, and an officer dressed in combat gear climbed out of the vehicle and stepped over to the two deputies.

"Good morning. I'm Colonel Rodgers. I command an infantry battalion based at Joint Base Lewis McChord. I have orders to provide security assistance to the airport because of the explosion."

He handed Derrick several pages of paper and waited while the man carefully read each one. If Derrick hadn't been distracted while carefully reading each page, he might have noticed Colonel Rogers slightly nodding to Sergeant Thomas.

Derrick handed the documents to his supervisor. "What do you think, Sergeant? Should I let them pass?"

Zach continued reading the stack of papers and handed them back to Derrick. "This looks legit. You're good to go, sir."

After the last truck had passed through the gate, Zach put his hand on Derrick's shoulder. "Just to be safe, you should notify the operations center. Can't be too careful."

## Operations Center, Boeing Field

Admiral Kurt Shaffer shifted his position in the hard plastic chair. At the same time, he listened to the Washington State adjutant general, Major General Cyrus Clements, share details of the ongoing rescue and recovery efforts. General Clements, a personal injury lawyer from Spokane responsible for the state's National Guard, had been appointed as the state's adjutant general because of his connection to Governor Gadman, his brother-in-law. After listening to Clements drone on for over an hour, Shaffer glanced at his watch and then briefly around the packed room. Also present was the chief of the Washington State Patrol and supervisory agents of the FBI, the United States Secret Service, and the Bureau of Alcohol, Tobacco, and Firearms. Chiefs of the local police departments filled other seats while the fire department chiefs stood against the far wall. The door opened, and an Army colonel in full combat gear armed with a 9mm sidearm stepped into the room and sat in the chair on

Kurt's left. General Clements appeared momentarily distracted and then continued with his presentation.

"Admiral Shaffer," Clements said, "I'm wondering what resources the Department of Defense will be able to provide to support the operation? I was surprised that the Pentagon sent someone of your seniority to assist."

Kurt Shaffer glanced again at his watch, stood, and joined the two-star general at the front of the room. "Thank you, General Clements, for the thorough briefing. Very informative. Before I begin, I'd like to introduce Colonel Sam Rodgers, United States Army. Colonel Rodgers commands the 2$^{nd}$ Battalion, 75$^{th}$ Rangers, out of JBLM. Taking over airfields is a traditional element of Ranger operations. Colonel Rodgers and his three companies of Rangers will provide perimeter security for the rescue and recovery effort."

General Clements looked shocked. "I believe you're mistaken there, Admiral. This is the state of Washington, and you have no jurisdiction here."

Admiral Shaffer removed a single-page document from a folder his aide handed him. "Quite to the contrary, General, I am the jurisdiction here. This document, signed by the acting secretary of defense, declares the explosion site as a National Defense Area, effective five minutes ago. President Hernández and Secretary of Defense Garrett are missing. I've been designated as the NDA incident commander. This location is now federal property until I release authority back to local control. I'll need everyone here to work with my staff for assignments. Questions?"

The FBI special agent raised his hand. "Admiral, what role do you want the bureau and the ATF to assume?"

Shaffer was about to respond when General Clements slammed his coffee cup on the table. "Now, wait a goddamn minute!" he shouted. "My troops aren't going to work for the feds. We're a Washington State force, and I report to the governor."

Shaffer handed Clements another document. "Not anymore, General. Effective immediately, you report to me. The president has federalized the Washington National Guard for this emergency. I suggest you read this document, take a minute, compose yourself, and then start working on helping me understand how best to use your troops. You're in the Army now, Cyrus!"

## Spencer Hale's Office, Hale Broadcasting

Zoey sat down in her father's leather chair and looked at the items he kept close while he worked through his day—an old black Swingline stapler, a coffee mug repurposed as a pen holder with an assortment of inexpensive ballpoint pens. She examined one to see the familiar tooth marks caused by his habit of angrily chewing on a pen when negotiating a particularly troublesome contract. She had tried to get him to stop the habit, but she quit complaining about it when she realized it was better than chewing on those terrible cigars. An obsolete Rolodex rotary file with hundreds of business cards sat next to the pen mug, something Zoey loved to kid him about. "Dad," she remembered saying, "I'm sure your assistant has all your contacts online. Why do you insist on keeping that old broken thing?" His response was always the same. "Because, my beautiful daughter, this old broken thing and I started this business together!"

Zoey picked up a small silver frame holding a photo of her with her father on the deck of an Alaskan fishing charter boat. They were straining to hold up the four king salmon they had caught earlier that day. The fishing trip had been more than twenty years ago, yet Spencer Hale had still treasured the memories of the time with his daughter away from the distraction of the business world. She slowly and almost reverently gathered the personal items and placed them in a cardboard box she had brought.

And then she began to cry. Memories of her childhood flooded back, and she finally let go. Her father had been a massive part of her life, more significant than she wanted or could admit. The one person in the world that she could turn to for comfort was just found dead. Colt and Zoey hadn't discussed any long-term plans for their relationship. The two busy professionals had been taking things day by day. But with the death of her father, Zoey began to wonder if she had been short-sighted regarding her personal life. Colt seemed a good match for her, but now she didn't have him, either. She noticed the broadcast feed on the monitor displayed a photo of her father and was about to turn up the sound when Sam Chun stepped into her father's office.

"Good evening, Zoey. Your assistant said that I might find you here. I want to discuss something with you if you have a moment."

Samantha Chun was a long-time member of Hale Broadcasting's board of directors and was the recently retired CEO of Chun Cosmetics, where she successfully led her company through a series of challenging acquisitions. Sam was a good friend of Spencer Hale and a familiar guest at Hale family events. She watched the broadcast monitor for a few minutes and then turned to Zoey.

"Dear, how are you doing? I can only imagine what you're going through. And they haven't found President Hernández or Secretary Garrett yet. Just terrible. I want you to know you can call me if I can do anything for you." Sam had heard rumors that

Zoey and Colt Garrett were involved but didn't think she should mention them.

Zoey smiled. "Thank you, Sam. I'm doing all right, I suppose. I just came here to get some of Dad's things before his replacement moves in. Have you decided when the special board meeting will be called?"

"That's why I came to see you. I've been speaking with the other directors, and we all strongly feel that you should succeed Spencer Hale as chairman and CEO. You know the company better than anyone, and with you at the helm, we believe Hale Broadcasting will have continued success. I know the timing's terrible, but we feel it's in the best interest of the shareholders that a new leader is in place before the markets open on Monday morning. Can I tell them that you will accept?"

Zoey wasn't shocked at the news but was surprised that the directors had already informally met. She was about to comment that it would be better to wait until after her father's funeral on Friday. But, she quickly remembered the board's first responsibility was to the corporation's shareholders. Business came first.

"You're right, of course. You probably know that Dad had been working on me to fill his seat at some point. I wish it didn't take him dying to place me there. I'd planed to benefit from his advice for a while."

She examined one of the chewed pens and then looked up at Sam. "You may let the directors know I'll accept the leadership of HBS should they elect me. When will the board meeting be held?"

Sam silently nodded her head and breathed a long sigh of relief. "Excellent. Wonderful. As for the meeting, the directors are waiting for us in the boardroom right now. I'll give you a chance to freshen up first, and then I'll let them know you're on your way."

Zoey looked at her reflection in a mirror and saw that her tears had ruined her makeup. As she did her best to get ready for the board meeting, Zoey thought once more about her father and how he had wanted her to succeed him. Closing the office door and walking down the hall to the boardroom, she thought, I guess he gets his way again.

# Day Seven

## The White House

Sunday morning was typically a slow day at the White House. Staff not needed for a particular task or activity were not required to be at work. That fact didn't prevent many West Wing staff members from spending hours at their desks rather than with their families this morning, even if they didn't have a work-related reason to be there. The president was missing and presumed dead. Each staff person assessed and calculated their chances of keeping their jobs in a Carlisle administration. It might improve their chances of staying on for the remainder of the term if they were noticed working on a weekend, particularly at a time like this. White House Chief of Staff Eric Paynter was under no such illusion. He had served in the role under two administrations, and that was a record for White House chiefs of staff. He and Joe Carlisle had known one another for years. In many ways, the vice president practically worked for the chief of staff. Carlisle had resented Eric Paynter's authority in the Hernández administration, and Eric was convinced that Carlisle would replace him the first chance he got.

It was probably for the best, he reasoned. Eric had no respect for Joe Carlisle and realized he had no interest in assisting the man in the likely gutting of the Hernández White House team. But he was still the chief of staff, and until Carlisle moved to fire him, he'd serve in the role as best he could. Eric nodded to the president's secretary and stepped into the Oval Office.

"Good morning, sir. I have some documents I'd like you to

review and sign. Nothing important, just some proclamations and such. I can pick them up later this afternoon. I have some details about today's schedule I'd like to review with you if you have time?"

Carlisle glanced up from his desk and scowled. "We can talk about the schedule later this afternoon. I want your thoughts about a press conference I called for this morning regarding our support for the QUAD."

Eric was surprised that Carlisle had called a press conference without his knowledge. He was even more astonished that Carlisle was planning on discussing defense policy without coordinating with the DOD or the National Security Council first. It was foolhardy and dangerous. Eric chose his next words carefully.

"Our support for the QUAD, sir? Are you planning on attending the San Francisco celebration of the UN? I realize President Hernández was planning on attending. Still, I assumed that given the explosion in Seattle was more than likely an assassination attempt, our top priority would be to protect you and the line of succession. The best place to do that is here."

Eric heard someone clear their throat and noticed that Travis Webb had been sitting on a couch at the other end of the office. Travis stood up and joined Eric in front of Carlisle's desk.

"I think we know what we're doing, Eric," said Travis. "And the president is not going to San Francisco."

Eric visibly winched when Travis referred to Carlisle as the president. "I believe the term is acting president."

Carlisle raised his hands in mock protest. "Quite right, quite right. We mustn't get ahead of ourselves. Now is not the time. But as acting president, I need to ensure that our allies clearly understand our position regarding the QUAD and our future involvement. Things are heating up in the Pacific, and we must pull back. I'm planning on making that clear at the press conference. The time has come to change our aggressive posture in the region and do more to promote peace. This will lead to stabilization and reduce the likelihood of conflict. Given the turn of events."

Eric was about to respond when he saw Carlisle reading directly from a blue folder on his desk. "Is that what you plan on reading to the press, sir? Can I at least have a look and share it with the press secretary? She'll need to be prepared to answer the inevitable questions. Particularly considering this is a significant change in President Hernández's defense policy."

Carlisle quickly closed the folder and placed it in his desk drawer. "You don't need to be concerned about my statement to the press, Eric. Travis and I will directly respond to any questions the press may have regarding this issue. And you should know President Hernández herself crafted this policy change. She discussed it with Travis and me before the Seattle trip and planned to announce the change in San Francisco."

Eric nodded. "Right, sir. I understand." He excused himself and left the office. Moments later, he sat at his desk and thought through what had happened.

He was intimately familiar with President Hernández's position on the QUAD and what she had planned to announce in San Francisco. He was sure of it. Something strange was developing, and he was determined to discover what Carlisle and Webb were up to. While he still had a job.

## Museum Maintenance Hangar

Chloe Ryan wrapped her arms around Wyatt's neck moments after he walked into the maintenance hangar. He could feel her body shaking when she said, "They still haven't found him, Wyatt.

I guess that's a good thing, right?"

Wyatt nodded and kissed Chloe on her forehead. "That's a great thing."

Wyatt learned from Chloe yesterday that her father was among the missing. The last time anyone had seen him was in the maintenance hangar touring the old Air Force One with President Hernández and her team right before they returned to the museum. She'd gone to Dave's house earlier this morning to shower and get something to eat and then returned to stand vigil while waiting for news of her father.

She led Wyatt across the hangar into an office where a small TV sat in the center of the room. "I've been watching the news all morning, and nobody's been found alive."

Wyatt watched the news broadcast that showed scores of rescue workers carefully sifting through the massive rubble that had once been the Museum of Flight. It reminded Wyatt of the images in the aftermath of the collapse of the World Trade Center. A loud horn sounded each time a victim was found, and all searching stopped. Wyatt stared at the screen as he saw six firefighters carefully and respectfully carry a white zippered bag containing the latest body found at the site. They moved the body past dozens of other workers, some solemnly saluting while others stood with bowed heads.

"They've found twenty-three bodies so far," whispered Chloe, "but only eighteen have been identified. Some admiral from the Department of Defense who flew in yesterday has taken over the entire operation. I hope to God that he knows what he's doing."

Wyatt had seen the message declaring the NDA and naming Admiral Shaffer as incident commander. He knew that Shaffer ran the Pacific Command and guessed that the senior admiral knew what he was doing but decided to keep the comment to himself and shift the topic. "No word about your father yet?"

Chloe shook her head. "They said more than 150 people were invited to the gala, but they don't know precisely how many were inside when the building collapsed."

"And no sign of the president or SECDEF, either?" Wyatt asked. "Not yet. The news anchor said it could take days to get through the rubble. I suppose they're going slowly in case someone is still alive. It would be terrible to injure someone in the process of searching for survivors."

Looking at the large pile of destruction and the still smoldering rubble, it was difficult for Wyatt to imagine how anyone could have survived that explosion and the resulting collapse of the building. He decided to keep that opinion to himself as well. Eventually, the rescue teams would complete their task, and the results would be known. Wyatt could imagine the pain Chloe was experiencing. He still recalled the anguish he felt that day in Whitefish when his father told him his mother had died. He was only twelve. Chloe was an adult, but Wyatt could tell that she was still suffering badly. He moved close to her and rested his hands on her shoulders.

"They'll find him soon. And he's a tough guy. My money's on Dave Ryan."

Chloe started crying again. "How about a cup of coffee?" Wyatt asked. "I saw a coffee maker over by the water cooler."

Wyatt found a tin of coffee and some filters in a cupboard and began to brew a new pot. He was thinking of the last time he saw Dave Ryan and how he'd planned to tell him he would continue seeing Chloe despite the man's objections. He remembered watching the man lead the president's team into the tunnel and back to the museum when a thought occurred. He remembered the president mentioning something about visiting an old shelter. Was it possible that the group had stopped there? If they did, might they have avoided the museum's collapse? He finished brewing the coffee and carried a steaming mug back to Chloe. Before raising Chloe's hope, he wanted to know much more about that tunnel under the runway and the fallout shelter.

## Fallout Shelter, Boeing Field

Colt awoke suddenly when the diesel generator sputtering echoed throughout the cold and damp shelter. He slowly rolled to one side, swung his legs out of the cot, and pushed himself upright into a sitting position on the side of the temporary bed. Years ago, Colt learned from a physical therapist that was the best technique for a man of his age with a sore lower back to get up from bed. "The preferred way to avoid injury is to do things slowly," he remembered her recommending. "No sudden movements." Colt hadn't slept well on the wafer-thin cot mattress and was covered by the scratchy, musty army blanket—a far cry from the comfort of his home bed. He tilted his neck, first to one side and then to the other, and was rewarded with the sound of a satisfying crack. His folded suit coat had made for a poor pillow. But Colt had spent many nights in terrible pipe berths on drafty Navy ships. He knew they were lucky to have found the cots; it beat sleeping on the cold, dirty concrete floor. And then there were the rats. They had gnawed into one of the food bins, and from the feces and urine on the floor, it was clear the rats had been living there for some time. He had just recalled that a group of rats was called a mischief when María Hernández murmured, "Good morning, Colt. Sleep well?"

Colt looked over at María lying on a cot near his. He'd admired the woman for years and believed she was perhaps one of the best persons to have served in the office. But he knew nothing could have adequately prepared her for this situation's challenges

202

or the decisions she needed to make in the coming days. He was glad that he could be with her in this dire emergency.

"Better than expected, given the accommodations, Madam President. I would have asked for a better room, but I don't have enough points for the upgrade." María giggled at his response but then asked in a severe voice, "Do you think we'll be found? I can't believe we're trapped here. We've got to find a way out!" She rubbed her eyes and massaged her temples. "I didn't sleep much last night, worrying about what might become of us. The food and water won't last forever."

Colt realized that the president wasn't asking for his accurate assessment of their chances for survival. At this moment, she needed reassurance and hope. Candor could come later.

"I think they'll find us soon, probably today or tomorrow. After we're not found in whatever that explosion damaged, the rescue teams will expand the search area. It's only a matter of time."

María stood up from her cot and attempted to comb her hair with her fingers when Special Agent DeSantis approached her. "President Hernández, I have the television working, and we can watch the local news stations. It appears that some type of bomb destroyed the museum. Workers are attempting to find survivors, including us. I have a chair next to the TV if you want to watch it, ma'am."

María, Colt, Dave Ryan, Anna DeSantis, and Cade Blanton sat transfixed as they stared at the images on the small television screen. Aerial and ground-level cameras broadcast pictures of an enormous pile of rubble described as the Boeing Museum of Flight. Colt watched as dozens of workers scoured over the debris. The TV screen displayed a red banner on the bottom stating forty bodies had been recovered thus far, but no survivors.

Along one side of the fenced-in area, red medic units and their paramedic crews waited and watched as bags of human remains were gently and silently passed from rescue workers to specialists from the King County medical examiner's office. The news reporter mentioned the remains would be transported to the medical examiner's facility at the Harborview Medical Center for forensic analysis and possible identification. Colt shuddered to think that he could have been in one of those bags, and then his heart sank when he realized what his grown children must be going through as they watched these same images.

The news reporter just shared that the US Department of Defense had declared the bombsite a National Defense Area and was reporting on how that might affect the recovery operations. Colt saw images of a gray-haired naval officer talking with a fire chief and was pleased to see that his good friend Kurt Shaffer had been assigned to lead the search efforts. Colt realized that Steve Holmes must have made that decision because of Colt's long-time relationship with the admiral. Colt also knew Shaffer would stop at nothing to find the president and his friend.

The news anchor interrupted the reporter. "Excuse me, Roland, but we have some breaking news. Acting President Joseph Carlisle is about to make a statement from the White House. We'll go there live right now." The small television screen showed the network's logo and then cut to a shot of Joe Carlisle in the Oval Office, sitting at the president's desk with his hands folded and looking solemnly at the camera.

"My fellow Americans, I wanted to speak with you directly this morning about the recovery efforts in Seattle and our search for President María Hernández. As has been reported, no survivors have been found yet, but we continue to be hopeful that there are people who may have survived this horrendous tragedy. I can tell you that President Hernández was not among the casualties that have been recovered. I will serve in an acting capacity as president in the near term. We have not yet discovered the cause of the explosion. At this point, there is no reason to assume the bombing was a direct attempt to kill President Hernández. I have directed that a National Defense Area be established in the immediate area of the explosion. I want to be very clear on one point with our allies and adversaries. The United States government is stable, and our defense capabilities remain fully operational. Pause."

Colt realized that Carlisle had mistakenly read aloud a note from the teleprompter screen. "It's a good thing it didn't say wave to the camera!"

María gave Colt an icy stare and turned back to the television screen as Carlisle continued his prepared speech after realizing his error. "Yes. Fully operational. To demonstrate our continuity of government, I want to take this opportunity to announce a policy change that President Hernández had planned to share at the United Nations celebration in San Francisco. For some time, tensions have been increasing in the Pacific. President Hernández and I believe that, to some degree, our country's involvement with an old and largely antiquated alliance has been at least partially responsible for worsening relations with important trading partners in the region. We have no interest in perpetuating this unfortunate situation. As a result, later this week, I will meet with representatives of India, Australia, and Japan to communicate our intention to withdraw from the Quadrilateral Security Dialogue. I realize that many will have questions about this policy change. National Security Adviser Travis Webb will be holding a press conference later this week after I have had the opportunity to meet with congressional leadership. I want to close by saying that Robin and I are praying for the safe return of President Hernández. Our thoughts and prayers are with her husband,

Ethan Davis, in this challenging time. May God bless you, and may God bless these United States."

María was beside herself with rage. "What the hell? I never agreed to that change in policy, Colt. Hell, I haven't even spoken with the vice president about the QUAD since the Camp David meeting. It makes no sense!"

Colt waited momentarily and then said, "Actually, I think it might make perfect sense, President Hernández. A DOD investigation has been gathering evidence of treason against your national security advisor for some time. You'll recall our conversation at Camp David. We knew there had to be some sort of leak in the intelligence community after the disasters in Cambodia and Vietnam. We knew Webb was the source but didn't want to proceed with an indictment until the proof was undeniable. The reporter said that a bomb with military-grade C4 caused the explosion. We know that Carlisle and Webb were strongly against you reaffirming our commitment to the QUAD alliance. What if the explosion was intended to prevent you from going to San Francisco and making that announcement?"

María was speechless. "Are you saying that Webb and Carlisle conspired to assassinate POTUS? For a policy change? I don't know. I'm not buying that, Colt."

"What if it wasn't just the policy change? We know the Russians and Chinese have been pushing to end the QUAD. We know that Webb has been working with the Russians. What if the Russians and Chinese are behind the bombing? And what if Webb and Carlisle are involved?"

"I can't believe that to be the case. Look, I have no faith in Carlisle, and I believe you when you say that you are certain that Webb has been feeding information to the Russians. But to attempt to assassinate the president? I think that's a step too far."

Colt was about to respond when Cade Blanton approached

them. "Excuse me for interrupting, but I must go on the record here. The Secret Service has no information that Mr. Webb has been leaking classified information. And we'd know if the vice president presented any threat to the president."

"Well," began Colt, "the Secret Service was explicitly left in the dark about the Webb investigation. We didn't know who to trust."

President María Hernández sat in a folding chair and crossed her legs. "It seems to me the only people I can trust are in this room!"

## Museum Maintenance Hangar

"What are you looking for, Wyatt?" asked Chloe. She found him sitting at a desk in the maintenance office, searching through the drawers.

Wyatt closed a bottom drawer and walked to a wooden bookcase. "I was thinking about the last time I saw your dad and remembered something President Hernández and her Secret Service agent discussed." He began pulling documents from the bookcase and putting them on the linoleum floor.

"What were they talking about? Why?"

Wyatt stopped sorting through the bookcase and decided to share his thoughts. "They were discussing if there was time to visit some sort of shelter on their way back to the museum. The agent said there wasn't time for that. That was right before they went back into the tunnel. I thought I'd see if Dave had a drawing or map of the tunnel system. It might show the shelter's location."

"Do you think they might have gone into the shelter?"

Wyatt slowly nodded. "Probably a long shot, and I don't want to get your hopes up, but it's a possibility. Help me look

207

through these files, and maybe we can find a tunnel map or some reference to a shelter."

Chloe picked up a gray flashlight from the shelf above the desk. She slid a switch, and a dim light glowed from the lens. "We don't need a map to find the shelter. I know exactly where it is! Do you think we should call someone and let them know what you suspect?"

"Let's just see if we can find it first. After you!"

Chloe led the way down the rusty metal stairway while Wyatt followed closely. He suggested they find a better flashlight before heading into the tunnel, but Chloe insisted they immediately head for the shelter her father had shown her years before.

"I had just graduated from high school, and Dad wanted me to see the fallout shelter he'd discovered while exploring the tunnels under the runway. He was thrilled to find the old relic from the Cold War. I remember him describing his military service during those years and how worried people were that the Russians might someday launch weapons at America. He told me that when he was in grade school, the kids would be told to duck and cover during bomb drills. Can you imagine? Frightening small children like that?"

Wyatt was about to respond when he tripped over a metal object and almost fell into Chloe. He bent over while Chloe illuminated it with her dimming flashlight. "Just an old socket wrench," he said, sticking it in his back pocket. They continued down the musty tunnel and followed it as it angled to their left.

Chloe abruptly stopped when she saw that several support beams had fallen from the ceiling and were leaning against a metal door. Wyatt could make out a Civil Defense sign on the door. "This is it," announced Chloe.

Wyatt pulled the rusty wrench from his back pocket and banged three times on the steel door. They both held their breaths and were startled when they heard someone banging on the other side of the door.

"Oh my God, Wyatt. There's someone inside! Help me clear this wreckage!" They struggled to lift and remove two heavy beams blocking the shelter entrance. After removing the last beam, the door slowly opened, bathing the tunnel in bright light.

"Dad!" shouted Chloe when she saw her father's smiling face. "Thank God, you're all right!" She crushed him with a bear hug. "I thought I'd lost you!"

Dave Ryan held his only daughter tightly. "I'm fine, honey. Come inside; I'd like you to meet someone!" Wyatt followed Chloe and her father into the shelter, where four others waited patiently. President Hernández thanked Wyatt and Chloe for finding them. She smoothed her hair and straightened her skirt.

"We must look dreadful, but I can't wait to get out of here and let the world know we're alive." She took a few steps toward the shelter door when Clay Blanton stepped to one side. He pulled his pistol from his belt holster and pointed it at Anna DeSantis's chest. Nobody's going anywhere." He carefully circled the others and slammed the shelter door closed.

"DeSantis, I want you to use your left hand slowly and gently remove your firearm from its holster and rest it on the floor. Then kick it over to me."

Anna did precisely as she was told, careful not to make a sudden movement that might cause the Secret Service agent to fire. Blanton picked up Anna's pistol and tucked it into his waistband at the small of his back. He motioned for Chloe and Wyatt to join the others in the room's center.

"What's this all about, Blanton!" demanded the president. "Put that gun away!"

Blanton smiled thinly. "I don't think so."

Colt could see that Blanton was trying to decide what to do

next. "The president asked you a question, Blanton. You seem to be the one in charge here."

Blanton looked around the room and performed a quick threat assessment. He disregarded the president. He'd known her for months, and she presented no danger. Garrett and Dave Ryan were old men. Perhaps they could have been a threat in their prime, but that was years, probably decades ago. Ryan's daughter couldn't weigh more than 130 pounds and didn't appear to be exceptionally athletic. The young pilot standing beside her was the pilot who gave the president the tour of the old Air Force One. Reasonably fit and a military guy, but pilots didn't typically have self-defense training. DeSantis was by far the most dangerous person to him. Now that she was disarmed, he needed to position her on his left to cover her more easily.

"DeSantis, exchange places with our pilot friend. I want to be able to watch you better." After the two swapped places, Colt Garrett said in a low, controlled voice, "Blanton, what the fuck is going on?"

Blanton was more relaxed now that he believed he had reduced the threat. He lowered his pistol a bit and looked directly at the president. "You were supposed to die in that explosion. That's why I was trying to get you back to the museum. The plan was for me to exit the building before the bomb was detonated."

"But why?" asked María. "For what reason?"

Blanton laughed. "Because you've been making some serious foreign policy mistakes, and there are people much more capable than you that should be in charge."

"People? Which people, Blanton?" asked Colt.

"It doesn't matter now." Blanton motioned with his pistol at the television screen showing Vice President Carlisle and National Security Advisor Webb taking questions from the press. "Those two, for example," he smirked.

Colt nodded. "How far does this go, Blanton? The cabinet as well?"

Blanton shook his head. "It's hard to say. I take my orders from Webb and Carlisle."

María couldn't believe what she was hearing. An assassination to affect a policy change? Who would benefit from that? But she stopped wondering about Webb and Carlisle's motivation when a more pressing thought occurred.

"I suppose you are not merely going to hold us here until Carlisle can do whatever he wants? Am I right?"

Blanton smiled again. "Unfortunately, you're correct. There isn't a scenario where any of you will leave this shelter alive. He watched DeSantis slightly nod, and he briefly wondered what that meant when something crashed against the far wall. He was closely watching DeSantis when he heard another noise to his right. He quickly turned, but it was too late as Wyatt Steele launched into his side and sent them both crashing to the floor. Anna DeSantis reacted first by grabbing her pistol from the floor and covering the two men. But the threat was over. Wyatt picked himself off the floor while Cade Blanton lay motionless on his back. He'd fallen on top of a small metal electrical outlet box in the center of the room. Blanton lay whimpering where he lay while the others gathered around him.

"I better tie his hands before he recovers," said Anna DeSantis as she pulled a zip tie from her pocket.

Wyatt looked at Blanton's crumpled body and listened to his moans. "I don't think that will be necessary. I've seen this before. His back's broken."

Colt Garrett breathed out. "I think we should get out of here and find our way back to the maintenance hangar. And for now, I suggest we all turn off our mobile phones. I need some time to think."

## Museum Maintenance Hangar Conference Room

"Alright, Mr. Secretary. Will you explain why you don't want us to turn on our mobile phones and let the world know we're alive? We could all use a shower and something to eat." The president was exasperated with her defense secretary and was eager to end the misery of the last two days. María thoroughly trusted Colt Garrett, but her patience was wearing thin. Wyatt, Dave, DeSantis, and Chloe waited for him to respond. María sat glaring at Colt with her arms crossed. "Well?"

Colt bit his lower lip and then began. "Our phones need to be off so they won't ping a local cell tower announcing our presence and location. There's lots we don't know, of course, but after watching Carlisle's press conference and based on what Blanton has confessed, I'm starting to understand our situation."

After the group returned to the maintenance hangar, Colt and Wyatt zip-tied Blanton to a small metal framed twin bed that Dave used whenever he stayed overnight. Wyatt had been right about Blanton's broken back. He was paralyzed below the waist, unable to feel or move his legs. He was in excruciating pain, and his cries only ceased after Dave gave him the oxycodone he had prescribed for his knee replacement. But not before Colt and Wyatt thoroughly questioned the Secret Service agent regarding the plot to assassinate President Hernández. She wouldn't have condoned the enhanced interrogation methods he used to encourage Blanton to answer his questions, but Colt decided that he'd deal with any repercussions later. Some might have called it torture, but Colt preferred enlightened encouragement. Blanton was resting peacefully now, secured to the bedframe.

"First," Colt continued, "we know that Carlisle has immediately moved to reverse your policy regarding our defense posture and alliances in the Pacific. Your absence from the UN celebration in the Bay Area gives him a perfect opportunity to change the policy. Second, Webb has been working with the Russians for some time, and both men appear to be working together. Third, the Russians and the Chinese have become much closer in recent months, publicly stating their shared global interests, particularly in the Pacific. Fourth, we know directly from Blanton that the Russians and the Chinese are working together on this operation. We don't know how widespread the conspiracy is or who we can trust. And we need to find a way to safely bring you into the public eye such that your survival is undeniable and you can assume your constitutional duties. We will need lots of press for that."

"But how could we do that? We're stuck here in this hangar without the ability to communicate with anyone who might help. And as you said, who could we trust even if we could reach out?"

Colt was about to respond to the president when Wyatt Steele said, "I have an idea, but it's pretty crazy."

María shrugged her shoulders. "Let's hear it, Lieutenant Commander Steele."

Wyatt pointed at Special Air Mission 970 parked inside the hangar. "Why not fly POTUS to San Francisco in the old Air Force One? I mean, look at that bird. Sure, it's a 707, but with that paint job and the presidential seal, most people would think it's the real deal. Can you imagine parking it on the SFO tarmac with the international press surrounding it as POTUS walks down the stairs? Instantly, the world would know that President Hernández is alive, and Carlisle would have to back down."

Colt stared at Wyatt, then at SAM 970, and then back at Wyatt. He looked at María and saw her nod. He asked Wyatt, "Does it fly?"

"Yes, Mr. Secretary, but with a hell of a lot of work," Dave

Ryan said. Her flight control systems are sound, mostly just cable and pulleys. The tires are new, and three engines have been tested. The biggest problem is engine number four, outboard on the starboard wing. It needs to be replaced, and we don't have one. The Air Force has more than a dozen sitting on maintenance carts at the military facility on the south end of the runway. They've refused to provide one, even though they own this aircraft."

"I suppose the big question is how long to replace an engine," Colt stated. "How long, Dave?"

Ryan rubbed his chin. "If I have the right team of mechanics, we could do it in a day, assuming we don't run into something unexpected. But I'd need that engine."

Colt turned to Wyatt and Chloe. "You two are the only ones who can be seen outside of this hangar. Wyatt, I need you to go to an ATM and withdraw as much cash as possible. Don't worry, you'll be reimbursed. Then, go to three different convenience stores and purchase a prepaid mobile phone from each store. Pay with cash. Bring the phones directly back to me here. Do not turn them on. Do you understand?"

"Yes, Mr. Secretary!" Wyatt turned and briskly walked out of the hangar.

"Captain Ryan, you're going shopping. Not for you, but for President Hernández. She'll give you her clothing and shoe sizes. She'll also give you guidance regarding style. You'll have to use your own money, also subject to government reimbursement, of course. Cash is preferred. Say you're shopping for your mother, who'll be attending a funeral. That should work well."

Chloe spoke briefly with President Hernández before heading out to the mall. Dave Ryan began making a list of things to be done before SAM 970 could safely fly while Anna DeSantis closely watched Blanton in the makeshift hospital bed. María Hernández joined Colt on an old, worn sofa.

"You know, I've been thinking. We're different, you and me. You seem most comfortable working through a pressing problem and then directing action to resolve it. You thrive on it. I prefer working on long-term issues and policies—the strategic versus the tactical, if you will. I watched you immediately grasp the feasibility of Wyatt Steele's idea and then put everything in motion to operationalize the plan. Quite impressive."

Colt was embarrassed at her compliment. He never considered his skill at solving issues particularly impressive or rare. He more commonly wondered why others couldn't see the path to resolution as quickly as he did.

"Thank you, ma'am. I appreciate your words. I'm wondering if I've missed anything."

María leaned closer to him. "There is one thing that might be helpful." She spent the next few minutes explaining to Colt how they might be able to prove that Carlisle and Webb were traitors. After he heard her idea, he couldn't wait to see if he could get the proof that would put Carlisle and Webb in federal prison for the rest of their lives.

Two hours later, Wyatt returned to the hangar, where he found Anna closely watching Blanton. Chloe was murmuring with President Hernández on the sofa. Colt and Dave leaned over Dave's desk and studied a set of aircraft schematics. Wyatt placed three white plastic bags on the desktop and waited for the two men to finish.

"Like I said before, Mr. Garrett," Dave reiterated, "it's technically feasible, assuming you can get me one of those Air Force JTD-3 engines. They keep them in storage in the military delivery hangar as spares for the Air Force AWACS birds and the Navy E-6 TACAMO airplanes they service there." Dave Ryan made a few more notes on the old blueprint before excusing himself to get another cup of coffee.

"Here are the cell phones you asked me to buy, sir. I didn't have any trouble getting them."

Colt put two bags into a desk drawer and opened the third. "This will work fine, Wyatt. Nice work." He handed Wyatt a single page of paper. I told you you'd be reimbursed for anything you purchased for this little project.

Wyatt carefully read the paragraph signed by the president and witnessed by Secretary Garrett. It appeared to be some sort of formal authorization for payment.

"I drafted it for President Hernández's signature. Chloe Ryan received one, too. I read that Thomas Jefferson gave a similar letter of credit to Captain Meriwether Lewis for the expedition's use."

Wyatt read the last sentence aloud. "And to give entire satisfaction & confidence to those who may be disposed to aid you, I, María Hernández, President of the United States of America, have written this letter of general credit for you with my hand and signed it with my name."

Colt, a former university professor, smiled. "It's a direct quote from the Jefferson letter," he proudly said. Wyatt reread the letter, carefully folded it, and slipped it into his shirt pocket. "I just hope I can use this!" he joked.

Colt found a quiet corner of the hangar. He pressed a series of numbers on the inexpensive prepaid cell phone and nervously waited for the call to connect.

"Steve Holmes. What can I do for you?"

Colt let out a sigh of relief. "Steven, listen very carefully. Do you recognize my voice? Just say yes or no."

Colt didn't hear an immediate response, and he was about to repeat the question when Steve quietly said, "Yes."

"Good. I need you to memorize this phone number and grab one of those phones in your lower right drawer." Colt looked at his watch. "Leave your cell phone on your desk and take a walk outside by yourself. Call me back at this number in exactly fifteen minutes. Got it, Steve?"

"Yes, sir."

Precisely fifteen minutes later, Colt's phone rang. Colt pressed a button and stated, "I need to bring you up to speed, Steve." Colt updated his deputy and good friend on what had happened to him since the explosion and how he planned to restore President Hernández's authority. After Steve shared his reservation regarding the plan, he ultimately relented. "What do you need me to do, Mr. Secretary?"

"First, I need you to order the Air Force to release one of their spare Pratt & Whitney JTD-3 turbo fans immediately to the Boeing Museum of Flight. Specify that it's for SAM 970 and mark it to the attention of Mr. David Ryan. He'll pick it up in person at their hangar in two hours. The Air Force still owns that aircraft, Steve. It's just on loan to the museum."

"This will raise questions, Colt. Really out of the ordinary."

Colt considered what his deputy had just said. "You're right. Let it be known that a Washington State Congressional Delegation member is on the museum's board and pushing for it to go through ASAP. They're using their position on the armed services committee to assist the museum."

Steve chuckled. "Okay, boss. That should work. What's next?"

"This one's tougher. The president says there's a system that records everything in the Oval. It's used to transcribe an official record of all executive actions. It's called the Presidential Online Dictation System, or PODS. Here's the kicker. Only the president and her private secretary can access PODS or are even aware of the system. Not the chief of staff, not the national security advisor, and not even the vice president."

"So, Carlisle and Webb are completely in the dark about this system?" Steve asked.

"We believe so. I have the president's user ID and password for you. I need you to get into PODS and download everything that's been said in that room since Carlisle moved in."

Steve whistled. "Oh, man. We'd have it all. But I do have a recommendation. I think we need to bring the president's chief of staff into our confidence. Eric told me he thinks something odd is happening between Carlisle and Webb. Carlisle already told him he'd be replaced as soon as President Hernández's body was found. And we will need him to work with the other cabinet members."

Colt considered Steve's suggestion regarding bringing Eric Paynter into the picture. "I'll have to get that cleared with the president and get back to you. I agree with you, Steve, but it's her call."

## Occidental Park, Seattle

In the heart of downtown Seattle and its historic Pioneer Square lies a small city park that attracts a wide variety of visitors. Built on a half-acre of asphalt in 1971 and famous for its Renaissance revival architecture, eccentric shops, art galleries, ethnic cafes, bookstores, and boisterous nightlife, Occidental Park provides a place for people to relax if they're in the mood for some low-impact outdoor recreation. Ping-pong tables and bocce courts are constantly used during Seattle's warmer and dryer days. During the daytime, office workers bustle through the park on their way to and from meetings. The lunch hour brings out a mixed crowd. Workers cram the small cafes or find room in one of the pleasant park benches to enjoy a sack lunch. Mothers bring small children to play on the park's climbing equipment or among the several totem poles on display. A firefighter's memorial is prominent in the park's center, honoring decades of those who lost their lives. Logs slid past this spot in the 1850s on the way to a sawmill, earning the slang name Skid Row.

But as the sun sets over Puget Sound, Occidental Park takes on an entirely different ambiance. Homeless encampments emerge with the associated crime and drug use. To alleviate law enforcement staffing pressures, the city partnered with the local business community to create the Downtown Seattle Ambassadors, a cadre of paid employees to improve public safety and establish a clean, safe, and welcoming environment for everyone. It's a massive job.

Professor Sheng Genji waited on one of the park's benches and watched what appeared to be some sort of drug deal take place less than twenty yards away from her. She became disgusted when she saw two Ambassadors calmly watch the drug deal go down. The two men seemed to be only moderately interested in the illegal transaction and remained sitting on their bikes when the dealer and his customer went their separate ways. The deep-cover Chinese operator felt this was just another example of the decay of Western society and why communism was far superior.

"Hi, Genji," said Lillian as she joined her on the bench.

"How are you doing, dear? I mean, since the museum's collapse?"

Lillian removed a soiled handkerchief from her coat pocket and wiped her runny nose. "I haven't been able to sleep since then. You told me the switch would just set off some smoke bomb or something. That was a real bomb, and people died! The news is saying even the president is dead!"

Genji took Lillian's hand while casually looking around the park. "I know, dear. You must be feeling terrible. Something must have gone wrong with the detonator. But at least Mr. Fawthrop is gone. That's something."

Lillian blew her nose again and sighed. She suspected that Genji knew it was a bomb all along, but she didn't want to accuse her. What would be the point?

"I do have one question, Lillian. Have you spoken to anyone about the museum? Anyone at all, dear? Anything about our plans?"

"No, of course not. I haven't talked with anyone about anything. You are my only friend."

Genji considered her response and handed Lillian a paper cup filled with coffee. "I brought this for you, dear. I thought it might help with your head cold."

Genji watched as Lillian sipped at the now lukewarm coffee. "Drink it up, dear. I'm sure it will help."

After Lillian finished the coffee, Genji offered, "Here. I'll get rid of that for you."

She deftly placed it into her handbag and turned back to Lillian. "Can you show me your bracelet again, dear? My neighbor asked me about them, and I told him you have one for your Narcan allergy. Please take it off so I can take a photo of it."

Lillian removed and handed Genji her small silver medical alert bracelet with a red medical symbol. Engraved with Lillian's name and naloxone allergy, it served to warn others of Lillian's hypersensitivity to the drug. Two years ago, Lillian had received the life-saving drug from a policeman who found her unconscious in a Seattle alley. An emergency room doctor determined she was allergic to the drug after she barely recovered from a week-long coma in a hospital bed. Genji pretended to take a photo of the bracelet with her smartphone and then slid it into her handbag with the coffee cup, hoping Lillian wouldn't notice. She shouldn't have been concerned because Lillian had slumped down on the bench. Genji scooted away from her now unconscious form and briskly walked to the two Downtown Ambassadors.

"Please help!" she shouted and pointed at Lillian lying on the park bench. That poor homeless woman asked me for money, and she passed out as I reached into my purse for my wallet! I think she must be on drugs or something!"

The two men dropped their bikes and ran over to where Lillian remained unconscious. Several months ago, they received an hour-long training on using naloxone. They determined the homeless woman must be suffering from an opioid overdose, and they applied a dose of naloxone to her nose. Seeing no immediate effect, they administered a second dose and then radioed central dispatch for assistance. Three minutes later, a Seattle Fire Department Medic One unit arrived, and two uniformed paramedics raced over to the bench with their bags of equipment.

"What do you have?" asked one of the paramedics.

"A homeless female about forty, likely opioid overdose. We've just given her the fourth dose of naloxone, but no joy. Glad you guys are here!"

The two highly trained emergency responders began assessing the woman's condition. "You say you suspected an opioid overdose. Why?" asked the older paramedic.

One of the Downtown Ambassadors shrugged his shoulders. "Some lady told us that."

He looked around the park. "She's gone now."

# Day Eight

## Maintenance Hangar

Cade Blanton was in extreme pain when he woke from a restless night. His right wrist remained tightly zip-tied to the top rail of the bed's metal frame, cutting into his wrist and severely limiting his ability to shift to a more comfortable sleeping position. He only had himself to blame for the pain because he'd been cheeking the medications that DeSantis had been giving him in the remote possibility that he would be able to escape somehow. He had been thinking of nothing else since he regained consciousness after breaking his back in the shelter.

While serving in the Army, Blanton attended the survival, evasion, resistance, and escape (SERE) course at Fort Novosel, near Montgomery, Alabama. The Army's website describes the three-week course as a program to "train service members, DOD civilians, and contractors who are identified as being at high risk of isolation on the Code of Conduct and tactics, techniques, and procedures of survival, escape, resistance, and evasion, enabling them to survive isolation and captivity to return with honor." Blanton reasoned he'd need to draw on everything he'd learned at SERE school if he were to have any chance at escaping from the bed and the hangar. During one of the few times that he was able to fall asleep, he had a horrific nightmare. He dreamt he was being held in a federal penitentiary somewhere in the South and was beaten and then gang raped in a prison shower stall. Prisons are inhospitable to former law enforcement agents. When he woke from the dream, he resolved to find some way to get out of that bed and get word of the president's survival and plan to Carlisle. It was his only hope of avoiding the realities of his nightmare.

Blanton looked at DeSantis sitting at a small desk on the other side of the room. She'd been assigned to serve as a combination nurse and guard while the others made plans to fly President Hernández to San Francisco. He'd carefully listened to their discussions and arguments, leading to their decision to fly the old Air Force One to California. The plan seemed far-fetched and unlikely to succeed, but he needed to let Carlisle know. He decided that he should continue to pretend as if he was asleep or knocked out from the pain meds. He might be able to learn something else of value.

Outside the office where Blanton lay, Wyatt, Dave, and Chloe gathered around a makeshift table formed by a large sheet of plywood resting on four stools. Over the night, Dave had prepared a chart listing all the tasks that needed to be completed before SAM 970 could fly. He had drawn lines and arrows to show the dependencies between the long list of tasks and circled some tasks with a red pen.

"I've highlighted the project's critical path in red. It's the longest path from start to finish. If any of these tasks take longer than expected, the entire project moves to the right. It's delayed."

Wyatt pointed to the first critical path task. "Okay, Dave. We've seen these types of charts before. It looks like several things are not dependent on others. That means they can be started immediately?"

"That's right. For example, if we have enough people to do both things simultaneously, we can remove the existing engine while waiting to get the new one."

"I'm not much of a mechanic, Dad, but I can work on the navigation system tasks. What are your thoughts?"

Dave pointed to his chart. "We need a functioning nav system and someone to operate it. The 707 was designed to have a dedicated navigator onboard. We don't have one. And if we did, I think the nav systems are shot. There's probably something in the power supply. Hell, even if we got it running and could find someone to serve as navigator, the systems are archaic and pretty much useless."

"Okay," commented Chloe. "I'll start thinking about the nav problem while you two get us a new engine. I've got a few ideas."

Wyatt turned to Dave. "How long do you anticipate the engine swap-out will take? Secretary Garrett wants us to be wheels up no later than 0730 tomorrow. It seems like the job's going take more than just we three."

Dave tapped his mechanical pencil on the chart. "The only way we can meet that schedule is to get more people," Dave agreed. "On a 707, you can have an outboard engine up in four hours if everything goes right and you have a maintenance crew that knows what it's doing. Inboard engine change-out takes about six hours because you always run into problems with the utility hydraulic system. The operations checks and trim adjustments can be completed in another eight hours if everything goes right, which is rare."

"It sounds like we might meet Garrett's deadline, barely. But Dave, where are we going to find a crew to help? People we are sure can be trusted."

"I already spoke with Mr. Garrett, and he approved me to bring in a small group of techs I've worked with on similar projects. They know what they're doing around these old engines. All five of them are licensed airframe and powerplant mechanics and have been working as AMT technicians since before you were born. The secretary said I need to keep them in the dark about our destination; I plan on telling them we're just getting her ready for a flight test over Puget Sound. We just need to ensure they don't see the president or Garrett."

"Sounds like a plan. I'll start working on removing the old engine right away. You need to find out if that authorization for the new engine has made it through the Air Force supply system yet and get it here ASAP!"

## Maintenance Hangar Conference Room

Colt grappled to open the plastic clamshell packaging that enclosed the second prepaid phone. Shoplifting and its impact on retail profit margins meant that most anything bought in a store was encased in a transparent blister pack, resulting in what Colt termed a struggle fest. He considered simply reusing the phone he opened yesterday, but he knew better than to tempt fate that some unknown entity might have intercepted his call with Steve Holmes. It was safer to endure the hassle of breaking into the plastic-entombed cell phone. As he used a box cutter to slice into the package, he reflected on seeing Blanton lying motionless on the bed earlier this morning when he opened the desk drawer to get the second phone. He thought he caught Blanton watching him at the desk and then reconsidered, given the large amount of pain medication DeSantis was giving him. Enough to knock out a horse, she had said. Colt finally freed the phone from the packaging and began the initialization process. He pressed a series of buttons and waited for the call to connect.

"Good morning. Zoey Hale. What can I do for you?"

Colt felt suddenly warm at the sound of Zoey's voice. Somehow, just hearing her over the phone made him trust things would turn out okay. Maybe the plan would work.

"Good morning, yourself. Don't mention my name, but I want you to know how much I enjoyed our time Thursday evening.

Would you mind walking down to our favorite coffee shop and calling me from there? You might ask to use their phone, like before. I need to bring you up to speed on several things, and I also need to ask you for a big favor."

Zoey's brain was bombarded with thoughts as she briskly walked down the hall toward the elevator. Colt was alive! Where? In what condition? Where had he been all this time? Why shouldn't she use his name, and why did she need to call him back on another phone? She knew about Colt's background in intelligence, but he'd never acted so mysterious. And she'd forgotten about President Hernández. What does Colt's sudden survival from that explosion mean for her? She stared at the lighted floor numbers blinking as the elevator descended, and she had to endure an eternity when the elevator stopped at floors on its long way to the lobby. It was pure agony, with a stop at almost every floor. Finally, the elevator reached the lobby, and the doors parted. Zoey elbowed her way past a group of noisy tourists and headed directly for the exit.

A casual, family-owned cafe was on a busy corner two blocks from the Hale Building. It was where Zoey had first met Colt when he bought her coffee after discovering she'd left her office without her mobile phone or handbag. Colt must have remembered that Zoey used the café's landline to ask her assistant to bring her phone so she could Venmo Colt the cost of her coffee. She remembered how they laughed at him, not knowing how to accept a payment. They agreed to meet for dinner, her treat. That's how their relationship had started. She thought about not wanting to miss a second chance at love when the person in line in front of her paid their bill and moved to the waiting area.

"Excuse me, Stephanie. Can I use your business phone? It's kind of an emergency."

Moments later, she finally relaxed when she heard Colt say,

227

"Hi. Miss me?"

"Colt! Thank God you're okay. You are okay, right?"

Colt spoke for twenty minutes, describing the events that led him to call her.

"I saw that your father's body was found. I'm so sorry. And that you've been named Hale Broadcasting's new boss. A lot for you to process."

"I'm doing all right, Colt. I suppose it helps that I know that Dad wanted me to succeed him. I just wish the circumstances were different." There was nothing more she could say. She wanted to discuss where her relationship with Colt might go in the future but wanted that conversation to occur in person.

"So," she asked, changing the subject, "is this a burner phone? I can safely call you on this number?"

Colt replied, "Yes. I think we can safely use this number today, and I probably won't need another anytime soon." He described the procedures he was using to avoid being detected or tracked. "It's vital that the fact that the president has survived remains secret. The whole thing should be over by tomorrow if everything works out."

Zoey was frightened when Colt explained the plan to fly the president to San Francisco. She thought too many things would go wrong, and Colt may be glossing over the risks.

"You mentioned that you need a favor from me. Name it!"


An hour later, Wyatt carefully climbed down from a ladder resting against SAM 970's right-side wing. He had been working feverishly on loosening stubborn bolts that secured the engine to its cowling, support pylon, and the massive swept wing. His arms ached from the exertion, and he was about to take a short break when he heard someone knocking on the hangar's main door. Sliding one of the doors just a crack, he was pleased to see a broadly smiling Dave Ryan sitting on an aircraft tug attached to a large wooden crate on a massive cart.

"Don't just stand there gawking," said Dave as he started the tug's motor. "Open the hangar doors, and let's get this monster inside before anyone notices."

Once the tug and its precious cargo were safely inside the hangar and the doors were closed, Dave skillfully maneuvered the airport tug to carefully position the crate directly under a chain hoist supported by the hangar's high overhead beams. With an experienced eye, he nudged the tug, first one way and then the other, until he felt completely satisfied. He disconnected the tug and parked it on the side of the hangar. Wyatt approached the crate and asked, "Any trouble with the Air Force?"

Dave shook his head. "Just the usual supply-type bullshit. Some worthless master sergeant with a shitty attitude wasn't happy about releasing the engine to me—typical ground-pounder. He even asked for my ID. He probably has nothing better to do than keep folks like me who have actual jobs from doing them. Why would anyone want to work in supply? He kept saying that the engines were spares for the operational airplanes they service. He said he didn't have time to deal with an old Air Force relic. It wasn't clear if he was referring to SAM 970 or me."

Wyatt knew all about the challenges of working with, and often around, the military supply system and the people who ran it. For some reason, it seemed that they felt as if they personally owned the supplies and equipment. Wyatt listened to Dave gripe about the supply sergeant for another ten minutes before asking, "Were you able to get ahold of your powerplant techs yet? I could use some help getting the old engine disconnected. It has been attached to that pylon for decades and doesn't seem to want a divorce."

Dave walked over to see how much progress Wyatt had made since he went to get the new engine. He was worried that the engine removal would take too much time. It was one of those tasks he had circled in red ink. "Yep, it looks like you need some help. The guys will be here by noon. Keep loosening those bolts, and I'll have two techs give you a hand when they get here. The others can help me uncrate the new engine and start prepping it for installation."

Contrary to popular opinion, a jet engine is much more elementary than the highly intricate piston-propeller powerplants they replaced. Pilots need not be concerned with mixture controls, cowl flap controls, propeller pitch levers, or manifold pressures. Some aircraft maintenance courses have gone so far as to describe the jet engine as a flying broomstick. The engines are attached to pylons, which are connected to strengthened wing ribs parallel to the direction of flight but diagonal to the central ribs, which flare outward. Much of the pylon is made of magnesium, so the pylon will burn through in the event of an engine fire, allowing the engine to fall away. Perhaps that's one of the reasons why property values under airport approach and departure paths are so depressed. It's not just the noise.

The Pratt & Whitney JT3D, or its military designation, the TF33, brought turbofan technology to the Boeing 707. The manufacturer added a fan to the front of a JT3C model to significantly increase each engine's thrust to 21,000 pounds. Pilots flying 707s equipped with the new engine often commented that it was like adding a fifth engine. The engine Dave received from the Air Force measured twelve feet long and four feet in diameter and weighed more than two tons. After the old engine was finally freed from its mounts and gently eased out and down onto an engine cart, Dave and his team of experienced powerplant technicians began the myriad of tasks to prepare the new engine for installation. They had been retired from Boeing for many years and were thrilled to get back into a hangar and get their hands dirty again.

Colt silently watched the work progress and continued to worry that it may not be completed before Carlisle and his associates discovered María Hernández was still alive. He hadn't heard back from Steve yet about the president's online recording system and hoped that it might reveal what Carlisle and Webb knew and what they were plotting.

## The West Wing

Appointed directly by the president and not subject to Senate confirmation, the White House chief of staff is responsible for directing, managing, and overseeing all policy development, daily operations, and staff activities for the president. The chief of staff's most important role is the creation of a structure of reporting and decision-making for the entire White House staff. Eric Paynter was thinking about his job description and how it didn't even remotely resemble what he'd been relegated to do since President Hernández went MIA in Seattle. Within an hour of Joe Carlisle assuming his responsibilities as acting president, he had made it crystal clear that he didn't want Eric to do anything without his direct authorization. The change in policy resulted in Eric needing to bring many mundane decisions to Carlisle for his approval and was causing unnecessary delays in the workings of the Office of the President. Eric had served under two presidents and decided he wouldn't work for a third. He'd typed his resignation letter and was about to ask for a meeting with Carlisle when Steve Holmes had unexpectedly dropped by his office earlier that day. The meeting couldn't have been more encouraging and enlightening.

Learning that María Hernández was alive lifted a heavy weight off his shoulders. He liked and admired the president, and the idea that Carlisle might replace her revulsed him. Steve had explained Carlisle and Webb's collusion with the Russians and Chinese to overthrow the government and President Hernández's concern that the plot might have extended to members of the Cabinet. Eric thought that unlikely because he'd worked closely with the more senior members and thought they were beyond suspicion. Still, he agreed with the president's directive not to share the facts of the insurrection with anyone. But his anger with Carlisle and Webb continued to build, and he was determined to do everything in his power to keep the two men from further damaging the country until President Hernández was safely returned to power and they could be prosecuted and punished to the fullest extent of the law.

Eric's thoughts were interrupted by a tone from his desk phone. "Mr. Paynter, Acting President Carlisle has requested your presence in the Oval. At your earliest convenience, sir."

"Thank you, Nicole. Let the president's secretary know that I'm on my way." He picked up his mobile phone and a bound notebook as he left his corner office. He turned right and headed down the short hallway to the Oval Office. Steve had warned him not to give Carlisle any indication that he was aware of the man's betrayal during their frequent interaction. He was supposed to maintain professional composure while attempting to obtain incriminating evidence of Carlisle's treason. And he was supposed to do all this while being aware that everything he said was secretly recorded. Sure. Easy.

"Hello, sir. I understand you wanted to see me?"

When Eric walked into the Oval, he found Carlisle reading a

document at the historic Resolute desk. He removed his glasses and closed the blue folder.

Motioning to one of the chairs facing the desk, he replied, "Yes, Eric. Please have a seat."

This was new. Carlisle had always kept him standing whenever they met previously. Eric had assumed it was some sort of power move. He secretly enjoyed that Carlisle obviously needed the compensating mechanism. Eric placed his phone on the desk, opened his notebook, and removed a pen from his shirt pocket. Waiting for Carlisle to tell him why he had been summoned, he watched as the man opened the blue folder and seemed again to read aloud from some document in the folder.

"Eric," began Carlisle, "you have had a long and distinguished career serving this nation and the Office of the President. You performed your duties with skills unmatched by those who preceded you in your position. As I am certain that you, more than anyone, can appreciate and understand, regardless of your professional capabilities, I need someone running the office and White House staff with whom I have a close relationship. For that reason, I'm asking that you tender your resignation to me no later than the close of business tomorrow. That will give you enough time to conclude any personal business and to prepare a list of outstanding actions for your replacement. Any questions?" He looked up from the folder and nodded once.

Eric Paynter sat silently, watching Carlisle close the blue folder and place it in the desk's top center drawer. Remembering the recording system capturing everything said in the office, Eric chose not to ask for additional reasons for his firing or who would be replacing him. He was about to say something that might sound noble but was interrupted by the president's secretary when she stepped into the office.

"Mr. President, you are scheduled to meet with Mr. Webb

and members of the House Appropriations Committee in the Roosevelt room. You asked me to remind you, sir."

Carlisle stood and thanked Eric for his service as they walked out of the office together. Eric was halfway down the hallway on the way back to his office when he suddenly stopped and returned the way he had come. He stopped at the presidential secretary's desk.

"Hi, Emma. Left my phone in there." She was on the phone and nodded as the chief of staff walked into the Oval Office and over to the Resolute Desk. He opened the top drawer, removed a blue folder, and briefly scanned the contents. He placed the folder in his notebook, picked up his phone, and left the office.

Emma was hanging up the phone as he passed her desk. "Did you find what you were looking for, Mr. Paynter?"

Eric showed her his phone. "I believe so," he answered, turning to walk back to his office.


## SAM 970 Flight Deck

Chloe joined Wyatt and her father in the plane's cockpit. They watched as Chloe unpacked several boxes from a large white shopping bag. After placing the items on the navigator's station directly behind the pilot's seat, she reminded the men of the problem she had been tasked to solve. "Here's the challenge. The 707 was designed to be flown by four aircrew: a pilot, a copilot, a flight engineer, and a dedicated navigator. Wyatt and I will be the pilot and copilot, respectively. Dad, you'll act as our flight engineer, sitting at the panel behind me. We don't have anyone trained as a navigator, and even if we did, the plane's nav systems would be inoperative due to the electrical fault we haven't isolated. And even if we solve the power problem, the nav systems are so old that most of the technology they were designed to utilize is no longer in operation."

Wyatt rubbed his chin. "Got it, Chloe. What's the solution?" She pointed to a small white device, slightly larger than a deck of cards.

"This is an Automatic Dependent Surveillance–Broadcast, or ADS-B for short." She attached the plastic box to a suction cup accessory and pressed the unit onto the copilot's side window. "It's battery-powered and can operate for eighteen hours continuously without recharging. If we need to recharge it, there's a USB port on the side."

Wyatt immediately knew where all this was going, but he decided to remain silent and let Chloe impress her father with the nav solution she had developed. He moved to the rear of the cockpit so that Dave could get a better view of Chloe's demonstration. She pulled two new iPads from the bag and attached each to a plastic mount with an articulated arm. She suction-cupped the iPads to the cockpit windows, one on the pilot's side and one for the copilot's use next to the ADS-B. Dave watched with interest as Chloe powered up all three devices. She launched an application on one of the iPads and began selecting configuration settings. Before long, the iPad displayed an aeronautical chart of Boeing Field with a small icon in the center. She zoomed in on the display. Dave was shocked to see that the small icon was in the museum's maintenance hangar. He turned to his daughter and asked, "How does all of this work?"

Chloe began putting the packaging material back into the white bag. "The ADS-B is essentially a receiver-transmitter that processes our position information and that of other ADS-B aircraft. It has an integrated GPS receiver, so it knows our position in the world. The device has its own Wi-Fi network, which allows it to connect to the two iPads. Do you follow me so far?"

Dave looked at the chart displayed on the tiny tablet computer and nodded. Chloe had given him an iPad for Christmas two years ago, but he used it only to play Mahjong and occasionally read a novel he'd downloaded from the public library. He could get on the internet to check personal email, but that was the limit of his understanding of this new technology. He had barely comprehended what his daughter said but decided his questions could be answered later. "Go on," he said.

"The iPads are very similar to yours, just newer and more powerful models with larger storage. I've loaded flight-planning software on them, and they have the Jeppesen electronic charts fully loaded."

"How much coverage? We'll be flying through both the Seattle and Oakland centers."

"The Foreflight software includes worldwide coverage."

Dave remembered many long flights when the navigator across from him unfolded unwieldy charts in the small space behind his flight engineer station, how he was constantly checking his charts to ensure he had the latest editions in his flight bag.

"Things sure have changed a lot. The navigators used celestial navigation with a sextant using stars or the sun, just like on a ship back in the day. They calculated the airplane's position using dead reckoning with a compass and stopwatch. One of the best navigators I ever flew with preferred to look at landmarks out the window. Anything else to show me?"

"Just two additional feature sets. I already mentioned the traffic-aware capabilities, but I wanted to make you aware of the altitude heading reference system. It gives us a real-time depiction of the aircraft's pitch and roll. We can use this as a backup means in the event of a failure of the plane's primary systems. Finally, we can use the system to electronically file FAA flight plans, both

VFR and IFR. We won't have to talk with anyone."

It was difficult for Dave to comprehend that the three small devices could replace a dedicated navigator and a full panel of navigation equipment. "What did all of this cost?"

Chloe handed him a stack of receipts. "I spent just under four thousand dollars. And what's even cooler is that Boeing companies manufacture both the ADS-B and the iPad's flight planning software."

Dave asked Wyatt to remain after Chloe left the flight deck to speak with María. "I wanted to continue discussing you seeing Chloe," he began. Wyatt had wondered if Dave had changed his mind about the pair's relationship, particularly after Chloe had clarified that it was none of her father's business. Wyatt waited for Dave to continue.

"You've impressed me over the last few days. You're an extremely competent man, and I believe you sincerely care for my daughter. But I want you to know that I think you and she are on two different paths. Chloe wants to settle down after her Air Force obligation expires. She wants to continue her education and pursue a career as a professional engineer. I know she wants to start a family, and she's been vocal about wanting to live somewhere in the Pacific Northwest." Dave paused, but Wyatt remained silent.

"Chloe is right about your relationship being none of my business. But her happiness is all that I care about in this world. Do you honestly see yourself making a home here? Buying a house and going to PTA meetings? And what would you do for a living? You said yourself that your Navy career had come to an end. You'll be forced out before you can earn a retirement. I suppose you could try the airlines, but I suspect that's not your path, either. You're a loner, and I think you know it, son. I don't want to see you two do something you both might regret. Okay,

I've said my piece."

He got up from the worn flight engineer seat and left Wyatt alone with his thoughts in the cockpit.

## Maintenance Hangar

Anna DeSantis finished cleaning up Cade Blanton after he let her know his diaper needed changing. His body's lower half remained paralyzed, meaning that he needed someone's assistance whenever he had a bowel movement. Anna understood why Secretary Garrett had assigned her to care for the injured Secret Service agent. Not only was she a highly trained special agent, but she also didn't have any of the skills that could be used to assist with getting the airplane ready to fly. And she had much more experience with changing diapers than anyone else on the team.

"How is Blanton doing?" asked Colt when he entered the small office and makeshift hospital room.

"Hard to say, sir. He's been fairly quiet, except for the occasional moaning. I've been giving him as much of the painkillers as I dare, but he still is in a great deal of pain."

Colt stepped over to the bed and confirmed Blanton was still secured to the metal frame. "How are you doing?"

Blanton responded with a guttural groan but nothing more. Colt wondered if the man would walk again once he had access to proper medical attention. Perhaps the paralysis was caused by something compressing a nerve. Colt didn't know but decided to put it out of his mind. Not really his problem. He reached down to the desk drawer and removed the remaining prepaid mobile phone. He looked at the sealed package and returned it to the drawer.

"I don't think anybody's looking for us. I think I can safely use the phone that's already initiated. Besides, I don't want to struggle with that packaging again."

Anna smiled at his comment. "You're probably right, sir. By this time tomorrow, this will all be probably over."

"I hope so. And thank you for keeping a close watch on Blanton. We need him healthy enough to stand trial for his treason."

Colt walked by the old 707 and watched the maintenance techs hover over the new engine. Things seemed to be going well, according to Dave Ryan. They'd run into a few unexpected problems with mating the new engine to the much older pylon and cowling—some electrical and hydraulic connections required retrofitting. Dave had made several trips to Boeing's repair facilities to secure the necessary parts. He'd said that he hoped to be able to start the engine shortly after midnight. That's when the testing phase could begin. The maintenance techs were in for a long night.

He walked through the hangar's back door and out onto the tarmac. It was good to get some fresh air finally. On this side of the hangar, he was concealed from the rescue and recovery operations at the museum. He pressed several buttons on the mobile phone and waited for Steve to answer.

"How's the work coming along?" asked Steve, standing on the back deck of his home in Arlington. "Any unforeseen difficulties?"

"Just a few," answered Colt. "They're going to try to start the new engine in a few hours. We'll know a lot more after that. I think we've solved the nav system problem, and the pilots are saying that they think we'll be ready to go in the morning, assuming the engine checks out okay. Were you able to get into the online recording system? We must get proof if we move to prosecute."

"We got them. Cold. I was able to access the system with
the president's credentials. It's clear that Carlisle's unaware
the system exists, and I was able to download audio files that
incriminate both the VP and Webb. Carlisle fired Eric. His last
day is tomorrow. I know you were expecting that. But get this:
Eric found a paper folder in the Oval with what appeared to be
notes for the entire plan in Carlisle's handwriting. He's secured the
documents with an old friend of his at the Justice Department.
He plans to meet with the attorney general tomorrow morning,
and I will be at the Pentagon in the NMCC. I think we have
everything covered."

Colt spent another thirty minutes working with Steve on the
preparations required for their plan to succeed. There was a lot
that could still go wrong.


**Maintenance Hangar Conference Room**

Colt found María sitting at the conference room table,
switching between the various news channels on a small TV. He
sat across from her and waited until she turned the set off.

"I'm just trying to remain current on world events," she
explained. "How are things going?"

Colt spent the next few minutes giving the president a detailed
update on the engine replacement and other systems that Dave
was repairing or replacing. "I'm sure you heard the engine start
up. That was a major accomplishment. The team will now
focus on putting the engine through a fairly rigorous series of
performance and stress tests to ensure everything was done
correctly. Sometimes, even new engines experience failures during
this phase. We'll just have to wait and see."

President Hernández considered the impact of what Colt had

just said. "I assume that if this engine doesn't check out, we'll have to delay our departure for San Francisco. How long would it take to locate and install another engine?"

"We know the Air Force has several more at the maintenance depot. I'd need Steve to authorize another transfer, but I'd be concerned that might raise more eyebrows than we want. I'm counting on Dave and the team to work through any problems they encounter and certify the engine for flight. I suspect they'll be working on it for several more hours. I'll keep you informed, ma'am."

María was about to ask another question about the engine testing but reconsidered. They would know soon enough. One way or another. "I saw our young pilots installing new equipment in the cockpit."

"Yes," Colt responded. "They've found a technical solution to our navigation problems. Seems very promising."

"I'll trust you to take good care of the two officers after all this is over. I mean, take care of their careers. This plan of yours wouldn't have a chance without those two bright and capable people. We'll owe them a great deal."

"I've been thinking about that, and I promise they'll be taken care of. Everyone who's helped us, for that matter. Can I brief you on my conversation with Steve Holmes, ma'am?"

"Yes, please. What did you learn?"

Colt walked her through his phone conversation with Steve regarding what he'd been able to download from the online recording system. Still, it wasn't until he mentioned that Eric Paynter had discovered and secured an incriminating document from Carlisle's desk drawer that her mood brightened.

"You meant to say he found the folder in my desk drawer, correct? I mean, I'm still the president!"

"Yes, ma'am," Colt corrected himself. "Your desk drawer."

She giggled and then stated, "It's hard to comprehend how someone could be so foolish as to have written proof of their treason. Amazing, really."

"Foolish and arrogant, a bad combination of traits in anyone. Steve also mentioned that Eric plans to visit with the attorney general tomorrow morning over at Justice. He reasoned that it would be helpful to sit next to the AG when we need law enforcement resources we can trust when we land at SFO. We just don't know how far the plot has spread within the Secret Service. Best to have the FBI, ATF, and the Marshals Service waiting for us."

María nodded in the direction of the maintenance office. "Speaking of the Secret Service, what about Blanton? Are you planning on taking him on the plane with us?"

"I'd rather not. Agent DeSantis has him securely bound to that bed. He's still paralyzed from the waist down, and she's kept him knocked out with pain meds. I thought we'd leave him here. I'll ask DeSantis to give him more pain meds right before we leave tomorrow morning. I'll make a note to call Admiral Shaffer after we land to send a team to arrest him."

María continued to be impressed with Colt's ability to manage complex problems. "I understand you're looking forward to leaving government service after my term expires, but that would be a grave mistake. You're very good at all of this. I know you hate politics, but that's the price of admission. I really can't see you checking out and just wasting away on that silly boat of yours. I hope you reconsider."

Colt considered what President Hernández had just said. There was an element of truth to it. He agreed to give the topic some more thought. But for now, he needed to stay focused on getting that airplane ready to fly.

## Maintenance Hangar Aircraft Bay

It was three hours past midnight when Dave finally certified the engine ready for a test flight, and his weary group of technicians left the hangar for a well-deserved rest. Colt glanced around at the assembled team members sitting in chairs near SAM 970. The president and Dave looked worn out, but the younger people looked like they could pull an all-nighter. Colt turned first to Dave.

"I understand the engine passed all your tests. Anything left to do?"

"Nothing else we can get done in the hangar. I can't refuel her inside, so a truck will be here at 5:30 to fill the tanks. It shouldn't take more than an hour. I could use Wyatt's help with that."

"No prob. I'll be here."

"Where are we with the nav systems, Chloe?"

Chloe Ryan referred to a notepad. "Good to go, Mr. Secretary. Everything checks out fine inside the hangar. I'll want to confirm the GPS reception after the plane is pulled out tomorrow morning."

"Good. Wyatt, anything to add as our aircraft commander?"

"Just this, sir, Wyatt answered. "I just filed our flight plan for a test profile over Puget Sound and then the Olympic Peninsula. It's pretty standard for this type of maintenance. Assuming the number four engine is running smoothly, and when you give me the word, I'll refile the flight plan in the air listing SFO as our new destination. Our schedule calls for everyone to be on board and seated no later than 0700. Assuming our preflight checks go as planned, we could be wheels up and on our way no later than 0800."

Colt clasped his hands together. "Anything else?"

Chloe handed the president a stack of clothing. "Here's the

outfit I have for you, ma'am. You should have everything you need there. I'll drop by before we board and help you with your hair and makeup. Secretary Garrett has warned us there will be press waiting for you after we land."

"Thank you, Chloe. I very much appreciate your help with all of this." She stood and faced the small team. "Tomorrow is going to be a huge day. Many things need to go well to execute this plan fully. But I want each of you to know how grateful I am for what you have done here. I won't forget it. Now, let's all try to get some sleep!"

# Day Nine

## Boeing Field

Colt Garrett strode purposefully onto the tarmac, his footsteps sounding on the fuel-stained pavement. It was a brisk morning, the air keen with the promise of a new day. He had witnessed countless sunrises in his hometown, but this was something else.

As he gazed down the runway to the southeast, a sight caught his breath mid-exhale. The first light of dawn began to seep over the horizon, a golden ribbon weaving through the inky tapestry of night. It caressed the snow-covered peak of Mount Rainier, casting an ethereal glow that seemed to awaken the dormant volcano.

Like sentinels guarding a treasure, wispy clouds danced around the summit. Colt watched in awe as the first rays of sunlight painted the snow a radiant shade of pink, then golden, before settling into a pristine, dazzling white. The mountain's majesty was awe-inspiring, and he couldn't help but feel humbled by nature's grandeur.

The scene gradually brightened, and Colt's face was warmed by the touch of the rising sun. He couldn't deny the nerves that gnawed at him. Today's flight was a matter of national importance, fraught with danger.

Yet, as the sun continued its ascent in the east, a strange calm settled over him. The world below came alive, a symphony of colors and sounds. The engine roars of departing aircraft, the city's distant hum, and birds' chirping melded into a harmonious rhythm. Colt knew the challenges that awaited him in the skies, the decisions that would shape everything for the nation's near- and long-term future. But at this moment, as the sun's rays kissed his face, he felt a glimmer of hope.

The beauty of the sunrise and the vastness of the sky stretching out before him reminded him of the resilience of humanity. This extraordinary sunrise reminded him that no matter the obstacles, he would overcome them.

Colt turned away from the mesmerizing vista and walked back toward the maintenance hangar to call Steve Holmes one last time before takeoff. The shadows of doubt that had haunted him earlier in the mission had receded, replaced by a sense of purpose. He would face the day head-on and couldn't help but smile. He knew that there was always a way forward in the face of adversity. He took the phone from his pocket and called Steve.

"Everything in place," Steve stated. "Lenny's here on speaker. I'll be in the NMCC on other matters and can help you from there if things go sideways. Do you want us to let your family know you're okay? Dan and Allie are having a very tough time. The press has been reporting there's no hope of finding anyone alive. We could tell them we might have some good news to give them later today."

For a moment, Colt considered agreeing that his grown children could be brought into their confidence. But then he changed his mind.

"Nope. No, sorry. Don't say a word to them or anyone else until this is over."

"Okay, boss, understood. Eric Paynter will be with the AG and law enforcement directors at Justice. There'll be local resources that can support you in San Francisco as soon as I give Eric the word."

"That's fine, Steve. Did you speak with Zoey Hale as well? Having the press there will be critical to our plan."

"She called me an hour ago. You should have plenty of press coverage. All the major networks have been tipped that something major will be happening at the San Francisco airport. They're guessing the California governor will make some big announcement about his political future." Colt spoke with Steve and Lenny for several minutes to address some last-minute concerns. He ended the call and stepped into the maintenance office.

"Have you given him the additional meds?"

Anna DeSantis nodded. "Yes, sir. About twenty minutes ago. They should keep him quiet until we're a long way from here."

"Thanks. You should probably find the president and see that she gets aboard the plane. I'll be along shortly."

Colt examined Blanton's restraint again and walked out of the hangar to find Anna escorting María to the plane's stairs. Colt was surprised to see the two pilots standing at the foot of the stairs wearing service dress uniforms. Wyatt and Chloe smartly saluted as President Hernández walked by them and up the stairs into the plane.

"What's with the uniforms?" asked Colt as he returned their salutes. "I expected you two to be in flight suits this morning. Maybe even leather flight jackets!"

Wyatt straightened his tie. "Well, sir, we figured this is Air Force One now, and we should be dressed appropriately."

"I hope we don't have to use that callsign until we arrive in San Francisco," Colt responded. "Until then, let's just use SAM 970."

When Colt entered the cabin, he noticed that Dave Ryan was also in uniform, complete with six rows of ribbons and the stripes of a chief master sergeant. "You too?" kidded Colt.

"Yes, sir, Mr. Secretary. It was Lieutenant Commander Steele's Idea. I earned the privilege of wearing this after my retirement, almost fits. I'll probably ditch the jacket tie after we secure the door, though."

Wyatt, Chloe, and Dave started their preflight checks as Colt sat near the president and DeSantis. He made another phone call to Steve before turning the phone off. After the call, he realized something was bothering him, but he couldn't put his finger on it. Had he missed something?

"Everything all right with Mr. Holmes?" asked the president. "You have an odd look on your face."

"It's probably nothing, ma'am." He looked up to see Dave close the cabin door and secure the locking mechanism. He could look forward through the open cockpit door to see the flight crew select several switches.

"Good morning, Madam President," Wyatt announced over the intercom. "We've just received clearance from ground control to taxi. We'll be using runway fourteen right, taking us southeast until we turn right and head out over the sound and then over the Olympic Peninsula. You should get a nice view of Mount Rainier out the left side of the aircraft. Request permission to depart, ma'am."

María wasn't interested in checking out the scenery on the trip. She just wanted to get to San Francisco. She peered into the cockpit from her seat and called out, "Permission granted!"

On the other side of the runway, Admiral Kurt Schaffer put the phone down and watched as the 707 accelerated down the runway and into the morning air. It was an odd sight, the old Air Force One leaving Boing Field while the remains of President Hernández lay undiscovered under a massive rubble pile. Shaffer watched the 707 exit the departure pattern and bank right to start the planned flight tests. He picked up the phone and said, "Sorry about that. Just airport noise."

## Maintenance Office

Cade Blanton lay motionless in the bed, listening for any sounds after the loud whine of the plane's engines gradually decreased and finally ceased. The pain he felt radiating from his upper back was excruciating, but his only possibility of escape was by not swallowing the pain medication that DeSantis had constantly administered since that pilot injured him in the shelter. He had never been more embarrassed in his entire life than when DeSantis cleaned him up after that first uncontrolled bowel movement. He watched the disgust on her face as she performed the revolting task. He didn't know if her attitude toward him was caused by her anger at changing his diaper, her hate for his treason, or a combination of the two. Three days had passed since that first diaper change, and Blanton was only slightly embarrassed by the necessary ritual. Besides, he wasn't the one who caused his injury.

He'd gone over in his mind for hours how he could have underestimated the guy's ability to be a threat. He wasn't armed and not very close to him. It all made sense when DeSantis mentioned the pilot had been a high school rodeo champion. Those cowboys were of another breed. The guy hit him like a freight train. Blanton was determined to return the favor to that tall pilot if he recovered from his injuries, as unlikely as that seemed at the moment. Maybe the right specialist in the right medical center could make him right again. But what would be the point? If the president successfully made it to San Francisco and told the world what had happened, he knew he'd be convicted of countless federal crimes and spend the remainder of his life in a high-security prison. And everyone knew what happened to law enforcement officers in prison.

Estimating that it had been more than an hour since he heard the plane depart, Blanton decided it was finally time to attempt to free himself from the bedframe. He'd worked out the plan during his long, painful hours staring at the ceiling. It was now or never. He moved his bound wrist so the rusted part of the bed frame was directly under the plastic cable Zip Tie loop. Then, slowly, and rhythmically, he moved his arm from side to side, carefully working the plastic band against the rough metal edge. Waves of pain catapulted up his broken back as he tried to cut through the solid plastic band. He needed to rest after a while, nearly blacking out from the exertion and the pain. Relaxing his arms to let the blood flow back into his wrist, he thought back to how his involvement in the plot to overthrow the president had begun.

Like most traitors, he wasn't the subject of a blackmail operation or even a honey pot scheme. He didn't have a gambling problem, and he wasn't interested in using illicit drugs. He wasn't interested in personal power or fame. He just wanted to be rich or at least financially comfortable. He yearned for a lifestyle that meant he could purchase one of those Georgetown penthouses and vacation wherever and whenever he preferred. None of that was going to happen on a federal salary.

While playing at the FBI National Academy golf tournament, he met Becci Quinn. The annual tournament was held at the Columbia Country Club inside the Chevy Chase Beltway. It raised money for the academy's foundation, which supported several law enforcement education programs. Blanton joined the organization after he attended the FBI's prestigious National Academy Program. Becci's LeDroit Society was one of the tournament's primary sponsors, allowing her to attend the luncheon and mingle with the golfers after they returned to the clubhouse. The attractive woman had eased into a chair next to his at lunch.

"Hi, Cade. I'm Becci Quinn!" she had said, offering her hand. "Did you have a good round this morning?"

He wondered where they had met before realizing she had merely read the nametag on his shirt. That lunch had led to a series of dates over the next few weeks leading to the moment Becci eventually confessed her interest in him was much more than romantic. She ultimately offered him a way to improve his financial position in a very short period dramatically. There was high risk, to be sure, but the opportunity to own that Georgetown penthouse was too much to pass up. But that would all go away if he couldn't free himself from the bed.

Blanton finally succeeded in cutting through the plastic tie. He rolled to his left, crashing to the linoleum floor below. Lying face down, he stretched his arms out in front of him and let out an uncontrolled scream from the unexpected pain that shot up his back. After taking several deep breaths, he started using his arms to inch his damaged body slowly and painfully across the highly polished floor. The effort to get to the other side of the room took all his waning energy and strength, but he knew he had no choice but to continue the agonizing crawl. It was this or prison for life.

At last, he reached a desk leg and struggled with great effort to pull himself forward and up to a sitting position. He used both hands to grasp the drawer knob and ease the drawer open. Looking inside, he was relieved to find a prepaid phone resting in the drawer's bottom. Only one challenge remained. How to free the phone from its plastic blister packaging in his condition.

**The Oval Office**

Carlisle and Webb sat facing one another on the two beige sofas in the historic office. "And there's still no sign of the president's body?" he asked. "Or of Garrett, either?"

Travis briefly scanned the document his staff handed him earlier in the day. "Not yet, sir. More than two hundred bodies have been removed so far, but no sign of her or Garrett. Admiral Shaffer is estimating the team has moved most of the rubble, including the stage where we believe the president was supposed to have been standing at the time of the explosion. They found the body of the Seattle mayor yesterday, and it was found lying next to the governor on the stage. It's hard to figure out what happened to her."

"Maybe her body was vaporized by the explosion. That's possible. That was a pretty large quantity of military explosives the Chinese team planted. Would that explain why they haven't found the body?"

Travis shook his head. "Doubtful. The bomb was supposed to be placed in a container on the other side of the room, opposite from where she would have been standing. Something else. I haven't heard a word from the Secret Service agent that was part of this. He was instructed to make certain Hernández was on the platform at the appropriate time and then get out of the museum before the bomb detonated. Maybe he didn't make it out of the building in time."

Carlisle stood and stepped over to the presidential desk. He opened a drawer momentarily and then abruptly closed it. Pressing a button on the desk console, he said, "Emma, do you recall seeing a blue folder on my desk? It was here yesterday afternoon."

"No, sir," she quickly replied. "I haven't seen it. Would you like me to check with the housekeeping staff?"

"Yes, Emma. Please do that immediately. There was some particularly sensitive information in that file. Instruct them not to open it if it's found."

Joe Carlisle began to think about the notes he had written

in that file and what could happen if the wrong person read them. He badly needed to find that folder. His thoughts were interrupted when Travis' mobile phone rang. Travis spoke softly into his phone for several minutes and ended the call.

"Travis, what's wrong?" asked Carlisle. "Bad news? You look like shit." He had gone three shades of gray and pale.

"Terrible news, sir. That was Cade Blanton, our Secret Service agent. He was calling from a hangar at Boeing Field. He's been seriously injured and in a lot of pain. He said that Hernández and Garrett were in an old fallout shelter during the time of the explosion, not injured at all. And he said that she and Garrett have somehow patched up an old Air Force One from the Johnson administration and are currently airborne and flying to San Francisco. We're talking about an old 707 from the museum. Somehow, they found a flight crew. I know. It's hard to believe. Apparently, she and Garrett know what we have done and our involvement with the Russians and Chinese. They've been watching the news, and she's planning on making a public announcement regarding the US reaffirming the QUAD agreement when they land. I'm assuming our involvement will also be exposed."

Carlisle dropped into the massive leather chair and stared at Travis. It was all going to come crashing down. Everything. Every possible scenario that he considered ended with him being convicted of the murder of hundreds and treason. The retired Navy rear admiral found himself wondering if a civilian could be shot for treason. Was the vice president subject to the Uniformed Code of Military Justice? He imagined that would be debated in the months to come. It might even go to the Supreme Court. He'd lose everything, of course. Reputation, fortune, and family. He considered that he might be able to protect his wife from prosecution if he pled guilty and saved the country at the expense of a trial. Carlisle rubbed his temples as a headache began to throb at the base of his neck and move to his forehead. He hoped it was the beginning of a stroke when Travis finally got his attention.

"I said I just spoke with Becci on the phone, and she has an idea of how we might get out of this."

The two men conferred and eventually prepared a statement for Carlisle to read. It had to be perfect. Carlisle walked over to the office door and opened it. "Emma, I need to speak with NORAD immediately! And do whatever it takes to find that blue folder!

He stepped back over to the Resolute Desk and sat in the chair. "Okay, Travis," he announced, "Let's see if we can fix this mess."

## Joint Base Lewis McChord, Washington

Colonel Kari Hunter had just changed back into uniform and started her lunch after her midday workout when the watch officer found her in the breakroom.

"Colonel, you need to come out to the watch floor. Tyndall is on the line for you, ma'am."

She gulped down the last of her coffee and followed the young lieutenant down the hallway, wondering what it could be all about. She grabbed the offered handset and said, "Colonel Hunter. To whom am I speaking?"

"Kari, General Cody. I have an odd one for you."

Lieutenant General "Wild Bill" Cody commanded the First Air Force at Tyndall, near Panama City, Florida. He was a friend of Kari's older brother, but more importantly, the three-star general was her boss.

"Yes, sir, General. What do you need?"

"What I need is for WADS to scramble a section of interceptors to intercept an old 707 on the way to San Francisco. We've designated it as hostile; your team should already be tracking it. Apparently, there's intel that the plane's loaded with plastic explosives, and the Islamic terrorists aboard intend to fly it into one of the Bay Area buildings. The target could even be something like a stadium or one of the bridges spanning the bay. It's all pretty sketchy. Regardless of the target, we have orders to take it down. Preferably over the ocean. And one other thing, Kari. This is coming directly from the president. The national security advisor was on the phone when he gave the order."

"What about forcing it down, General? Lots of options short of splashing it into the sea."

"I hear you, but the tasking is clear. Knock it out of the sky. That's an order, Colonel Hunter."

"Yes, sir. Knock it down."

Kari turned to the watch team and asked, "Where's the southbound bogey now?"

"Radar holds the bogey just south of Portland, ma'am. The 114th out of Kingsley looks like our best option," a young sergeant responded. "Do you want me to alert them?"

"Hell, yes," Kari ordered. "And we better start working on getting some tanker support up ASAP. I think some KC-135s are working down south with a section of C-17s. Reroute them!"

The sergeant nodded and keyed several commands into his workstation.


## Klamath Falls, Oregon

Driving north on Highway 97, travelers are greeted by a

new sign welcoming visitors to Oregon's City of Sunshine, a town known for having more than 300 days of sun per year. The Rotary Club of Klamath County partnered with the city to renovate the sign and added a message inviting tourists to return. It was just another example of local service clubs working with elected officials to improve their community. Rich Manning served as the club's current president. He was using this Tuesday morning to identify the club's next service project by working with the city council to survey Klamath's small population regarding areas of need. Service clubs had learned it was best to ask the community rather than assume the club knew what the city needed.

"Darn it, Jerry," exclaimed Rich, "I just don't understand why you are opposed to conducting a survey. I have the form ready; we just need the city's permission to email it to the community."

Mayor Jerry Farmer was elected in November by a landslide. He wanted to work with the other service clubs in town, not exclusively with the Rotary Club. His position was difficult because he was a Rotarian himself.

"I just don't feel comfortable excluding the other service clubs, Rich. They've been itching to build a spray park beside the river. And a lot of their members are your customers."

Rich owned Manning Mortgage on Second Street. "Hell, Jerry, everyone in town is my customer."

Jerry wanted to change the subject. "I hear you have duty today, Major. Are you calling me from the air base?"

"Yep, I'm sitting in the ops building as we speak, sweating in a flight suit and speed pants. Very glamorous."

Rich held a commission as a major in the Oregon Air National Guard. Once a month, he pulled rotational duty as an alert intercept pilot at Kingsley Field. He'd resigned his commission in the Air Force after fulfilling his mandatory service commitment.

He had joined the Air Guard to keep flying while serving the required years to receive a military pension. And what flying it was, because Rich Manning was an eagle driver, fully qualified to fly and, if necessary, fight the F-15C Eagle. The single-seat interceptor could track fourteen and simultaneously engage six targets with medium and short-range missiles. Or the pilot could use the 20mm cannon. With a top speed of Mach 2.5, the Eagle could get anywhere it was needed in a hurry. He was about to take another run at convincing the mayor to partner with his club when a loud horn blasted throughout the building. The loudspeaker blared, "Scramble, Scramble, Scramble. Alert crews to their aircraft. We have enemy inbound. Scramble, Scramble, Scramble!"

Rich yelled, "Gotta go!" into his phone and dropped it on the table before racing out of the room and down a hallway. He was running down a flight of stairs when he was passed by his wingman, Captain Ernie Mathieson, call sign BERT, who was zipping up his flight suit as he reached the foot of the stairs. The two pilots opened a metal locker and quickly donned survival vests and parachute harnesses before grabbing flight helmets from a top shelf and racing for the double doors. A large white van with its engine warming up was waiting for the pilots directly in front of the building. The pilots climbed into the van, and it immediately accelerated away toward the alert hangar, less than fifty yards away. No one said a word as the pilots put on their helmets and gloves and adjusted their oxygen masks. They draped communications cords over their shoulders and looked out the window as the van stopped in front of the alert hangar with two F-15C Eagles inside. It had been only forty-five seconds since the alert horn first blared its alarm.

Rich climbed the temporary ladder into the open cockpit and immediately started the engines. While the turbo jets wound up, he snapped his harness into the seat and connected his comms cable and oxygen hose to their receptacles. Next came connecting the air inflation hose for his anti-g suit to help prevent loss of consciousness during high-g maneuvers. When he closed the canopy and enabled the ejection seat mechanism, it had been just over two minutes since the alert sounded. After several hand gestures with the plane captain to ensure everything was ready, the ground crew pulled the wheel chocks free, and the fully fueled and armed F-15 rolled out of the hangar and turned right onto a taxiway to follow BERT to the active runway.

At the three-minute point, BERT keyed his microphone. "Hey, LUNCHBOX, any idea of what this is all about? We were scheduled to be off duty at 1600, and it was my turn to pick up the kids after soccer practice."

Rich had acquired his callsign after his squadron mates noticed that he brought a sack lunch when he had the duty. At first, it annoyed him, but he eventually rationalized that some pilots received worse ones.

"Sorry, BERT. No idea. They'll tell us soon enough." Rich acknowledged the tower's clearance, and the two fighters turned onto the runway and accelerated at full speed using afterburners. The fighters rotated before reaching the runway's end, going full vertical to reach their assigned altitude and initial heading. The moment they were in the air, they were no longer under Air National Guard authority. At that moment, they became Air Sovereignty Alert assets of the United States Air Force.

The WADS air controller vectored the two lethal fighters toward the southbound 707 to take an advantageous firing position behind the large airliner. Within a few minutes, the fighters had made the simple intercept. Rich keyed his mic when he had the airliner lined up for a missile shot.

"WADS, this is Saber Leader, Saber 104 with Saber 215. We

have a tallyho on your track five one three four, wings level at angels three two. We have radar lock, over."

BERT moved his fighter into a combat spread formation to get a better angle on the bogey. He selected the squadron frequency and said, "LUNCHBOX, are you sure about this? I mean, it's frigging Air Force One! Look at that airplane, Major! I know it's a relic, but she looks like the real deal to me!"

"Roger, BERT. You hang back while I slide up for a look see."

Rich eased his plane forward, reasoning the threat from the airliner was minimal. He noted the plane's tail number on his kneeboard and then nudged the fighter further forward until his cockpit was even with the Boeing's nose. He could see the crew flying the 707 and was surprised to see the pilot wave at him and motion to his headphones. Rich maneuvered the fighter back to his previous position and verified he was still on the squadron frequency. He suspected someone had received twisted intelligence.

"BERT, unless terrorists have started wearing US Navy uniforms, I'm not certain WADS knows what we've got up here. I'm gonna reconfirm. I'm the on-scene commander. I won't shoot down anybody until we straighten this out!"


"I'm telling you, WADS, you've got it wrong. Or the intel is wrong. Something's wacky. Does the tail number I gave you check out?"

Rich's frustration grew as he attempted to get the WADS controller to understand what he was trying to communicate. He was about to lose his temper when another voice came over the circuit.

"Saber Leader, this is WADS Actual, Colonel Hunter. You've been tasked to eliminate that airplane. Tell me, Major, what the hell is going on up there?" The two Air Force officers discussed the situation and decided that Colonel Hunter should speak directly with the airplane. She directed the comm specialist to select the air distress frequency and keyed the mic.

"Boeing 586970, this is Western Air Command. You have been designated as hostile and will not be allowed to land. Alter course immediately to 270, descend to 12,000 feet, and await further instructions. Do you copy, over?"

Colonel Hunter relaxed a bit after the fighters confirmed that the 707 had turned to the west and started to descend. She had bought herself more time to determine who was in that airplane and what they might be planning. But calls with NORAD didn't resolve her doubts about 970's identity. The tail number checked out as a decommissioned Air Force One on loan to some museum in Seattle. NORAD maintained that the airplane was hostile, specifically citing intel provided by the national security advisor. NORAD said the shoot-down order was coming directly from the acting president in the Oval Office. Colonel Hunter's orders were crystal clear, but she resisted. She needed something more before she would authorize the plane's destruction and the deaths of those on board.

"970, this is Colonel Hunter at Western Air Command. Who is onboard that aircraft?"

Colt nodded at Wyatt and keyed his mic. "Colonel Hunter, this is the secretary of defense, Colton Garrett. President María Hernández is on board, and we are headed to SFO. Do you recognize my voice, Kari?"

Kari Hunter processed the message. Was President Hernández alive? She began to piece the information together. There was a bombing in Seattle, the president's body not found, and a plane that took off from Seattle with SECDEF onboard, claiming POTUS was alive. The voice sounded like Garrett's, but she needed to be sure. A thought occurred to her; then she keyed her mic.

"Secretary Garrett, tell me about COOTS!"

"That's your brother's call sign!" he replied. "It stands for Constantly Overestimating Own Tactical Significance!"

Colonel Kari Hunter made the most critical decision of her career. Both elements of the National Command Authority were on that plane.

"Roger that, 970. You are confirmed. I will notify NORAD, ATC, and the Pentagon that 970 has changed its callsign to Air Force One! You are cleared to SFO direct. Break. Saber Leader, assume armed escort of Air Force One. We are vectoring tanker assets to rendezvous with you along your track. WADS out!"

## The Oval Office

Joe Carlisle couldn't believe what was happening. Just as he thought he might be able to survive the catastrophe that was the Shanghai Protocol, the plane carrying María Hernández was a little more than an hour from landing at SFO and ruining his life forever. He knew having the Air Force shoot it down on his order was a long shot, but it was worth a try because he was out of options. He considered ending his own life rather than facing the consequences of his actions, conspiring to kill the president of the United States, murdering hundreds of others. But he could never do that. He was too much of a narcissist to select that solution. Travis was on the phone, shocked to see Carlisle tearing the hair from his head.

"Excuse me, sir. I have Becci Quinn on the line. She has one more idea that might solve our problem. Can I put her on speaker?"

Carlisle looked up at Travis and hissed, "If you must."


## MV Orion, North of San Francisco

Major Tang nervously and helplessly watched as the huge crane lowered two containers onto a cleared area of the massive ship. Even a slight mistake by the crane operator would immediately end his mission before it started. The containers had been welded together to create a hidden but serviceable hangar for the small attack helicopter that became visible when the crewmen opened the container's front doors. They slowly rolled out the aircraft until its tail rotor cleared the makeshift hangar, allowing the overhead crane to reposition the containers near the ship's bow. The Harbin K-19 helicopter, a licensed-built Chinese version of the Airbus AS365, was remarkably like another Airbus derivative, the US Coast Guard MH-65 Dolphin. But this aircraft featured a two-person, tandem cockpit configuration, and its pylons were loaded with missiles, rockets, and a 23mm gun. Major Tang climbed into the rear seat after the maintenance technicians completed their setup procedures. He watched Lieutenant Lou strap into the weapons officer station directly in front of him. Tang started up the two turboshaft engines, and within a minute, the attack chopper was airborne and heading for its inbound target.

Tang glanced at the small photograph of his wife holding their dog taped to the instrument panel. He'd taken the photo last summer when on leave near the coast. His wife had named the Pug Frank after seeing a bootleg copy of *Men in Black*. They secretly loved watching American movies but were careful not to share their preference for the forbidden Western media with neighbors or family members. One never knew who might report them to the authorities. He continued to fly the intercept profile when the lieutenant announced, "Major Tang, I have the target, and we are locked on. Do I have your permission to fire, sir?"

"Yes," Tang replied. "Two missiles."

The guided missiles launched from the helicopter's pylon and pitched up to acquire the target. It wasn't far away. "Sir, we have two successful hits. The target continues to fly, but it is falling."

Tang watched the tactical picture in his head-up display and quickly decided. "Designate and fire the two remaining missiles, Lieutenant. We need to be certain the airliner falls into the sea."

Above and behind Air Force One, Rich watched with horror as a missile destroyed the 707's number two engine and another detonated near the tail. The big 707 began to descend and roll to the left when Rich yelled, "We've got a bandit that's locked onto Air Force One! It looks like a helo! Stay with Air Force One, BERT!"

Rich instinctively designated the hostile aircraft and fired two Sidewinders at the threat before slamming his throttles forward and pressing forward for a follow-up shot. It wasn't necessary because the helicopter erupted as the two AIM-9 missiles obliterated it.

## Air Force One, Northwest of San Francisco

"Wyatt!" Chloe screamed as the number two engine exploded, broke off from the wing, and fell to the sea below. The big Boeing airplane shuddered with the missile's impact, immediately yawed, and rolled left while it pitched down into a steep dive. Wyatt had momentarily left the flight deck to use the restroom and had been speaking with Colt about how they narrowly

264

avoided being shot down by the Air National Guard interceptors when the two Chinese missiles detonated.

Wyatt rushed back to the flight deck and strapped into the pilot's seat. "My airplane!" shouted Wyatt as he applied right rudder and right aileron to return to wings level. He gently pulled back on the control yoke to reduce the nose-down attitude because he needed to reduce airspeed before the plane exceeded its design limits. He was fighting to control the airplane when he turned to Chloe.

"Retard the throttles to idle. We need to reduce this yawing and rolling. I'm going to continue the descent and try to stabilize her.

"The fuel to number two is cut off," Dave announced. "No fire indications yet. I'm still checking for other damage. The fuel tanks look good.

Colt buckled into the navigation station behind Wyatt and across from Dave. He watched the two pilots fight to control the damaged airplane. He remembered something a pilot had once told him. "Altitude, airspeed, and brains. You can't lose any two and survive." This wasn't the first time Colt had witnessed the difference a skilled pilot could make. The difference between life and death. After the emergency had passed, Colt wondered if they should be looking for a place to land. "Wyatt, do you think you can make SFO? Are there closer options?"

Wyatt waited until he had the plane in stabilized flight before responding. He scanned the instrument panel and looked over his shoulder. "I think that SFO is our best bet, sir. A twelve-thousand-foot runway will give us room for error if anything else goes wrong. I recommend SFO, Mr. Secretary."

Colt looked back at the president sitting in the main cabin and nodded. "It's your decision, Wyatt. You're the pilot-in-command. Make the call, son."

"Okay, then. SFO it is. Chloe, let ATC know that we're declaring an emergency into SFO and that they need to be ready with the trucks and medics. Mr. Secretary, you better get back into the cabin and make sure that everyone is safely buckled in. Okay, let's get this bird on the ground."

Twenty minutes later, Wyatt keyed the intercom. "Mr. Secretary, SFO approach just informed me that Mr. Paynter wanted you to know that everything has gone as planned, and federal agents are waiting for us when we reach the terminal. I have the runway in sight, and our landing is assured. We'll be on the ground shortly."

After a period of what Wyatt would later describe to investigators as "doing some serious pilot shit," the plane crossed the threshold and landed on the runway numbers. It touched down so abruptly that Chloe's makeshift navigation equipment detached from their suction mounts and crashed to the flight deck floor. She was about to complain to Wyatt but stopped when she saw the broad smirk on his face.

"Oh, sorry about that, Chole. That's how we land in the Navy."

### University of Washington Medical Center, Seattle

Veteran Police Officer Ted Decca sat slumped in an uncomfortable chair while he listened to an audio version of the latest Tom Carroll novel through an earbud inserted in his right ear. The middle-aged, overweight, and out-of-shape patrolman rationalized that he needed only one ear to perform his security duty guarding a prisoner in a room on the hospital's eighth floor. Ted had jumped at the chance to pull a double shift and earn the time and a half pay. He considered it easy money, just sitting in a chair outside the room guarding a man who wasn't going anywhere soon. The prisoner was paralyzed below the waist and had been handcuffed to the hospital bed. And the meds that they had been pumping into his arm would have kept a racehorse unconscious.

The FBI had asked the UW Police Department to provide prisoner security during the night, and Ted needed the extra money to help him make the payments on his new Dodge Challenger SRT. The $80,000 sticker price was more than he could afford, and the monthly payments and insurance premiums were killing him. His family and friends had warned him that he should consider making a more sensible purchase, but Ted Decca was not in the habit of taking advice from others. He was finishing the last of a chocolate milkshake when yet another masked medical assistant came by to check the prisoner's vital signs. Ted thought someone had just done it an hour ago, but that was none of his business. He waved the short woman through without looking at her and concentrated on listening to the book.

Genji closed the hospital room door and put on a pair of blue nitrile exam gloves. She removed a small pistol with a suppressor from her bag and pressed the muzzle against Cade Blanton's left temple. She coughed twice as she squeezed the trigger, effectively muffling the sound of the 22-caliber bullets, silencing Blanton forever. She slid the pistol under the hospital bed and quickly left the room.

Officer Ted Decca didn't look up as Genji briskly walked down the hall on her way to the stairwell. He had fallen asleep in the chair and wouldn't awaken until hours later when the charge nurse screamed, "Help! He's been shot!"

# SHANGHAI PROTOCOL

## Ritz-Carlton Shanghai, China

Minister of State Security Sun Ping gazed through the windows of the Carlton Suite on the hotel's 58ᵗʰ floor. He preferred to stay in the suite whenever he traveled to Shanghai because it offered a magnificent view of the nearby Oriental Pearl Radio and Television Tower. It was situated in Lujiazui, in the heart of Shanghai's commercial, financial, and upscale retail center, only an hour from Shanghai Pudong International. It was very convenient for his purposes on this trip. He moved to the ornate art deco-style desk, opened his personal MacBook, and launched a banking application. After verifying his identity through passwords, biometric safeguards, and two-factor identification procedures, he transferred his entire investment portfolio from the Agricultural Bank of China to banks in Montreal, the Cayman Islands, and Zurich.

Once he confirmed the banks had received his funds, he reserved a business-class seat on the Air Canada 777 scheduled to depart for Vancouver at 6:15 that evening. Sun had always known that the operation to assassinate President Hernández had a high risk of failure. It was only prudent to plan for that eventuality and be ready to leave at a moment's notice if necessary. And now, it was most necessary. After issuing the orders to have the Orion launch its helicopter and destroy the president's plan, he had spent his afternoon making final preparations for his escape from arrest, conviction, and punishment. The firing squad, no doubt. When he received the news that the helicopter attack had failed, he ordered room service and packed a bag for the flight.

Sun opened his leather briefcase and removed a Canadian passport bearing his name and photograph. China didn't recognize dual citizenship, but Canada did. He'd been investing millions of Canadian dollars in real estate throughout Vancouver.

He had even purchased a shopping mall and a hotel in the downtown core. His investments in real estate outside of China had not attracted any attention from his government. He was personally responsible for state security, and many other high-ranking Chinese officials had similarly invested in overseas real estate to diversify their portfolios and reduce exposure to government nationalization of personal assets. It had happened before.

Sun used a service elevator to reach a dark alley behind the hotel. He walked around a corner to find a row of ride-share cars waiting for fares in front of the hotel.

"Excuse me," he said to a young man leaning against a white sedan. "I'd like to go to the airport, and I'm late for my flight. I am willing to pay extra. Do you accept cash?

# Epilogue

## Severomorsk, Kola Peninsula, The Russian Republic

The owner of a small café perched on the edge of a cliff overlooking the massive naval base nudged the slightly built woman—the shabby-dressed worker who had been staring out the window since ordering a cup of black tea. The owner didn't appreciate one of her few tables being occupied by someone who didn't order food and might be unable to pay for the tea. The local workers knew how she felt about them using her café as a shelter from the wind. It was rare to find one of them here.

"Would you like to order something to eat? I have a delicious sandwich with boiled sausage if you are hungry."

"No," the stranger replied. The owner refilled the woman's teacup and noticed her hands were not rough or oil-stained like others in the small village. Instead, they more resembled the hands of her daughter, who worked in a bank close to town. The cafe owner shrugged and shuffled back to the kitchen to prepare another batch of potato and mushroom leek soup.

Rear Admiral Sofia Orlov let out a small exhale after the café owner left the dining room. In the weeks after the failure of the plan to assassinate the American president, the military intelligence officer felt she was living on borrowed time. President Hernández had survived the bombing and had returned to Washington, determined to discover and prosecute the guilty. Colt Garrett managed to survive, as well. Not only had Carlisle and Webb been arrested and charged with treason, murder, and a score of other offenses, but the entire GRU operation

**271**

in Washington had been blown, and most of the officers were being held in federal custody pending trial or deportation. Minister Sun had disappeared, and the Chinese were disavowing any involvement in the assassination attempt. The minister had gone rogue and been acting alone. After Admiral Kornilov had been suddenly summoned to the Kremlin, Sofia decided it was time to take the two-hour flight to the Kola Peninsula to inspect Russia's Northern Fleet headquarters unannounced. Just before disembarking from the Ministry of Defence executive jet, she stressed to the flight crew that she would be remaining in Severomorsk until the end of the week, and they should return on Saturday to bring her back to Moscow. She glanced again at the waterfront below, finished her tea, and asked for the check. She paid in cash.


US Navy Captain Colin Irwin furiously paced back and forth across the bridge of the USS Michael Monsoor, a Zumwalt-class guided missile destroyer of the US Navy. Named for Petty Officer 2nd Class Michael Monsoor, a Navy SEAL posthumously awarded the Medal of Honor for his heroic actions in Ramadi, Iraq, the Monsoor was completing the last day of a week-long visit to the Russian naval base. The ship was scheduled to get underway at 1300 and was thirty minutes behind schedule. All services between the ship and the pier had been already disconnected, and port-provided line handlers waited next to the mooring lines on the steel-reinforced pier. The only thing that kept Monsoor from departing was the slow but steady line of workers carrying fresh provisions across the gangway and into the ship for storage.

"God damn it, can't they move any faster?" Nobody on the packed bridge answered the captain's rhetorical question. "Now what?" he asked when a messenger tapped his arm.

"Captain, Senior Chief Frost asks that you meet him in the wardroom. He says it's important, sir."

"What now?" the exasperated captain shouted as he stormed off the bridge and headed for the deck below. Irwin opened the wardroom door to find his chief master-at-arms and two armed sailors standing beside one of the workers.

"What do you have, Senior Chief? Catch someone with sticky hands?"

The worker removed a woolen hat to reveal the face of an attractive woman with piercing eyes. "Hello, Captain. Please forgive my appearance, but it was necessary to board your ship unobtrusively. I am Rear Admiral Sofia Orlov of the Military Intelligence Directorate of the Russian Navy. I am formally requesting political asylum from the United States of America. I have information that your defense department would find extremely valuable. While you confirm my identity with your intelligence services, I suggest you depart Severomorsk as soon as possible. I may have been followed."

Captain Irwin looked at the woman's passport and the other documents on the table. He'd read about the assassination attempt and Russia's involvement. He looked at the woman once again and then made up his mind. He stepped over to a console mounted on the bulkhead. "Bridge, this is the captain. I want to be underway in five minutes."


## Skyline Drive, Shenandoah National Park, Virginia

Wyatt Steele was admiring the spectacular scenery of Skyline Drive as something briefly caught his eye. He crushed the brake pedal and stopped the rental car just in time to avoid hitting a whitetail doe and her fawn standing in the middle of the highway. The two beautiful animals stared at Wyatt momentarily before bolting off the roadway and disappearing into the dense, poplar forest. "What a way to start a new assignment," he said out loud, chuckled, and continued the drive along the crest of the Blue Ridge Mountains. The one-hundred-mile highway was the only public road through the Shenandoah National Park. Wyatt was shocked and delighted with the spectacular vistas and waterfalls that appeared after each roadway turn. While accelerating the small sedan along the scenic byway, Wyatt reflected on the events that had brought him here.

It had only been a few weeks since he barely landed a badly damaged Air Force One at San Francisco International Airport. The attack on a sitting president shocked the nation and the world. Everyone wanted answers, and they wanted to know who was responsible. The Air Force had immediately rushed Wyatt and his copilot, Chloe Ryan, away from the heated press surrounding President Hernández and Secretary Garrett before the reporters could notice and identify the pilots. Exhaustive and endless interrogations (the Air Force called them interviews) followed at a remote Colorado base. Last week, the Air Force finally allowed Wyatt and Chloe to leave the hidden base, but only after signing a stack of national security forms documenting their obligation to keep the incident to themselves. Forever. Wyatt remembered watching Chloe climb into her father's SUV as it drove down the winding mountain road—and out of his life.

It wasn't as if he hadn't expected it. The weeks holed up at the isolated base allowed Chloe and him to discuss their new relationship and where it might lead. She was clear about starting a life away from the Air Force, perhaps pursuing another career entirely. It would mean more years of school for her to obtain another degree. As usual, Wyatt wasn't confident about what he wanted out of life but knew he wasn't ready to settle down yet. Chloe was heartbroken with the news, and they hadn't spoken for the last few days. A handwritten note left for him under his door stated that she needed time to think. Wyatt knew it was over.

He was surprised that he hadn't heard a word from Garrett or anyone from the president's staff since San Francisco. After all, he'd been crucial to saving the president from an attempt on her life, not to mention the plot to overthrow the government. Garrett seemed genuinely and sincerely appreciative of his effort to land the old 707 safely, and Wyatt thought the secretary might reward him somehow for his role in the incident. He supposed Garrett was more concerned with his career than a washed-up pilot's future. And what would happen to former Vice President Carlisle and National Security Advisor Webb? A public trial would be unlikely—probably some plea deal in exchange for providing evidence of the Chinese and Russian plot. Lots of heads would roll.

"Here are your orders, Lieutenant Commander Steele."

Wyatt took the yellow envelope and returned the Marine's crisp salute. When he returned to his quarters, Wyatt was surprised to read that the orders required him to meet with someone at a location in the Shenandoah National Park in just a few days: a man's name and an address. There was no further information other than to wear casual civilian clothes. All very strange.


## Harry F. Byrd, Sr. Visitor Center, Shenandoah National Park

After driving another twenty miles, Wyatt saw a large wooden sign proclaiming, "Visitor Center Entrance." He turned the sedan into an expansive, mostly vacant parking lot and exited the car.

Wyatt first heard and then saw a small drone circling about three hundred feet overhead as he walked toward the only building in sight. I wonder who's flying that, he thought as he scanned the lot, searching for someone holding a controller. Wyatt disliked drones and thought the technology might someday replace real pilots like him. He approached the building entrance and saw an older man in a park ranger uniform sitting on a bench with several children and adults around him.

"That's right, sir," the ranger said. "The Civilian Conservation Corps built most of the park's original infrastructure. Nearly seven thousand boys who worked here during the Great Depression constructed the picnic grounds overlooks and most of the landscaping along Skyline Drive. Those CCC boys only earned thirty dollars a month and had to send twenty-five dollars home to their parents."

The small group of tourists left the ranger alone on the bench as they corralled their children and herded them through the visitor center's entrance. Wyatt was about to follow them, but he paused when he spotted the ranger's brass nameplate.

"Mr. Pellew?"

The middle-aged man looked up at Wyatt from under his broad-brimmed campaign hat, the trademark of a park ranger. "Yes, sir. I'm Oliver Pellew. How can I help you?"

Wyatt studied Oliver Pellew more closely. The man wore the field uniform of a National Park Ranger: gray shirt, green pants, and the famous tan campaign hat, like those worn by many state troopers and, of course, Smokey Bear. Oliver appeared to be about seventy years old, with a stomach that severely stressed the seams of his uniform shirt and forced the man's belt buckle to roll forward. Wyatt noticed the man's sad, gray eyes and broad face badly weathered and aged by the sun. But there was something else about those eyes. They seemed to pierce through

Wyatt as Oliver gave him his full attention.

Wyatt glanced around briefly. "I was, uh, asked to meet Oliver Pellew here this morning." He paused and then continued, "My name's Steele."

The park ranger nodded and then lowered his gaze. "I suppose you have some sort of identification, Mr. Steele?"

Wyatt reached for his military ID but stopped when Oliver raised his hand and said, "I didn't ask to see it, Mr. Steele. I merely shared an assumption. It would help if you listened more closely. It's a habit I've developed over the years that's served me well. Now walk with me, Mr. Steele. But first, could I trouble you to hand me those hiking sticks."

Wyatt was surprised by Oliver's comments but was also curious to learn why the Navy had ordered him to meet with this man. He picked up the two aluminum hiking sticks from the bench and handed them to the ranger, wondering, What the hell is this all about?

"I shouldn't call these hiking sticks, but that sounds better than walking sticks. Please allow me the illusion." Oliver chuckled as the man did his best to walk down the path.

Wyatt could see what the ranger meant. The man used the two sticks to fully support his body as they strolled, side-by-side, along a paved path next to the visitor center. The ranger wasn't going to hike anywhere soon.

"Let's start over. I'm Assistant Director Oliver Pellew of the United States Secret Service." He handed Wyatt a black leather case opened to the official credentials and gold badge of a special agent of the Secret Service. He continued with a laugh, "It's been nearly forty years, and I still get a kick out of saying that!"

Looking closely at the highly polished badge, Wyatt saw it comprised a silver, old-fashioned five-pointed star set onto a more traditional gold law enforcement shield topped by an eagle with outstretched wings. "A bit of history in that badge," Oliver commented. "That star was the first Secret Service badge issued in 1875. That star is the official emblem still used today by the Secret Service. The star's five points represent the agency's core values: justice, duty, courage, honesty, and loyalty. This badge remained unchanged until we adopted a new design in 1971 to promote consistency among federal law enforcement agencies. The badge you're holding was first issued in 2003."

Wyatt handed the credentials case back to Oliver.

"But what's with the costume?" He touched Oliver's shirt.

"Oh, this uniform? Well, it's just another illusion, I suppose. We have a covert field office in a cavern deep beneath the visitor center, and most staff wear park service uniforms to complete the deception. Our security forces dress as law enforcement rangers. It explains the weapons they carry."

Wyatt glanced at the two law enforcement rangers standing twenty feet away and noticed they appeared to be the most physically fit rangers he had ever seen.

Wyatt and Oliver continued to stroll along the path and gently descended into the valley. Wyatt noticed the drone again, but this time, it seemed to follow the men while they slowly walked down the hill.

"Don't concern yourself about the unmanned aircraft, Mr. Steele. It's one of ours. Our physical security is subtle but extremely effective. Now, tell me what you know about the Secret Service."

"I know you protect the president, her family, and other important government officials. I think you also investigate counterfeit currency crimes. Aren't you a part of the treasury department?"

"Not anymore, Mr. Steele. Most people know us as the people who guard the president. Still, we're one of America's oldest federal law enforcement agencies—created in 1865 to stamp out rampant counterfeiting to stabilize America's new financial system. At that time, nearly one-third of all currency in circulation was counterfeit. The country's financial stability was in jeopardy, so the Secret Service was established as a bureau in the treasury department to suppress widespread counterfeiting. Keep in mind that the Secret Service predates most other agencies. Over the years, the FBI, CIA, and other three-letter agencies assumed many of our missions. We currently live within the Department of Homeland Security. And yes, our primary missions are executive protection and counterfeit investigation. But that's not why you're here today. Let's sit for a moment."

Wyatt held the older man's arm and eased him onto a park bench. He waited for Oliver to continue.

"I assume you've heard of the Posse Comitatus Act of 1878?"

Wyatt nodded. "Yes, a law that prevents the president from using the military as a domestic police force. It was enacted after the Civil War to prevent federal troops from enforcing local laws in the South."

"Close, but not entirely accurate. The Posse Comitatus Act prohibits domestic law enforcement from the Army or the Air Force. However, the act's specificity refers to military forces. It says nothing about the Navy, the Marine Corps, the Coast Guard, or the National Guard. For this reason, the courts have held that the Posse Comitatus Act doesn't apply to the Navy or the Marines. Nevertheless, it's been DOD policy for many years to operate as if Posse Comitatus also applies to the sea services. Policy, you understand, not law."

"Okay, but I'm not following how this involves me."

Oliver removed a white handkerchief from his pocket and wiped the sweat dripping from the back of his neck. "Some people in government, and by that, I mean the highest levels of government, felt constrained by Posse Comitatus. Many years ago, a presidential decision directive created a special, off-the-books organization to provide a small, tactical element of highly trained individuals within the DOD to act when others could not or would not. The unit recruited naval officers as operatives because Posse Comitatus wouldn't apply. The president could use this capability anytime, anywhere. And it worked. But there was one roadblock: The naval officers in the special program didn't have arrest powers within our borders. As a result, the program was modified to provide the naval officers with credentials as special agents of the Secret Service. The administration created a special budget in the DOD to fund the Secret Service program covertly. I'm responsible for the program, which we have codenamed BROADSWORD."

Wyatt looked at the strange man on the bench next to him. He had never heard of the program, but he supposed he wouldn't have.

"And this brings us to you, Lieutenant Commander Steele. Your naval career has not been stellar, and if you'll forgive me, promotion seems unlikely, particularly after that unfortunate incident on the USS Portland. Your flying skills are average, despite your recent heroic efforts to land the president's plane, and you don't seem to tolerate the Navy's bureaucracy. A brief tour of duty with the border patrol proved that you are a brave man. You don't follow regulations. For example, this morning, you decided to wear a pistol under that jacket, even though you know that carrying a concealed weapon within a national park is a felony. But rules are for people who can't think for themselves. Am I right?"

"I guess that's true, Mr. Pellew. You seem to have me all figured out."

Oliver ignored Wyatt's sarcasm and continued. "You don't

play well with others, and most people don't like you. You don't have a strong sense of morality unless, of course, it suits you. You have the uncanny ability to get yourself out of trouble that most people would never get into. You're a loner, and you like it that way. You don't care about anyone other than yourself. You probably have some daddy issues, but those will remain unresolved now that he's dead."

Oliver paused and then asked, "How did I do?"

Wyatt stared at the concrete path beneath his feet and felt his rage build. This strange little man had reduced his life to a series of failures and implied he had no worth or value. Most of what Oliver said was true, but hearing it out loud made him seethe, and he wanted to strike out. He had enough and was about to announce it when Oliver stated, "And that's why we want you, Mr. Steele."

Wyatt was shocked. "You want me in your program after everything you just said? I don't understand."

"We are a minimal cadre of exceptional people with particular skills, Mr. Steele. We know who you are and what you are. The Navy might not be interested in you, but we are. I'm offering you unmatched special operations training and the opportunity to work and operate only with the best."

Oliver gazed over the valley below and then continued. "We aren't the Boy Scouts, Wyatt. There's no code of ethics or rules of any kind. There's only one thing that matters: the mission. The mission that we give you. These assignments will require you to operate under deep cover and for extended periods. Sometimes, you'll be on your own, and sometimes working as part of a team. If you accept, you'll immediately be promoted to commander in the United States Navy. After completing the special training I mentioned, you will also receive credentials as a special agent of the United States Secret Service."

# SHANGHAI PROTOCOL

Oliver turned his head and looked directly at Wyatt. "What's your answer, young man? I need to know right now."

Wyatt looked up at the drone circling above and the white clouds beyond. Oliver Pellew was offering him a new life, a second chance. He'd be promoted to commander and be able to retire after twenty years of service. It was an easy decision. He looked Oliver Pellew in the eye. "I say yes."

Oliver grasped Wyatt's shoulder and warmly smiled. "Welcome to Broadsword, Commander Steele!"

## The East Room, The White House

"Okay, Madam President. We're ready."

President María Hernández stepped through the door and into the East Room, packed full of the White House Press Corps, several members of her cabinet, and the senior leadership of the House and Senate. She paused for several moments and recalled the room's history while several photographers captured her image. George Washington designed the East Room to hold public meetings, but Abigail Adams hung her laundry there during the winter of 1800. Meriwether Lewis used the room for sleeping quarters before departing to lead the Corps of Discovery with William Clark. Union troops were bivouacked in the East Room during the Civil War, which would serve as the location for President Abraham Lincoln's funeral. This morning's announcement would be less sad than that occasion, and María hoped it would help the nation come together again. María realized everyone was watching her, and she spoke into the microphone.

"My fellow Americans, these past few weeks have tested the very fabric of our democracy. The attorney general, a group of federal marshals, and FBI agents placed former Vice President Joseph Carlisle and former National Security Advisor Travis Webb under arrest for their respective roles in an attempted but unsuccessful overthrow of this government. The attorney general will hold a press conference at the Justice Department later today to discuss the specific charges against Mr. Carlisle and Mr. Webb and his plan for prosecuting those charges. That will be all I have to say about that subject for now."

Several reporters raised their hands, but President Hernández shook her head. "Please hold your questions until I've concluded my remarks. Joseph Carlisle has tendered his resignation as vice president, effective immediately. I have accepted that resignation. After conferring with the cabinet and congressional leadership, I am pleased to announce that my nomination for vice president of the United States is Colton S. Garrett."

Colt Garrett stood up from his chair and joined the president behind the podium while the room erupted in applause and shouted approval. After the commotion died down, the president continued.

"Secretary Garrett has a long and distinguished career serving the United States. I believe he is best suited to serve as vice president during these extremely challenging times. I have consulted with the Speaker of the House, the majority leader of the Senate, and the ranking members of both legislative bodies, and they have assured me of a swift confirmation process for Secretary Garrett. Deputy Secretary of Defense Steven Holmes has agreed to serve as acting secretary of the defense department while the confirmation process is completed. Ladies and gentlemen, may I present the next vice president of the United States, Colton Garrett!"

After the second round of applause, Colt scanned the room and spoke into the microphone. "Madam President, Mr.

SHANGHAI PROTOCOL

Speaker, Mr. Leader, members of the cabinet, and perhaps most importantly, the citizens of this fine country, I was surprised and deeply honored when the president asked me to accept her nomination as vice president. As many of you know, I have never pursued political office, preferring to serve those duly elected. I've lived long enough to understand my strengths and weaknesses and remain convinced I am not a politician. But I was moved by the president's call to service and to assist her in restoring order and trust to our government that all of us were shocked and saddened to see threatened. Therefore, I have accepted the president's nomination to serve as vice president of the United States for the remainder of her first term, understanding that she will select another person as her running mate when she seeks a second term. With that, I'd be pleased to take any questions you might have."

After President Hernández and Colt Garrett left the East Room, the Speaker of the House and the majority leader remained to answer reporters' questions regarding the abbreviated process to confirm Colt as vice president. Minutes later, the news networks reported that Colt Garrett would be confirmed on Monday afternoon by a joint session of Congress. Immediately after, staff would escort the newly minted vice president to the Senate floor, where the president pro tempore would install Garrett as its new president. After meeting with President Hernández, Colt left the Oval Office and spoke with the Secret Service director when he noticed an old friend sitting on an upholstered bench beneath a portrait of John Adams, the second president and American Revolution leader. Colt gracefully excused himself and greeted his old colleague.

"Oliver Pellew! No, don't get up, Ollie. I'll join you. I've been standing for hours." Colt sat on the bench and clasped Oliver's hands in his.

"Did you ever imagine that one day we'd be sitting on a bench here in the White House? Perhaps it's ironic that Adams only served one term also."

"Congratulations on your nomination. Well deserved, sir, and I know you'll do very well here, no matter how long you choose to remain."

Colt saw that his friend still had that distinct twinkle in his eye, as if he knew more than he was willing to share. "Thanks for coming today, Ollie. It means a lot to me. Did you get a chance to talk with Dan?"

"I did. He mentioned he's leaving the Navy soon. Something about a vision problem: he's a smart and competent young man. You don't need to worry about his future. But I want to talk to you about another subject. I met with Wyatt Steele earlier today, and he's agreed to join our program. Thank you for recommending him to me."

A serious-looking man in a dark suit wearing an earpiece stepped forward.

"Mr. Garrett, the White House communications director would like you to stop by her office when you can, sir."

Colt Garrett stood to leave and rested his hand on his friend's shoulder. "Take care, Ollie. And do keep an eye on young Wyatt for me. I owe him a great deal." As he headed for the communications director's office, he thought about Commander Wyatt Steele joining BROADSWORD. He hoped he was ready for it.

*About the author*

Captain Tom Carroll served thirty years of combined active duty and reserve service in the United States Navy, specializing in Special Intelligence and Surface Warfare. Shanghai Protocol is the third novel in the Colt Garrett series. His first book, Colt's Crisis, was published in 2020. Colt's Cross was published in 2021. He owns an information technology firm in Olympia, Washington, where he lives with his wife and their golden retriever, Halsey.

Visit www.tomcarrollbooks.com and www.facebook.com/TomCarrollBooks for more information.

Made in United States
Troutdale, OR
06/18/2024

20661613R00181